THE 14TH COBBLESTONE

Agio
PUBLISHING HOUSE

PUBLISHING HOUSE

GABRIOLA, BC CANADA V0R 1X4

THE 14TH COBBLESTONE
ISBN 978-1-990335-24-2 (PAPERBACK)
ISBN 978-1-990335-26-6 (CASEBOUND)
ISBN 978-1-990335-25-9 (EBOOK)

Printed on acid-free paper. Agio Publishing House is
a socially and environmentally responsible company,
measuring success on a triple-bottom-line basis.

10 9 8 7 6 5 4 3 2 1

DEDICATED TO

Good friends Sherry and Stu –
We will always have Paris and Metz

Other Books by H.B. Dumont

THE NOIR INTELLIGENCE SERIES

The Black Hat

Spine of the Antiquarian

Kiss of the Death Adder

Assassin in My Bed

Gunpowder Treason and Plot

The 14th Cobblestone

THE 14TH COBBLESTONE

A Novel

H.B. DUMONT

CHAPTER 1

A ndrew Dupont approached the concierge, Philippe Abreo, at the entrance to the lobby of Novotel Paris Les Halles on Place Marguerite de Navarre in the 1re arrondissement, Paris. "Excuse me, monsieur. I have a request, one that you have probably not received before."

"I will do my best to assist you," the concierge replied with a welcoming smile. He was curious. "Please call me Philippe. If I cannot assist you, I am confident I will be able to introduce you to another member of staff who can."

"Is there somewhere we can speak in private?" Andrew asked anxiously in a low voice.

Philippe guided Andrew to a small nondescript office off the lobby. The door displayed neither a name plate nor a number. Inside, the furnishings and décor were spartan at best, limited to a petite secretarial-style chair and table with a computer monitor and keyboard.

"Do you know *an avocat* – a solicitor close to the hotel who speaks English?" asked Andrew. "I deeply regret I do not speak French sufficiently well, although I once did many years ago when I lived in Paris with my parents. My vocabulary back then was mostly limited to slang that I had absorbed from street kids in addition to the proper French grammar I learned in school."

"There are several law firms within walking distance. Can you explain what type of legal services you require – civil, criminal? Rest assured your request will remain confidential."

Andrew slid his hand into his pocket and retrieved his wallet. "My name is Andrew Dupont. I arrived in Paris late yesterday morning from Toronto, Canada." From his wallet, he withdrew a lottery ticket which he had purchased yesterday afternoon. "I believe I have won a considerable amount in last evening's lottery draw. I do not know how to claim my winnings or open a bank account here in Paris. I understand there are special procedures for a foreign national, a Canadian citizen, to follow."

Philippe typed in a search sequence and compared the ticket number against the numbers listed on the concierge's monitor. With a controlled smile, he replied, "You are correct, Monsieur Dupont. Congratulations! By chance, I can email my sister, Monique, who graduated from the Sorbonne-Asses International Law School with a degree in business law. She recently joined a prestigious law firm located adjacent to the Au Pied de Cochon restaurant, a seven-minute walk across the square from this hotel. She speaks English fluently."

Philippe confirmed Andrew's status as a registered guest in the Novotel before contacting his sister. "I note this is the third time you have stayed at our hotel. If I may ask, is your wife accompanying you on this trip to Paris?"

Andrew's smile vanished. "I regret not," he replied in a soft voice. "She died two years ago from injuries sustained in a car accident just as we were about to leave on a vacation to attend the 50th anniversary celebrations of D-Day on 6 June 1994." He felt very much alone having to explain her absence despite the fact it had been two years ago.

The concierge extended his hand, responding to the revelation. "Oh, I am so sorry for your loss, Monsieur Dupont. Please do not hesitate to contact me or any of our staff at reception. We would like to make your stay as pleasant as possible, given this news. With your permission, I will annotate your file."

"Thank you, Philippe, for your heartfelt condolences," Andrew replied as he took a deep breath to control his conflicting emotions. He was jubilant about the lottery win yet profoundly saddened that his late wife, Lynette, was not here to share in the excitement. Lynette and he had travelled extensively in Europe on business trips as well as personal vacations. The City of Light had become their favourite destination and Novotel Paris Les Halles their accommodation of choice.

"As you can appreciate, it is essential that this windfall be held in strict confidence. A winning lottery of this magnitude would attract unwelcome attention from a criminal element. No offence intended toward the citizens of Paris!"

"No offence taken, Monsieur Dupont." Philippe looked down at an incoming message from his sister. "My sister, Monique, can meet you here momentarily. If you would like to have a seat in the lounge, I will introduce you to her when she arrives. I will also advise our reception and security staff to provide VIP treatment with appropriate concern for your safety and security, especially any suspicious enquiries regarding your status as a guest. They will not know the details of the need for additional discrete surveillance and protection."

"Thank you," Andrew responded, still nervous about the impending lottery fortune. He was confident there was nothing suspicious about Philippe's intentions. He sensed he could trust him despite the brevity of their discussion and Philippe's offer to introduce him to his sister, Monique. There was just something familiar that gnawed at him. He maintained eye contact with Philippe as he scanned his memory as he would a Rolodex file without a specific index for a long-distant association. Something was hovering on the periphery of his consciousness though, perhaps stimulated by the prospects of what opportunities his lottery windfall might present. Understandably, he was conscious of his heightened awareness.

Within moments, Philippe approached. "Monsieur Dupont, I would like to introduce you to my sister, Monique."

Andrew stood up and held out his hand cordially. She reciprocated with a poised professionalism that partially calmed Andrew's concerns about her trustworthiness. He maintained eye contact with her as he had with Philippe. There was something familiar but distant about her, too, that held his attention. *She and Philippe could have been twins*, he surmised.

The greatest gift Paris presented to the world was its beautiful women. Monique met the standard for that truism. He found her attractiveness to be as compelling as most youthful Parisienne women but not coquettish.

Where had he crossed paths with her and Philippe, if at all? He chuckled to himself at what he perceived to be Monique's shy smile – quite the opposite of a cunning Cheshire cat grin. It was another elusive clue that teased his memory.

"Monique." He allowed her name to drift before repeating it in an attempt to disperse the mist that shrouded his memory. "Monique, how long have you been practising law?" He hoped she would interpret his query about her experience as the customary question of a potential client under the circumstances, as opposed to any crassness of interrogation.

"Just six years," she replied. "Prior to that, I had been employed in the tourist industry since graduating from *Lycées Baccalauréat Professionnel*, what you would refer to as high school with an academic emphasis. Subsequently, I attended the Sorbonne – l'Université de Paris."

Perhaps they had met on a previous trip he and Lynette had taken to Paris, he wondered, but that would not explain his sense of familiarity with Philippe. Again, he lamented the fact that Lynette was not with him. Her memory of events and people had always been far superior to his. He would have ample time to ponder, but for now he would attend to his personal priority, claiming his lottery windfall and opening a bank account.

CHAPTER 2

After claiming his winnings at the lottery office, they returned to Novotel Paris Les Halles. There, Monique helped him open an account at a bank on Place Marguerite de Navarre. He withdrew 10,000 francs cash, gave Monique 7,000 and kept the balance for himself.

"Thank you," she replied, "but this is far too much. I cannot accept it."

He was impressed by her integrity. "Consider it a retainer fee for future legal services. I may purchase a home in the Saint-Germain-des-Prés district of the 6e arrondissement. Now that my wife is no longer with me, there is nothing keeping me in Canada. Lynette and I had talked about retiring in Paris many times. With the financial benefits from this lottery, I can now pursue that dream more seriously rather than just fantasizing about it over exquisite cognac, which entertained us on many occasions."

Monique raised her eyebrows and asked, "Are you familiar with the 6e arrondissement district? If not, I can show you around. I lived in Saint-Germain-des-Prés as a child. I can introduce you to a good friend who has just qualified as a real estate agent, recently retired from the Police nationale as a capitaine. Her name is Natalie Corban."

"Thank you for your kind offer. I also lived there as a teenager," Andrew commented, "although my recollections are slightly less clear due to the passage of time and distance. My father was a military attaché with the Canadian Embassy in the late 1950s and early 1960s." He hesitated for a moment as if a pause was necessary while holding Monique's gaze. *Could it be?* he conjectured. He tentatively asked, "Do you have an older sister, Babette?"

It was Monique's turn to stare back. "Yes," she replied slowly as her smile migrated from her lips to her eyes. "Andrew Dupont? I believe we lived next door to you in Saint-Germain-des-Prés." Perhaps on another occasion she would mention that Babette had died shortly after he had returned to Canada.

"That is where I remember you and your brother, Philippe." He recalled Philippe as being more scholastic and Monique more interested in non-academic activities. "I thought I recognized you both. It has only been thirty-five years and much water has passed under the bridges in Paris. I was planning on inviting you and Philippe to dinner this evening at Au Pied de Cochon restaurant to thank you for your help and to quietly celebrate my good fortune. We can get caught up on all the years. May I ask you to forward your email address to me?" He gave her both his Canadian cell phone number and email address, and his European number and e-address that he had established on a previous trip to Paris. The latter was more convenient for travelling in different countries in the Europe. It was also considerably cheaper than paying roaming charges to his Canadian internet provider."

"Dining together would be lovely. Thank you. On my way back to the office, I will stop at Au Pied de Cochon and make reservations for 7 p.m. in my name," Monique stated. "I will first confirm that Philippe is available. In the interim, I can e-introduce you to Natalie, my real estate agent friend. You may recognize her also as she lived across the street from us." *It is fortunate he has won this lottery*, Monique mused, because property values in Saint-Germain-des-Prés on the left bank centrally located adjacent to the Latin Quarter and the Université de Paris had increased exponentially since the early 1960s when we were neighbours. It is now one of the most prestigious and, as a result, expensive real estate markets in Paris.

After claiming his winnings at the lottery office, they returned to Novotel Paris Les Halles. Andrew went to the front lobby only to find Philippe absent from his concierge station at the entrance. He enquired at the front desk. Philippe's shift had ended, he was told. The receptionist was cordial yet she seemed reserved, which left Andrew feeling a tinge of caution for reasons he could not fully comprehend. When he had explained to Philippe that Lynette had passed away, Philippe had extended his most sincere condolences and mentioned he would advise the staff to be empathetic to his circumstances. At this moment, the response of the receptionist to his enquiry regarding Philippe's absence seemed somehow less so.

He hesitated for a moment, bowing his head slightly while maintaining eye contact over the rim of his eye glasses. He had initially felt uneasy approaching Philippe and asking for assistance to claim his lottery ticket. Lingering traces of that feeling of apprehension once again enveloped him like a subtle lowering of the barometric pressure and a premonition of the approach of an offshore ocean fog bank. He was all too familiar with such almost imperceptible changes in weather having most recently lived in Halifax on the Atlantic coast of Canada, in addition to some of his formative years in Bristol on the west coast of southern England. Perhaps he was overreacting because of his heightened sensitivity due to the lottery win. When nervous, he had a habit of wavering between rational analysis and overthinking emotional stimuli. Lynette's presence had always been a calming influence.

Andrew's cellphone vibrated with an incoming email from Monique. "Do you remember the document we found in the basement of your house? We divided up the pages. I still have my half, somewhere. If I recall correctly, you told me that you had hidden your half in a safe place. It might be an agenda topic for discussion this evening. Very much looking forward to the first of many dinners *ce soir!*"

He replied, "Yes, I do recall the document, now that you mention it, but cannot remember where I hid it. That was so long ago!

You thought the language might have been an eastern European dialect of some sort, perhaps even Arabic. We never did work out what the pages represented or the words meant." He allowed his thoughts to marinate in hopes something pertinent would percolate through the mental mist to the surface. Destiny seemed to be tapping him on the shoulder.

Like a sand dune ever shifting in a wind-swept desert, Andrew had moved frequently as he grew up – post after foreign post as his father's diplomatic career dictated. It left him comfortable with making acquaintances easily. He had few good friends, vaguely familiar from previous places they had lived. There were memories, though, stretching back through friendships, a few enduring but most fleeting, some linked to sadness and loss. Serious liaisons were a novelty. In retrospect, there was only one love throughout his teenage years: Monique! If names or shared experiences, like those with Monique and Philippe, were hazy, he was comfortable with it. *C'est la vie.*

CHAPTER 3

Andrew arrived early at the Au Pied de Cochon restaurant. He was anxious to renew acquaintance with Philippe and Monique. She had made the reservation for two, not three. A note left with the restaurant concierge explained that Philippe could not attend at such short notice. Andrew was shown to a table in a secluded alcove on the second floor where he ordered an aperitif, Dubonnet, pending the arrival of his childhood friend. He had thought about the document and where he might have hidden it, but to no avail. He was confident the evening's conversation would help to jog his memory.

By 7:15 p.m., he was sipping his second aperitif and remained the sole guest in this private section of the dining area. The waiter approached with a second communiqué, this time from Philippe who apologized for his absence and requested that Andrew return to the hotel straightaway. There he was to ask at the front desk for the hotel manager. A shiver ran down his spine. He got up immediately. He paid for the two aperitifs and left a generous gratuity.

The square was filled with people who might witness his quickened pace. The crowds would camouflage the approach of any characters who had somehow become aware of his recent lottery winnings claimed only hours before. The feeling of elation at the prospect of his fortune had become a curse, an emotional millstone around his neck.

Oh, how he missed Lynette on occasions like this, another set of trusting eyes to support his natural caution and her rational words to calm his emotional state. But if she were here, beside him now, he would be consumed with worry for her safety as he always had been when he perceived vulnerability and certainly on other occasions when they were apart, even for brief periods.

"Hotel manager, please," Andrew asked the receptionist at the front desk as he presented his room card for identification. His gaze followed her to a closed door with a gold plaque that read: Directeur de L'hôtel. She gently knocked before stepping inside, returning as promptly as she had entered, followed by Philippe Abreo dressed in a professional three-piece dark-blue pinstriped suit, different from his conservative concierge attire.

"Please come in," Philippe requested.

Andrew followed him in, perplexed by Philippe's appearance. He was as familiar with the office as his role as the hotel concierge. With a welcoming gesture, Philippe invited him to sit in one of three high-backed leather chairs surrounding an ornate gold inlaid mahogany meeting table. On a side table was an antique teak Malaysian clock encased in brass. As a childhood hobby, Andrew had researched grandfather clocks. He estimated this one had been manufactured in France in the 1790s by Antide Janvier. The atmosphere of the office spoke of similar excellence.

"The plaque on the door read Directeur de L'hôtel," Andrew said guardedly.

"Allow me to explain. You may recall from your schooldays the legend of King Arthur, Excalibur and the Knights of the Round Table. With the wizard Merlin by his side, young King Arthur wandered the mythical realm of Camelot in order to assess for himself the status of the land and its inhabitants. I am the hotel manager, King Arthur so to speak. Novotel Paris les Halles is Camelot. I occasionally work a shift as the concierge to assess the pulse of operations and the mood of our guests, the inhabitants of the kingdom."

Andrew stared with furrowed brow, appraising Philippe's fairytale analogy. He pointed to the ornate table they sat at.

"Exactly, for the Knights of the Round Table when I hold court, meetings with my staff," Philippe confirmed with a smile as he tilted his head.

"And Monique?" Andrew queried, "Queen Guinevere?"

"No. Legal counsel to King Arthur, a.k.a. manager of Novotel Paris les Halles. Yes, she is my sister." He hesitated momentarily before continuing. "Let me provide you with some background and explain why I summoned you to my office. Monique is in the throes of a nasty divorce from her abusive husband. She is in hiding at this time because he assaulted her late this afternoon as she was leaving the Au Pied de Cochon restaurant after making the reservation. The police are attempting to track him down and execute an arrest warrant for a previous assault and breach of a court order. That is why, regrettably, she was unable to keep your dinner reservation this evening."

Philippe ended with a nod, tightening his lips. All the while he maintained direct eye contact with Andrew who dwelt on the circumstance behind his highly anticipated but sadly interrupted dinner plans.

"Can I help and, if so, how?" Andrew enquired. His lottery windfall had opened up options that were not available when he awoke this morning. Throughout his adult life, he had abhorred violence and cruelty perpetrated by bullies. He was not ignorant of the magnitude of spousal abuse in North America and some European countries he had visited with Lynette. Either there was an increase in domestic violence or the media was obsessed with reporting spousal assaults, in addition to other forms of cruelty. Clearly, there was more money to be made publicizing incidents of violence. Peace did not pay dividends to the same degree. He concluded the increasing incidents were more than likely a combination of both. That had become the tragic truth.

With Philippe's account of Monique's circumstances, he was reminded first-hand of how violence in a family interrupts lives outside the domestic domain. He let out a long breath as he rested his chin on his steepled fingers and considered the possible outcomes.

Philippe handed him a piece of paper with Natalie Corban's email address. "Monique asked me to give this to you. Please contact Natalie soon and arrange to meet her. She will update you on Monique's condition and how you might help her."

In his wildest imagination, Andrew had not considered the events of the past twenty-four hours as possibilities in his conventional lifestyle – meeting childhood friends not seen for thirty-five years and having reservations at one of the city's most exquisite restaurants abruptly cancelled, in addition to a fleeting introduction to the modern-day fairy-tale Camelot of Paris, Novotel Paris les Halles.

Now he was following instructions to attend a surreptitious *rendezvous* with an enigmatic eccentric concierge and/or hotel manager in a four-star hotel playing the imaginary role of the mythical King Arthur. He was about to contact another childhood acquaintance whom he could not readily recall yet was about to ask her for help in a real estate transaction. In addition, he was about to become involved in a rescue mission of a mutual friend, a victim of spousal abuse. Intrigue and blind trust had replaced prudence for reasons wholly unknown and uncommon to him.

Within moments of sending Natalie an email, he received a reply asking him to meet her at Les Deux Magots café at 6 Place Saint-Germain-des-Prés at the intersection of rue Bonaparte and boulevard Saint-Germain. He remembered the café well because he had met his mother there on different occasions after school. She had sipped cappuccinos with fellow aspiring writers hoping to absorb inspiration from the spirits of accomplished expatriates and local authors from decades past such as Ernest Hemingway, Gertrude Stein and Jean-Paul Sartre who had frequented Les Deux Magots for the same purpose. Here he was, about to meet someone with common cultural interests. *Un déjà-vu, peut-être* – an event previously experienced, possibly.

CHAPTER 4

"Andrew?" a welcoming voice enquired in a soft tone. He turned around not knowing what to expect and gave a non-committal reply, "*Oui*, yes."

He had wondered how a retired Police nationale capitaine now a real estate agent might look. He had misjudged her completely. Instead of a dominant stature with a strong physique and commanding presence, he gazed down at a petite unassuming *Parisienne*. There was nothing about her presence or mannerism that stood out. Nothing he would have expected, certainly nothing he recognized. *The perfect cop for clandestine or undercover surveillance work,* he presumed.

"Monique described you perfectly," Natalie breathed softly, not wanting to draw the undue attention of other patrons of the café.

"How is she?" he asked promptly in a lowered voice.

"As well as can be expected." Natalie raised her head, a small smile on her lips. She motioned to a waiter who nodded subtly in response. They wove their way to a table in the far corner of the café supervised by figurines of les deux magots mounted high on the wall. Natalie sat with her back to the wall. Old habits were hard to break. Good habits to be retained, she supposed.

"Cappuccino or something stronger?" she asked.

"*Thé vert*, green tea," Andrew replied, still assessing the ambience. It had not changed in thirty-five years. He appreciated the quality and excellence.

The waiter confirmed his request. "And your regular, madame?"

"*Oui*," she replied.

Andrew presumed it was a frequently visited haunt in her previous career. *But why, and why the familiarity with the waiter? Curious culture,* he pondered.

Natalie discreetly scanned the room and its occupants before returning her attention to Andrew.

"Monique sends her most sincere apologies for not being able to meet for dinner at Au Pied de Cochon. She so looked forward to catching up with you. She is confident there will be other social occasions, other dinners especially if you purchase a home here in the Saint-Germain-des-Prés district. In this regard, there are a select few properties of superior quality for sale that are not publicly listed. We can discuss your preferences this evening and view offerings tomorrow morning if that is convenient."

"That would be fine, but first I would like to know how Monique is doing," he repeated in a more determined tone. "Her brother, Philippe, said that you would bring me up-to-date. By the way, do you have a business card?"

The intent of his uncompromising glare and curt tone was clear. Natalie would need to confirm Monique's status or there would be no real estate discussion this evening, verbal or otherwise, or any showing of properties tomorrow.

Natalie seemed to be evading his enquiry for reasons he couldn't understand. If she was a good friend of Monique, her manner did not appear to reflect a caring long-term relationship. Then again, perhaps she was protecting Monique by being evasive. He surmised that Natalie might be understandably distant with him under the circumstances. After all, they had neither met nor spoken since they were teenagers if, in fact, they had spoken when he lived in Paris. He had no recollection of her. He only had Monique's word and Philippe's validation of Natalie's status as a childhood friend and retired Police nationale capitaine. He would have to come to his own conclusion in the fullness of time. The events of the day thus far seemed surreal, a *modus operandi* he was neither accustomed to nor particularly comfortable with.

"My apologies," Natalie responded to his abrupt challenge. She would need to replace her confrontational police demeanor and deportment with more pleasant businesslike etiquette. She handed him a business card with a welcoming smile. "My apologies," she repeated sincerely.

Andrew scanned her name and credentials. Now was not the time to call to confirm what he had read with the real estate company or her previous status as a capitaine with the Police nationale.

"Physically, Monique is showing signs of facial bruises, nothing that some foundation cosmetics will not cover up. Emotionally, she is fearful of her husband, hopefully soon to be her ex-husband. It is nothing that a period of rest and relaxation cannot resolve. That process has already been initiated, including offsite employment with the aid of her more recent employer." Natalie paused. "It is not the interpersonal violence that is so worrying but the fact that domestic violence has become so natural, even acceptable."

Andrew echoed her cordial business and personal manner with his own relaxed posture.

"I have just been informed that the police have executed the arrest warrant for her husband, Claude Laurent. He is an administrator with the 8e arrondissement where the Élysée Palace is located, thus he has some influence as a bureaucrat. Unfortunately for him, his aspiration exceeded his talent. I mention his name because you will more than likely cross paths with him if you associate with Monique. The courts have denied his request for bail so I can take you to her right now if you would like or wait until tomorrow morning. She is in our old neighbourhood of Saint-Germain-des-Prés in a house that I planned on showing you tomorrow. It is an unlisted property, one of the private sales I mentioned."

"Now would be reassuring," he replied with a note of urgency.

Natalie emailed Monique notifying her of their momentary arrival, while Andrew paid the waiter for their drinks.

Enroute, Natalie explained that the property had an eclectic but limited history. The courtyard was enclosed behind a traditional high stone and stucco wall and opaque metal gate that could be locked electronically. It was originally built in 1814 and refurbished in 1920 as part of the post-World War I Treaty of Versailles stipulations. It had been occupied by the Nazis from 1940 to 1945, and completely refurbished again in 1954 as part of the post-World War II restoration efforts to eliminate any overt symbols and memories of the brutality of the Nazi occupation. She muttered under her breath her disgust of the *Boche*, a derogatory French expression for German soldiers, with roots reaching back to World War I. *You can tear down and rebuild structures but not haunting nightmares and relentless memories*, she reflected.

Andrew sensed the profound repulsion and lingering sentiments of her animosity. Even in 1960, some structures had not been repaired because of the associations with the war such as the conduct of the Waffen-SS graduates of the Wewelsburg Castle in addition to some of the Wehrmacht. The memories were still too raw for some.

Natalie continued after a momentary hesitation. "It is now an approximate 2,900 square-metre three-bedroom, two-bathroom residence on two principal floors. It has a detached double-car garage that was once a stable and carriage house. There is a basement with a wine cellar and finished garret suite with its own bathroom suitable for separate accommodation. All appliances and furnishings were updated recently. The property is part of a divorce settlement that has been ongoing for over two years. The original asking price has been steadily reduced. It could be reduced further, I sense. Only recently have the respective lawyers convinced the estranged husband and wife to agree to the next offer, which is you, if you want it. Their lawyers have power of attorney to settle promptly."

Andrew pursed his lips with an expression of reserved interest. "Thank you. As you say, an eclectic history dating back to Napoleon's defeat at Waterloo in 1815."

Natalie pressed the intercom button installed on the ten-foot-high wall adjacent to the steel-plated gate. A security camera which scanned the road leading to the entrance and tracking their approach now focused solely on them. The lock on the steel door automatically opened and locked again with an audible clunk after they had entered the manicured courtyard, quite large by Parisian standards. They walked up the winding cobblestone path to the pillared front doorway.

"In some respects, this courtyard reminds me of the place I lived in with my parents thirty-five years ago," Andrew commented. He grew quiet as he admired the quality of the shrubbery and the façade of the house, both typically Parisian as he recalled from his childhood and visits with Lynette to the city of lights.

CHAPTER 5

The front door opened and Monique appeared a few steps back from the door, her identity masked in case of surveillance from neighbouring properties. The front door closed with a distinct thump like the front gate and locked automatically behind them. *High security for the sellers. Curious?* Andrew pondered. Perhaps they had also won a sizeable lottery and were conscious of criminal elements, for good reason known only to them. He hadn't considered security as a criterion for purchasing a property. On second thoughts, he could take advantage of their foresight.

Monique and Natalie hugged and whispered. Andrew overheard part of the conversation, "*Il est en prison pour la nuit mais peut être libéré le matin* – He is in jail for the night but may be released in the morning."

Monique gazed at Andrew who nodded pleasantly as he returned her cautious smile. He reached toward her and shook her hand, holding it for slightly longer than normal. Despite Natalie's assurance that a little foundation would cover the bruises, her injuries were considerably more serious.

"Look around," Natalie encouraged Andrew. "We can return tomorrow to view the courtyard, exterior and interior in the light of day. Monique and I have to talk about some priorities to confirm how she will escape from her husband before he is released from custody."

"Can I help? If so, how?" he suggested, feeling compassion for Monique's circumstances.

"Possibly but not sure just how," Natalie replied.

"Thanks for your offer," Monique added. "For now, your gracious retainer fee from earlier today is timely, most generous."

"With pleasure, Madame." His relaxed smile reflected his genuine concern for her physical and emotional wellbeing.

After surveying the interior with its vaulted high-ceilinged rooms and Romanesque windows, including the refurbished garret suite, Andrew returned to the library on the main floor as the ladies appeared to be concluding their plans for Monique's escape from her abusive relationship with Claude. He gazed around the room as he sighed pensively. There was nothing about the 19th century furnishings or décor that displeased him. Lapsing into introspection, he took a few moments to peer owlishly at what seemed to be an extensive yet select collection of books in a floor-to-ceiling bookshelf against one wall. *Curious*, he thought. He read some titles which appeared to be in volume series like the Brothers Grimm fairy tales. A few he recognized as being single titles such as *Les Misérables* by Victor Hugo. The bindings were hand-stitched and appeared to be similar, all seemingly shrouded in shadowy seclusion, begging to be explored and exposed for the stories they held within their distinctively bound covers.

"Initial thoughts?" Natalie enquired as she transferred her attention to him.

"I like absolutely everything. There is nothing I would want to add or change." He paused before adding, "I don't think I need to see any other properties unless they are significantly superior."

Natalie nodded as she smiled calmly. "I have a non-binding expression of interest document that we can complete right now. I appreciate the lateness of the hour but I can email the lawyers for the two parties and present the expression of interest, a tentative offer. If the lawyers agree, which I am confident they will, I can email an attached signed contract to them first thing in the morning, after we view the property in daylight, which I strongly recommend. I know them both from my time with the Police nationale. They are both honourable and stand by their word."

"I agree. Please proceed with a tentative offer of interest. Emphasize non-binding," Andrew directed. "The final price is to be negotiated tomorrow."

Natalie cast a warm glance at Monique and then at Andrew. "Excuse me for a moment while I send your expression of interest to the two lawyers."

She glanced down at an incoming email. "One lawyer has agreed to your expression of tentative interest on the condition that the other lawyer replies accordingly. Hopefully, we will hear back from her soon." Natalie's cell phone buzzed again with a second incoming message. A broader smile said it all. "Possession date tomorrow subject to a closer inspection in the daylight and negotiated price. Is that agreeable, Andrew?" *Faster sale than any of my more experienced real estate colleagues have ever made*, she giggled to herself.

"Tomorrow is just fine," he replied. "Only the Bastille, were it still standing, would be more secure with interior and exterior close circuit TV cameras, motion detector alarm systems, and electronic gate and door locks."

"One final request," Andrew asked.

"Certainly."

"Can you get a copy of the blueprints with a full description of the property?"

"I will request them from the sellers' lawyers," Natalie confirmed.

Natalie looked at Monique and then at Andrew. "You asked how you could help Monique? Can you accommodate a tentative temporary tenant for immediate occupancy?"

"And Langue?" Monique added on the heels of Natalie's request.

"Given the possibility that Claude may be released in the morning, I strongly suggest that we go to your house immediately or latest by early tomorrow morning and retrieve all your personal belongings, especially your passport and other identification documents," Natalie advised.

"And Langue?" Monique repeated.

"Langue?" Andrew repeated inquisitively.

"My dog," she explained. "He had been a police dog in training but was judged too mild mannered and friendly so he was rejected. He tended to greet new people he met, including some suspected criminals, by licking their hand. Hence, he was given the name, *Langue*, French for tongue."

"Yes, absolutely to both," Andrew chuckled. The house and courtyard could accommodate an affable mutt. "Having failed preschool, how is his sense of self-esteem? Has he received counselling from a dog psychologist?" Andrew asked.

The smile on Monique's face broadened in response to his light-hearted question.

"May I recommend a lawyer to represent you in this real estate transaction?" Natalie suggested to Andrew jovially. "I understand her rates are negotiable."

The release of tension in Monique's stance was palpable.

⧏ ⧐

AS AGREED, ANDREW MET NATALIE at the house in the morning. A quick inspection of the interior and exterior confirmed his commitment to purchase the house. He was particularly drawn to the finely detailed wrought iron railings on the balconies. They brought back fond memories of the house he had lived in with his parents.

"I appreciate that price may not be an issue for you but I have negotiated a reduced sale price," Natalie confirmed.

Andrew smiled gratefully. She was correct, money was not an issue. He simply felt very comfortable with the house and property, and more importantly, safe.

The written contract was signed and emailed to both lawyers of the divorcing parties, Luc and Estella Moreau. Pending the receipt of their ratification, Andrew strolled through the gardens. The apple and Mirabelle plum trees and raised vegetable garden beds enclosed by cobblestone paths also reminded him of the house he had lived in with his parents all those years ago. He especially remembered the harvesting of the Mirabelle plums, the scent of the fermenting fruit and wine being brewed, the wicker-wrapped casks and the racks of the bottled wine and liqueur left to mature in the coolness of the basement. On the eve of their return to Canada, the owner of their property had given Andrew's father a bottle of each. The corks on some other bottles had been popped previously and the contents sampled on special occasions including Christmas.

"Andrew," Natalie called out to him, waving her cell phone. "Congratulations on the purchase of your new Parisian home in the Saint-Germain-des-Prés district of the 6e arrondissement. The wine in the basement stacked against the cobblestone wall comes with the purchase as does a 1985 Renault parked in the garage. We will get the registration for the car transferred to your name soonest."

"We should open a bottle to celebrate," Monique suggested gleefully. Her relaxation was reflected in her deepening breaths with the realization that she had some stability in her precarious life, albeit short-term. She was most grateful for small gifts and caring friends who had her best interests at heart.

Throughout his working years Andrew had always thought holidays and weekends were very important, as had Lynette. He was confident that she was smiling down on him like a winged cherub proud of his most recent achievement. He reflected on the lives they had lived and lives they had talked about living. Now he could put into place some semblance of those dreams. But first he would celebrate the purchase of his urban estate with a childhood friend he had not seen for decades though he had certainly thought about her more recently.

They proceeded down the worn stone steps of the winding staircase as many other occupants had done over almost two centuries, some with wooden clogs that left imprints. Today, they would select a celebratory classic vintage. As they deliberated on which wine to select, Andrew paused and stared at the wall supporting the floor to ceiling wine racks adorned with dust. "I remember," he uttered to Monique.

"You remember what?" she prompted him.

"Where I hid my copy of the document we found as teenagers. The basement of the house we lived in was much like this one with similar cobblestone wall construction. The top row of cobblestones which capped the wall also supported a wine rack. It was the 14th cobblestone from the left!" he emphasized. "The centuries-old mortar had started to fall out. Well, I helped it to release its grip on the old stone. Behind that 14th cobblestone, I carved out a space where I stashed a small metal cookie tin. That's where I stored the document pages! All we have to do now is get permission from the current occupants to reclaim my secret treasure."

He looked mischievously at Natalie.

CHAPTER 6

"I suppose I could approach the owner with a cold call on the premise that I have a client who has expressed a keen interest in the property," Natalie responded to Andrew's shrewd if devious enquiry. "This is truthful. I could explain that my client lived in the house in his youth many years ago. This is also truthful. I could enquire if the property was for sale. If not, whether my client could visit the property one final time, particularly the basement where he played as a child." Natalie stared inquisitively at Andrew not as an interrogator but as a co-conspirator seeking endorsement of her scheme. They would need to have a well-rehearsed exit strategy in the event the plan fell off the tracks, so to speak.

"And?" he hesitated. "How can I help you to be more convincing?" His *modus operandi* during his working career had never been to deceive clients or colleagues, although he had to admit he had wondered about being more adventurous by pushing the limits. "My dearly departed Lynette always encouraged me to step out of my conservative box when circumstances permitted. She would approve." He chuckled under his breath. *It is interesting what millions of francs can do to liberate an orthodox soul*, he thought.

Natalie elaborated. "Give me as accurate a description as you can of all the rooms and their permanent fixtures. Being an early circa 1900 vintage, there must have been a laundry room in the basement at least with *un lavoir*, a stone washing pool for laundry that emptied into open floor drains leaving a lingering scent of caustic cleaning soap that permeated the place. There would have to have been other storage rooms of some sort, each with decades, if not centuries-old, locks. There might have been a coal-burning furnace when it was built but more than likely in a late nineteenth or early twentieth century renovation. There certainly would have been substantial stone fireplaces in most of the common rooms on the main and upper floors. Anything unique, distinctive. We are only going to get one opportunity, short of breaking and entering, which is not a viable option."

Natalie stared at an incoming message on her cell phone and then at Monique with a sense of urgency as she tapped in a reply, "Delay as much as you can, as long as you can," her reply read.

"Monique, one of my police colleagues just advised that Claude is about to be released from custody. We have thirty-five minutes, at most, before he is out of the jailhouse door. We'd better go to your house right now to pick up all your identification papers, and any personal stuff we can move in one trip from your *banlieue* suburban house in Neuilly-sur-Seine. Langue will be anxious to see you."

Monique's growing anxiety was apparent. "We will be tight for time. It will take us twenty-five minutes in good traffic to get there. Rarely is it not congested though. Claude always uses the front door so we should enter via the back. We can park in the lane for a quicker getaway."

"What can I do to help?" Andrew asked.

"Best if you stay here and monitor the CCTV," Natalie answered. "If Claude gets there before we leave, we don't want him to associate you with Monique. This will give you more safety and security, plus Monique as a tenant in your house. It is times like this that a gated property under electronic surveillance has tremendous value. When the cameras track our return, open the gates and immediately lock them after we enter the courtyard. Also, monitor any other vehicles that may be following us. I will text you when we approach and if I see any suspicious vehicles following us."

Natalie hesitated for a moment. "Do you mind if Monique and I take your Renault? If Claude sees us, he won't recognize the car. One less detail to worry about."

"Not a problem," Andrew replied. "We first need to be sure the battery is charged and nothing seems to be rattling where it should not be." He followed them into the garage where his recently registered chariot of fire started without hesitation or protest.

As Natalie drove in a way she had operated a police pursuit vehicle, she strongly recommended, more than mildly suggested to Monique, that she would put Langue in the car while Monique gathered what she wanted to take away. "I'll make a second trip back inside to cover our exit and secure the back door if we have time."

"There is a big smile on your face. I think you miss the excitement of your previous profession!" Monique stated as only a close friend could.

"I do, probably always will," she replied. "But it is good to be out of that rat race."

"There is an old Yiddish expression," Monique muttered half-heartedly, *"Man plans and God laughs."*

As Natalie parked in the lane behind her house, she caught a glimpse of a police patrol car stopping on the street. The driver of the patrol car made eye contact, urgently pointing at Natalie repeatedly. She understood the signal to leave in a hurry. "The Gods may be laughing, but not wholly at us," she whispered to Monique. "We need to get in and get out fast! No second trip."

Langue met them as they came in the back door. Natalie sprinted to the front window and stared into the street through the Alsatian lace curtains which impaired the view of anyone on the street. She recognized the second officer leaving the patrol car as one of her previous colleagues who had warned her of Claude's imminent release. She was now speaking with Claude as he got out of a taxi.

"Claude is in the front yard. Police are talking to him trying to delay his entry," she yelled at Monique. "Get the absolute minimum you need, valuable papers only, your passport. Forget your clothes. We can buy a new wardrobe which he won't recognize. Grab Langue and get out, fast. I'll be two steps behind you. I'll lock the back door."

Monique went pale. She hesitated as the injury Claude had inflicted on her spiked in pain. Her heart pounded and her chest heaved.

"Move now, fast!" Natalie shouted. Her glare said everything necessary.

In less than a minute, Monique called that she had Langue on his leash and was leaving the house as fast as she could.

Natalie monitored what appeared to be a heated exchange between the police officer and Claude as they approached the front door. She sprinted out of the back door and locked it. She bolted into the lane and the awaiting 1985 Renault which she prayed would start instantly and take them to the sanctuary of Andrew's house.

As they sped away, they heard Claude yell at the top of his voice, "Monique!" He realized she had gone with Langue. He had a strong hunch who had been an accomplice in Monique's getaway. He ran to the front door in hopes of hiring the taxi. But it had left as had the patrol car and the two gendarmes who had interfered with his tactics for speedy access to the house. He was left with no hard evidence of his wife's whereabouts, but he knew where to start his search.

He speed-dialed Natalie's cell phone. There was no answer, not that he expected her to respond straightaway. In the heat of the moment, he left a voice message: "I'm coming for you, bitch." The moment he said it, he regretted it. He knew the police would be after him again, this time for uttering threats. He didn't care. His focus was simple. He was after Monique and anyone who was aiding or abetting her escape. It was all her fault and she would pay. There was nowhere she could go or hide that he would not find her. Nowhere.

He went down the stairs to the basement where he retrieved his MAB PA-15 9mm semi-automatic pistol from its hiding place in the rafters. He ejected the 15-round magazine and confirmed it was fully loaded. He then replaced it and cocked the weapon. Under control, he allowed the hammer to move forward slowly. He left the rest of the ammunition in the box. He was confident he could achieve his objective without having to reload. He only needed two rounds, one for each of them, perhaps a third if there was another accomplice, like her brother. Philippe had never liked his brother-in-law and had encouraged Monique to initiate divorce proceedings. Philippe would have to go if for no other reason than his constant interference.

As he waited for Monique and Natalie to return, Andrew took the time to consider how his life would change since claiming his lottery win. He contemplated becoming a *flâneur*, a man of leisure, an urban observer, a connoisseur of the tree-lined boulevards and parks, of strolling through the connecting streets and back lanes, and sitting without an agenda at cafés in the City of Light. He recalled the words of an Italian friend celebrating the first day of retirement, *il dolce far niente* – the sweetness of doing nothing.

For now, he scrutinized the approach of Monique and Natalie on the CCTV monitor with Langue in the back seat. He opened the gate and locked it after they had entered the courtyard. He then scrutinized the lane to confirm they were not being followed. There were no vehicles. He doubted they would be shadowed by any pedestrians. Regardless, he continued to scan the courtyard until Natalie had safely parked the car in the double garage. He opened the front door as they walked quickly and entered the lobby with Langue. Andrew then electronically locked the garage door. Langue greeted him at the front door, whining excitedly as he licked Andrew's hands. His tail wagged so much that his back legs seemed to dance across the smooth granite floor.

Andrew took some deep, slow breaths. His initial urge was to hug them both. But instead, he smiled, expressing his sense of relief at seeing they were safe within the secure confines of his house and the enclosed gated compound. Lynette would be looking down with a reassuring smile. His decision to purchase this Parisian urban estate was wise.

CHAPTER 7

"**M**ission a success?" Andrew asked.

"Mission a success," Natalie confirmed, looking a bit harried. "The Renault performed as requested. It is in dire need of a complete tune up if you plan on keeping it, and a thorough cleaning inside and out regardless."

"Mission a success but not by much," Monique added. "I'll explain later. For now, we should sample some fine wine from your cellar to celebrate. I noted a section reserved for some fine Pinot Noir from the Côtes du Rhône region."

Andrew could detect a sense of anticipation in her voice.

Natalie checked an incoming text message from the patrol colleague who had warned her of Claude's imminent release. She had delayed him in the front yard of the house as best she could.

"All safe?" The text read.

"All safe. I owe you one," Natalie replied.

"I figured he would go berserk. We have intelligence suggesting he has a stolen handgun in addition to a store of contraband illegally acquired on the black market. Intelligence, as you know, is rarely sufficient evidence to warrant a request for a search warrant at this time. More worrying, he has been affiliating lately with known terrorists in the Saint-Denis region where there are more rogues than saints not that far as the criminal crow flies from where he works in the 8e arrondissement."

"You were correct in your assessment of him. He left a voice message threatening me. I am forwarding it to you now."

"Just received it. Will lay new charges of uttering threats and have an arrest warrant issued. Given this incident on the heels of the previous warrant, he may not be released as quickly. Will keep you informed."

"Much appreciated," Natalie answered. "Note that I will no longer be using this phone. I will resurrect my original phone number. Confirm *post-haste*."

Natalie retrieved and activated her backup cell phone from a concealed side pocket in her satchel. The most recent message read, "Confirming *post-haste* as requested."

"Ack," Natalie replied. She then advised all those on her VIP list of the change, including Andrew. This was not the first time she had been forced to use her second cell phone in an attempt to thwart the efforts of criminals to find her GPS co-ordinates and hunt her down.

That lifestyle had cost her a promising marriage. Although separated, she and her ex remained legally wedded. There was hope that they might get together again now that she was a licenced real estate agent. But then again, the erratic hours could be just as unpredictable and frenzied. She would tell Andrew about Claude's background and sociopathic behaviour. For now, she would not divulge all the details of her police career and personal life.

Natalie sent a photo of Claude to Andrew because she believed, as did the police, that he was in possession of a handgun and may be stalking Monique. She failed to mention that Claude may be targeting her too, in addition to anyone else known to be associated with Monique. That included Philippe and possibly Andrew.

Monique stared down at the remnants of her disastrous life – little more than her government-issued identification papers, the most important being her passport. *Ç'est dommage*, how sad, she ruminated as she slipped into her familiar state of despair, which had become all too frequent. She swallowed a sob. Natalie had always been there to help prop up her emotions. Perhaps her landlord's presence and the safety of his gated house could bolster her optimism, and then there was Langue.

As circumstances permitted, she would replace her wardrobe

as Natalie had suggested. She enjoyed shopping and was confident that Andrew would be a good judge of fashion. From the first moment they met in the lobby of Novotel Paris les Halles, she perceived that he was taken with her Parisienne style and charm. This was in complete contrast to Claude who always criticized her choices in dress and deportment saying she looked like *une prostituée*, a prostitute. Such verbal outbursts more often than not ended with slaps across her face or worse. Oh, how she longed to hear words of praise and admiration.

⌐ ⌐

ALTHOUGH THE RENAULT NEEDED MAINTENANCE, it was sufficient to get Natalie and Andrew to his childhood home. He waited in the car until Natalie came back with permission to view the main floor and the basement. The disabled owner had had an elevator installed in the alcove of the concave stone staircase with a stained-glass window and 19th century wrought iron Napoleon décor railing. She would not allow Andrew access to the upstairs because a boarder was there.

He followed Natalie back into the house where he graciously thanked the elderly lady for granting permission. Wonderful memories of living there with his parents flooded back. He first looked around the main floor, the grand foyer, the spacious living and dining rooms and the kitchen, which had accommodated a small cooking staff in the previous century.

"May I see the basement?" he asked.

"Certainly," she replied. He did not have to pretend to be grateful. His smile said it all.

He recalled as a child the feeling of the exposed electrical wires secured to the stone wall with wooden pegs pounded into holes in the deteriorating mortar, and of carefully turning on the old porcelain light switch. On occasion, he would experience a shock if he allowed his small fingers to touch the unprotected terminals.

The elderly lady cautioned him, explaining that she hadn't been down to the basement for decades, certainly not since she had become semi-disabled. Only one ceiling light of low wattage guided him. The wine cellar was virtually dark. He estimated he had approximately two minutes so as not to draw suspicion. Not able to see clearly, he reached above the top shelf of the empty wine rack and felt along, counting until the 14th cobblestone. It was loose but too high and awkward to reach easily. As a child, he had stood on an up-ended wine crate.

He located what appeared to be a similar wine case leaning against the wall. Although rickety, he turned it on its side, stepped up, pulled the cobblestone out, and placed it on the top shelf of the wine rack. He reached for the tin box. As he pulled it out, the crate began collapsing under his weight. He grabbed the wine rack for support but it started to topple. Letting go of the box, he barely managed to arrest the rack's momentum with both hands. The tin box fell between the wall and the wine rack as did the cobblestone, with a loud thud. Quickly squatting down, he reached in gingerly, removed the box's lid and withdrew the document.

"Is everything all right?" the elderly lady called out.

"Yes!" he replied, as he reached out for the hand rail to guide himself as he climbed up the winding stone stairs and out of the basement. At the top of the staircase, he reached to the left as he had done many times all those years ago and turned out the light by rotating the old porcelain light switch.

"Thank you," he replied as he again shook her feeble hand in gratitude. He smiled graciously as did Natalie who had kept the elderly lady distracted in his brief absence.

"Did you get it? I heard a noise," Natalie enquired quietly as they hastily walked toward the Renault.

"Yes," he replied. "It's tucked under my sweater. Good thing she is disabled and can't navigate the winding stone stairs into the basement to retrieve her evening bottle from the once replete racks of wine. Now the racks hold mostly dust accumulated over the decades. It is unfortunate for her," he commiserated, "but a blessing in disguise for us."

CHAPTER 8

"Andrew, I contacted *mon père*, Gaston," Monique explained, "and mentioned that he may remember your father from around 1960 when your family lived next door to us. I told him that your father had been a military attaché at the Canadian embassy. My father said he would like to meet you very much. I sent a text to Philippe and asked him to take you to our parents' home in the 1re arrondissement, within walking distance of Novotel Paris les Halles. I explained that due to the circumstances surrounding Claude's recent arrest and ongoing threats, I should remain in hiding here in your new gated urban estate. Everyone understood. Philippe agreed to make the introduction this evening if that is agreeable."

Andrew held her gaze, reflecting on the serendipitous circumstances that had brought them together in 1960 when they lived beside each other in Saint-Germain-des-Prés and now again with the lottery windfall that had them living under the same roof as tenant and landlord, although no rent changed hands. "I would be pleased to meet your father. But please do not go out of your way."

"I have a hidden motive," she winked. "I also asked Philippe to retrieve my copy of the document which I had stowed away in the bookshelf in my old bedroom. Although he was not with us when we found the document, he recalls trying to decipher it with us. He said he had always been intrigued. Now that you have found your copy, he is keen to review them both once again with the aid of the knowledge and skills he acquired at university when studying linguistics."

⊰ ⊱

"Papa, I would like to introduce you to Andrew Dupont," Philippe said as he hugged his father warmly.

"You look very much like your father when we first met," Gaston said as he shook Andrew's hand that merged into an equally sincere embrace. His heartfelt welcome left Andrew with the impression that he had been received by an Old Testament prophet. Gaston then spoke of Andrew's father with genuine fondness as one would a dear friend of many years.

"You seem to know my father well," Andrew said inquisitively, thinking that they had only met once in 1960.

"Did your father tell you about our relationship?" The question seemed to be baited. Andrew suspected that his lack of a comprehensive understanding of French culture might be at the core of his doubt.

"Nothing specific. When I asked him, he would only say there are some things you do not talk about. He only faintly alluded to the war. I learned about most of his exploits from my mother. Not much other than he flew a Mosquito aircraft with the RAF and was shot down over France somewhere a few weeks before D-Day. The *Maquis* smuggled him back to England in time to fly his beloved Mosquito over Normandy on D-Day."

"You are correct." Gaston gazed at Andrew at length before continuing. "What I tell you now I do so with a serious caveat. You are not to discuss what I am about to reveal outside this house. Do you understand, completely? It is not based on concocted conspiracies about *Maquis* exploits which run rampant at times like a lethal gossip mill. As a result, it leads to the death of too many honourable people who do not know why they are targeted. Instead, it is grounded in verified fact passed from one trusted *Maquis* member to another."

Gaston seemed to look far away for reasons Andrew did not understand. Nonetheless, he nodded, acknowledging the solemnness of the warning and the need for absolute secrecy because there are some things you do not talk about.

"Your father and I met during the war in the late spring of 1944. I was working with the French Resistance, the *Maquis,* in Caudebec en-Caux. Your father's plane had been shot down west of Rouen. I was younger than he was, just a lad who helped him and other downed Allied airmen to escape. I accompanied him to Honfleur on a barge where the local *Maquis* hid him in a safe house in the village on the Normandy coast. Ironically, it was in the warden's house adjacent to the old jail until he could be smuggled back to England on a fishing boat." A reed-thin smile filled Gaston's weathered face. "Even today, I chuckle at the audacity of our strategy, hiding him and other Allied airmen under the noses of the Nazis, so close they would have been able to smell them had it not been for the fishing nets and rotting bait hanging out to dry in the yard."

Andrew's expression mirrored Gaston's amused smile. "I recall one of my father's favourite expressions, *de l'audace, encore de l'audace, et toujour de l'audace* –audacity, more audacity and always audacity. My father explained to me that a teenage boy who helped him to escape had repeated this phrase many times. That must have been you."

Gaston replied, "*C'est vrai, c'était moi* – it is true, that was me."

"When your father returned to Paris in 1960 as a Canadian military attaché, we were living in the house that Monique mentioned. He had not changed. He was as elegant and charismatic as ever with the same prodigious memory. We drank some excellent cognac together and talked about his harrowing escape and the brief time we spent together. The war years were a time when youth and innocence unavoidably collided with suspicion and betrayal in the murky subterranean world of security and intelligence. After the war, we both continued to work in the tradecraft of espionage, I for France and he for Canada. We pursued the early years of the Cold War with the same tenacity and precision. I found it interesting, astounding, that the Canadian government did not have legislation for Canadians to spy outside Canada. Canadian military attachés could, but not officially. Very strange."

Gaston grew quiet again. His posture was neutral, although his call for caution was clear. "I repeat, young Andrew, do not discuss these details outside this house because the war is not over even after all these years. For some, it will never be over. There are tangential events that occurred on D-Day and in the final weeks and months of the war that affected the lives of many *Maquis* members a few of whom are still alive, in addition to their close friends and relatives, like my Monique and Philippe. Because of your recent association with them, you must be conscious of these relationships."

Andrew said nothing but merely nodded while noting Gaston's stern yet friendly stare.

Gaston continued, "Some people died by means other than Nazi bullets on the battlefield with comrades in arms or against a wall with colleagues in the resistance. I cannot tell you more because I do not know more. Be very wary of these and other people who support different political persuasions and ideologies and are them-selves sworn to secrecy by their superiors. Meet with Monique and Philippe only in strict confidence and then only in their offi-cial business capacity. Away from Novotel Paris Les Halles and Monique's new law firm, be very vigilant."

As Gaston and Andrew continued to talk, Philippe confirmed with Monique that he had located her document. "I have scanned the pages and conclude that some are written in what appears to be Russian Cyrillic script while other entries appear to be Old German text. Still other entries are written in open French text. They men-tion names of some former high-ranking French bureaucrats which I am aware of. A few are dead, others are still alive but retired. Some additional names I do not recognize. The connotations are ominous, something related to a conspiracy. We need to talk as soon as possible. As Papa has told us on many occasions, we need to be very careful who we share information with because the war is not over."

As a parting gesture, Andrew inclined his head in a salute of respect for reasons he was not fully aware of but knew deep down were appropriate, as one would do in the presence of a knight.

As they left Gaston's home, Philippe elaborated on what his father had shared. "My mother, Angelique, lived in Honfleur. Mon papa, Gaston, was from Caudebec en-Caux. When war broke out, he worked on the barges that delivered goods to Le Havre mostly but also Honfleur and brought canned fish and other marine produce back. Downed Allied airmen were hidden in a false hull constructed in the bow below the waterline. That is how your father was smuggled to the channel coast. It was a torturous journey for the stowaways due to the cramped quarters and numbing cold, in addition to being fraught with the constant danger of spies and Nazi informants. If discovered by the Gestapo, all the barge crew and Allied airmen would have been unceremoniously executed on the spot and their bodies thrown overboard. Increasingly, some of the marine members of the *Maquis* were being captured. There was a leak within the *Maquis*. Mon papa explained that there was one SS Gestapo major who was particularly vindictive. He took great pleasure in first torturing and then shooting all prisoners personally."

Philippe continued after a pause. "Ma mama was barely in her teenage years. She had also worked for the *Maquis* carrying messages and taking care of logistics as it was less suspicious for young girls and older women to be seen out on the streets with shopping baskets than men. Angelique had been captured by the Gestapo on 5 June 1944. Her torture began that evening. In the confusion of the D-Day invasion on the morning of 6 June, Papa and members of the *Maquis* rescued her and other Nazi Gestapo prisoners as they were being transported by truck to the regional headquarters."

Andrew's stare grew more intense as Philippe provided more detail than his father had divulged. It put into context Gaston's warning not to speak to anyone because the war was not over for those who had survived the days, weeks and months following D-Day. Andrew could only imagine what Gaston had alluded to.

Philippe continued to provide additional details less from his father and more from his own efforts to fill in the blanks. "The Carlingue, the French Gestapo, was composed of sociopathic criminals and corrupt police officials in German-occupied France, including the Vichy district. The French Carlingue had been formed as a counterinsurgency organization against the *Maquis*. Later on D-Day, this SS Gestapo major who had tortured ma mama was found floating in the Seine, in addition to other vicious Nazis under his command. The traitor who had infiltrated and betrayed the local *Maquis* cell was also found floating face down in the Seine. After her rescue, Mama identified this collaborator. There was a second collaborator who had escaped capture. Papa did not mention this to you but you need to know these details because, after all these years, there are those who continue to seek reprisal for what they perceived had been D-Day revenge killings. Mama and Papa had been and continue to be targets of former members of the French Carlingue Gestapo group that operated out of Normandy, for their part in the deadly Honfleur reprisals against the Nazis. This is what Papa refers to when he says the war is not over."

Andrew acknowledged Philippe's explanation of the D-Day events with a nod.

Philippe expounded on one final connecting detail. "It is important that you understand that ma mama met mon papa in Honfleur. He always volunteered for missions with the *Maquis* that would take him to Honfleur and to see her. Theirs has always been a relationship based on absolute love and devotion that grew out of those perilous *Maquis* missions."

"How did he manage that?" Andrew enquired. Again, he reflected on the unforeseen meetings with Monique when they lived beside each other and again when Philippe introduced them at Novotel Paris Les Halles. It almost seemed that destiny was playing a role in their renewed relationship.

"Where circumstances permitted, which was not always possible, mon papa timed his trips to Honfleur on the barge with the outgoing tide and his return to Caudebec en-Caux twelve hours later with the incoming tide. That schedule would maximize their infrequent and brief *rendezvous amoureuse* – romantic liaisons."

"After her rescue, mon papa considered taking her back to Caudebec to hide her from her captors and betrayers. He was forced to abandon this plan because the confusion of the D-Day invasion caused the Nazis to set up multiple road blocks. Perhaps more pressing, the captain of his river barge decreed that it would be too dangerous to go back up river for fear that Allied Mosquitos and Spitfires might mistake them for Nazi transport and attack with guns blazing. Instead, Gaston hid her in the same safehouse in Honfleur in which he had hidden the downed air crew pending their transport back to England on the fishing boats. It is for this reason this eleventh century seaport on the southern bank of the Seine estuary became sacred ground to them as the beaches of Normandy became for Allied troops on the morning of 6 June 1944."

CHAPTER 9

Andrew read a text message from Natalie with mixed emotions. "In response to your request for a copy of the surveyor's blueprint for your recently purchased house and property, the sellers' lawyers advised that neither of their respective clients reported ever having seen such a document, although Estella thought she might have. But she could not recall where."

"Recommendations?" Andrew requested. His intuition suggested that what seemed to be a simple request was looking as though it would be a difficult task for some reason.

"Our best option would be to search the Land Registry and City Planning Department for any records. Note that Paris probably would not have had such government organizations in 1815 when the house was built. Emperor Napoléon III commissioned Georges-Eugène Haussmann, a visionary urban planner, to complete a vast public works program in the mid-1850s by widening the main boulevards, planting trees and creating great public parks in an effort to rid Paris of the sprawling medieval slums. Many houses were destroyed in the process. It is possible that all original records would have been destroyed – if they existed in the first place."

"Can we hire a surveyor to research and, if no official records can be located, can the surveyor undertake an examination of what information might be available and complete a summary report? Thereafter, can this surveyor prepare an up-to-date blueprint of the house, all outer buildings including the double garage and garden shed, and the perimeter walls?" Andrew asked.

"Certainly. Will do," Natalie responded. "We have a surveyor on contract with our real estate firm. With the large number of buildings constructed before the city had an urban planning department and started keeping permanent records, such a request would not be out of the norm. After the Hausmann reconstruction more accurate records were kept of houses, commercial buildings and secondary structures. Many of these historical records noted pre-nineteenth century construction without names of the builders, addresses or original owners. Such legitimate provenance increases value today," Natalie replied. "It will be expensive, though."

After she sent her reply, she had a second thought. Price would not be a factor.

CHAPTER 10

Andrew, Monique and Philippe reviewed their rediscovered document several times. Only the names in French seemed obvious because, for whatever reason, they did not appear to have been coded. Monique and Philippe had a working knowledge of Old German grammar taught in school. The Russian Cyrillic script remained a mystery though.

Each subsequent review exposed sharper translations. It became apparent that they were dealing with a conspiracy to influence the 1946 election in France which had been called by the provisional French government led by General Charles de Gaulle. Its mandate had been to create a constitution for the post-war Fourth French Republic.

It was clear that a considerable number of the authors of their discovered document were proponents of the French Communist Party with tentacles reaching back to post-World War I and the leaders of the 1917 Russian Revolution. The creation of the first French Communist Party in 1920 was a consequence. There would be nothing democratic about the French Communist Party manifesto that this rediscovered document proposed. It outlined a strategy for the assassination of General Charles de Gaulle as the first temporary leader of the postwar provisional French government or any another non-communist leader.

Equally evident was the strategy to appoint communist-leaning bureaucrats to influence elected officials in the first postwar French National Assembly and subsequent administrations. In the decades following the war, those retired from these formal government positions were to be appointed as board members of quasi-public and lucratively contracted private sector communist-leaning organizations. All would exert a backroom influence in ongoing public policy decisions. A few of these bureaucrats were implicated in political scandals linked to corrupt key officials in the Fourth and subsequent Fifth French Republics. The quickly organized French Communist Party was not without its foibles, just like any other party. The major difference was its primary source of funding which came from Moscow through indirect channels. This lucrative link remained intact.

"We need to involve Natalie," Monique suggested. "When she was with the Police nationale, she had worked with some interesting people, doing interesting things in interesting places. I don't know exactly what she did. She never discussed the details with me. I am aware that she can read and speak Russian. How fluently, I am not certain."

"We also need to speak with Papa," Philippe suggested. He had worked with the French counter-intelligence in some capacity after the war. It was another of those unspoken activities related to his time with the *Maquis* during and after the war that remained a mystery to this day.

First on their agenda was a meeting with their father. His response was cautious but that was nothing new in their household. As a child raised in your father's house you were grateful for any information he shared and did not ask for clarification. It was just understood that if you needed to know, Papa would tell you. More importantly, anything mentioned in the confines of the house was not to be shared with anyone outside the house. Papa was to be informed immediately if anyone outside the family made enquiries, with the emphasis on *immediately*.

"Your lives will not necessarily be richer as a result of being in possession of this document, my children," Gaston began. "Instead, there is a greater probability that they will be more stressful and could even be shorter." Gaston stared at each of his children and

Andrew. Philippe and Monique looked down, an obedient learned response.

Gaston paused to accentuate the seriousness of what was to follow. "Now is as good a time as ever to explain that your mother and I have been playing a deadly game of geopolitical cat and mouse with some of these communists, former Gestapo agents and the most zealous Wehrmacht Nazis who remained in France after the war formally ended. Our lives and, as our children, your lives, remain linked to our service with the *Maquis*. This all goes back to events related to *Maquis* activities just prior to and on D-Day in and around Honfleur, notably the killing of the SS Gestapo major who captured and tortured your mother on the 5th of June 1944."

Gaston's demeanour became stone cold. Philippe and Monique had witnessed this transformation several times over the years after he returned from surreptitious meetings with people they had never formally met nor ever wanted to cross paths with. More troubling to them was the transformation of this otherwise warm loving man to a distant figure they did not recognize. The torture of Angelique was the trigger.

"Let me clarify that all communists during the war were not Red Russians. There were many foreign immigrants who held communist beliefs. They fought against the Nazis alongside the French resistance fighters or as members of their own resistance organizations. Just as there were those branded as traitorous French *Maquis* collaborators, there were communists who spied for the Nazis. These communists tended not to be harassed as a group by the Nazis until after Nazi Germany invaded Russia – Operation Barbarossa in June 1941. Thereafter, they were rounded up and either executed on the spot or shipped off to concentration camps. When I say the war is not over, I mean just that."

Monique and Philippe were quiet. They had learned not to

challenge their father following such curt accounts. They remained silent with heads bowed in compliance. Andrew merely observed.

"The war continues to this day as evident with the identification of those who authored the document you unearthed with the revelation of the names and the influence they have wielded. As your parents, our greatest fear has always been that you would become targets. Perhaps it was inevitable. Monique, you need to contact your friend, Natalie. She knows people who can help you, protect you, if anyone can."

At that succinct directive, Monique raised her head and stared at her father in wary bewilderment. Her expression communicated the discussion she had never had with him. She suspected her acquaintance with Natalie was more than a casual acknowledgement of childhood neighbours and friends that seemed to grow over the years.

Gaston transferred his sombre gaze to Andrew. "You are your father's son. You may have thought you could retire here in the City of Light and live the life of a *flâneur*, a leisurely but also passionate connoisseur of the Parisian culture enabled by your newly acquired wealth. Alas, your reconnection with Monique and Philippe, old friends from a more innocent youthful time, is more than historical. Your mutual rediscovery of this document has caused your compass bearing to turn to a new magnetic north set in play by forces linked to the 1917 Russian Revolution, the 1933 German election of Adolf Hitler, and your father's service with the RAF in World War II and thereafter."

CHAPTER 11

Natalie's cellphone danced across the desk in her real estate office. The message from Monique was succinct. "Papa sends his compliments." Her reply was equally terse but abundantly clear, "Home of the Renault."

"*Oui*," was the reply. "On my way."

With paraphrasing by Monique and Philippe of the Old German text and Natalie's patchy translation of the Russian Cyrillic script, it became apparent that the content of the communiqué in the document required the confidential services of additional colleagues.

"I have friends," she said. Natalie mentioned her two old childhood friends and the acquaintance of her new real estate client. She pressed a code for speed dial. While she waited for a reply, she met Monique's stare. "I return your Papa's compliment. He is wise in his autumn years." She then tapped in a confirmation code to the incoming reply. The first word read: "couple," followed by an alphanumeric sequence. That was followed by the address of her current location. Her coded means of communication was as secure as any. The location of the furtive rendezvous with all the CCTV surveillance cameras, motion detectors and electronically locked gates would provide the requisite security. The final word was: "uncouple," followed by a second alphanumeric sequence. "My friends will be here within the half hour," she informed those assembled.

She transferred her gaze to Andrew. "On a related matter, Andrew, the surveyor you asked me to hire has discovered a document in the city archives and another in the National Library that mentions your property. It is not a formal surveyor's blueprint but it does provide some credible provenance. The original owner in 1815 was a confidant of Napoléon Bonaparte. He couriered messages for the self-appointed ruler within and beyond the borders of the fledging French Empire born out of the 1789 revolution and the storming of the Bastille. There is some indication of an undisclosed secret door. This evidence is tentative and, as such, difficult to confirm. The surveyor has not yet been able to find any survey maps to validate this information. Whatever the secret entranceway was may have been built over or filled in by now. It echoes the plot of *The Tale of Two Cities* by Charles Dickens and the romantic exploits of the daring protagonists brought to life by the quill of Alexandre Dumas. Our surveyor will get back to me as his research continues."

Monique grunted in acknowledgement. "Intriguing, given our initial translation of the document in the context of our family connection to the *Maquis* and its struggles against the traitors of the French Carlingue Gestapo and Nazi Gestapo. More bothersome is the communist conspiracies to interfere in the first postwar French election and geopolitics."

Philippe interjected, "It is ironic that democracy as a political philosophy allows communism to flourish with a published manifesto to disrupt everything that granted it unfettered freedom to function."

"To disrupt, yes, but not necessarily unabated," Natalie retorted. "Your parents have stalwartly stood guard on the ramparts day and night since the end of the war. As your papa reminds us, the war is not over. Others have taken up the standard against the ever-continuing onslaught of the 21st century Communist Russians and Nazi Germans with deep roots reaching back to the amalgamation of the Kievan Rus' and Teutonic Hun tribes. Both had been engaged in the business of war for centuries. You do not change that narrative overnight or at all." She lingered for a moment before summarising, "The Gallic culture remains superior to both."

"We should talk," Andrew quietly proposed to Natalie as he gazed at her over the rim of his crystal wine glass.

"With regard to…" her voice trailed off. The search for background information was becoming increasingly opaque for reasons unknown. Provenance addressed some questions but raised others. Yet without provenance, its pedigree would remain unknown.

"We should talk about a co-beneficiary of my new affluence, and property with its roots reaching back to the original owner and his clandestine connection to Napoléon Bonaparte. Rue Bonaparte is just around the corner from my urban estate. A coincidence by chance, in addition to Les Deux Magots where we first met, and a waiter who, I sense, has his own connections and influential associates?"

"Astute observation," Natalie replied with a subtle smile. "Yes, we should talk."

CHAPTER 12

Andrew scrutinized the approach of a vehicle on the CCTV monitor. It stopped at the gate. A male passenger got out and pressed the call button on the wall by the outer gate.

"Daan Segers to see Natalie Corban. I am accompanied by doctors Alexandra Belliveau and Paul Bernard," he announced in an authoritative yet friendly tone. A short silence followed.

"Please drive in," a careful voice replied. The surveillance cameras continued to monitor the vehicle and its three occupants as the gates swung open and closed immediately once the vehicle had entered the compound. Other cameras monitored the three as they left the vehicle and walked along the cobblestone path to the front door which opened as they stopped at the 18th century front door. It was similar to what one would expect to see at the entrance to any of the Versailles estate buildings.

Langue was the first to greet the guests to his new home. He stood motionless, ears erect. He whined briefly, a prelude to his cautious welcoming gesture. Then he stepped forward wagging his tail and sniffed each person before licking their hands.

Natalie extended her hand in a warm professional greeting to all three. "Daan, always good to see you. Alexandra and Paul, it has been a while, too long. May I introduce you to Andrew Dupont, the new owner of this property."

"With an impressive CCTV and motion detector security system," Daan commented more as a compliment than a criticism, as he angled his head ever so politely and extended his hand.

Andrew reciprocated with a firm handshake and an amused smile. His initial impression of Daan was that of a Swiss banker, professional and thorough. Andrew concluded he would be easy company without any need for awkward banter. "The security system was installed by the previous owners. I am not sure what prompted them to invest in such an advanced multi-layered security configuration," he added.

Daan blinked in acknowledgement. The less said at this juncture the better.

"We can talk about that later if need be. But for now, let us adjourn to the dining room where we can examine the document in detail." Natalie directed the agenda.

As they entered, she introduced them to Monique and Philippe as the children of Gaston and Angelique Abreo.

"I know your parents professionally and personally," Daan acknowledged. "I am impressed by their history with the *Maquis* and their courage in battling against the French Carlingue and Nazi Gestapos, in addition to the Wehrmacht, during the war. It was even more impressive given the fact they were just young teenagers."

Natalie explained, "Andrew, Daan is the head of the European Union Intelligence Unit whose mission is to gather intelligence to protect the European Union from internal threats. The jurisdiction of the EUI Unit is solely within the borders of the European Union. There are affiliate organizations beyond the borders who work with us. Alexandra and Paul are two of the most experienced EUI Unit agents and they are married."

Andrew nodded in acknowledgement, as did Monique and Philippe.

"I sense that I have known you a long time, Daan, although we have never been formally introduced," Monique said. "My father would explain his absences as business meetings with colleagues like you. I would never probe for details and he would never expand beyond describing them as corporate associates."

"A bit of a background first," Natalie continued as they sat around the table. "Andrew lived with his parents here in Saint-Germain-des-Prés around 1960. His father was a military attaché with the Canadian Embassy. Quite by chance, they lived next door to Gaston and Angelique. Monique and Philippe were childhood friends of Andrew. Andrew and Monique found the document I'm about to show you. Not understanding the significance of the content, they divided it up, each retaining half. Upon returning to Paris and serendipitously reuniting all these years later, they located their respective copies and, with a more mature eye, they realized their importance. They discussed the content with Gaston who immediately referred them to me and I to you, Daan."

With their collective translation skills and background knowledge, Daan, Alexandra and Paul reviewed the content of the papers that lay before them. A silence consumed Daan. It was all there, who was involved, who wasn't or perhaps purposely who was not mentioned. The planned details. The contingency plans to be followed explicitly. That was the Stalin signature, obey without question or else. Such was the landscape of paranoia.

Daan broke the silence. "We were aware of the communist conspiracy dating back to the final months of the war but we never knew who was involved. We had heard rumours that such a document existed and are surprised it has survived after all this time. France may have been the initial target of Moscow's aggressive Cold War incursions but many others followed as the Allies liberated Nazi-held nation states that redefined pre-1939 borders. The bi-polar prism of the Cold War distorted all subsequent perspectives of conflict. To say the least, its existence will re-write the history of global intelligence and redirect current and future geopolitics. Alexandra and Paul, your thoughts?" Daan invited.

Alexandra gazed upward in deep concentration, pursing her lips and frowning. "First, we need to digest the full spectrum of the implications and their impact on current East-West relations. Second, we need to develop a strategic plan. In doing so, we must decide who should be on the distribution list and the consequences of *not* sharing the content of this document with those we exclude."

Paul nodded at Alexandra and at those gathered around the table who were not members or affiliates of the European Union Intelligence Unit. "One of my primary concerns at this juncture is the safety and security of Monique and Philippe as children of *Maquis* parents who remained unharmed for reasons we are unaware of, given the vindictive actions of their parents' enemies. It is imperative that we keep their identity, involvement and knowledge of the contents an absolute secret. Andrew has only tangential affiliation as the child of a former Canadian military attaché. His connection with Monique and Philippe raises his profile. In the City of Light, there are just too many people with eyes and ears on too many competing payrolls."

"I agree with both your observations," Daan concluded. "Being children of Gaston and Angelique, there are far-reaching implications. As Gaston has astutely noted, World War II is not over. The Cold War is still in its relatively early stages and may erupt like Mount Etna if we are not strategic in our actions."

"Not to pour fuel on a volatile situation," Natalie added, "there is another variable that we need to be aware of. Monique is in the throes of a nasty divorce from Claude Laurent who is on the Police nationale terrorist watch list. He is suspected of being in possession of illegally obtained firearms in addition to other prohibited contraband. And, worryingly, he has demonstrated symptoms of mental instability. He poses a threat to Monique and all others associated with her, including Andrew."

"Good to know," Daan replied. "Keep me informed. We have resources we can deploy to intervene if circumstances warrant that level of response in order to maintain security at the highest levels."

"I approve of appropriate pest-control measures," Natalie mused.

"Due to the international implications of the intelligence in this document, I will need to consult with my superior, Yolina Lambert, at the European Union Headquarters in Brussels," Daan advised. "For your information, Yolina helped create the European Union Intelligence Unit shortly after the EU was created in 1993. She approves funding, authority and direction for all our missions. Releasing intelligence such as the contents of this document to all members of the EU, especially those who were former members of the Soviet Union, would have dire consequences. In addition, there are other dubious associates who sympathise with Moscow. Such relationships have precedent in some cases we have been involved in. Still others, like supposed NATO Allies, continue to operate on both sides of the Cold War fence."

"Regarding Andrew's identity," Natalie elaborated, "I am confident that no one beyond those assembled here are aware of his involvement, with the exception of reception staff at Novotel Paris Les Halles."

Philippe interjected promptly. "I personally interviewed all employees who have access to guest information and conduct ongoing security assessments regularly. This is necessary because there are a few guests whose identities must be protected. The reputation of the hotel depends upon it. As a result, I can speak for the integrity of these members of my staff. Andrew is in the hotel database with his former wife, but as a tourist only."

"Perhaps to our advantage," Natalie added, "he is free to stroll the tree-lined boulevards of Paris unrecognized except as a *flâneur* or other rich retiree. His only concern is being a recent lottery winner. Any suspicious individuals will not know his name if he uses cash for all minor purchases such as beverages at cafés and meals at local restaurants. Accordingly, his credentials cannot be searched easily on a foreign database."

Daan nodded slowly in approval. This would be one less priority to have to consider in this high-priority file. Natalie could be his handler and trainer.

"I will get back to you with directions from Yolina," Daan confirmed as he gazed at Andrew. "In the interim, maintain a low profile."

CHAPTER 13

A ndrew rose to scrutinize the perimeter of his estate on the CCTV monitors before his quests departed. Langue lifted his head, ears erect. He escorted the guests as they approached the front door.

Sensing no reason for alarm, Andrew opened the gates. For a short while after Daan and his colleagues from the European Union Intelligence Unit had left, he continued to monitor the street activity. Philippe and Natalie departed shortly thereafter, all also under Langue's vigilant scrutiny. With ears erect, he then returned to his post on the Persian rug near the front entrance while keeping a watchful eye on his recently adopted master.

"Good boy," Andrew spoke warmly as he leaned down and patted Langue's head. The Police nationale dog trainer may have awarded him a failing grade on aggression but Andrew had no doubt he had received first-class grades in physical security classes.

"The two of you appear to have bonded," Monique commented, perhaps with a tinge of envy in her voice.

"It seems so," Andrew replied, "and I welcome his companionship. Cameras and other surveillance systems provide a sense of security, but this alert fellow is second to none as his intuition kicks in far sooner and remains active much longer."

With Langue by his side and Monique as his boarder, Andrew was becoming less worried about being stalked by felons after his lottery coup.

"A glass of Pinot Noir?" Andrew offered with an amiable smile.

"*Mais oui*," Monique replied. Before Andrew had become the owner the house seemed lonely. It was large by Parisian standards. She felt she rattled around from room to room and floor to floor. *Good physical exercise*, she supposed. The growing loneliness gnawed at her mental state, though. Andrew's substantial presence helped to alleviate that feeling of cabin fever.

He poured two glasses and returned to the living room. Monique held his gaze as he passed one to her.

"Thoughts? What's on your mind?" he enquired. He too was seeking company and stimulating conversation.

"May I tell you something personal?" Monique asked.

"Yes, of course." He sat back looking forward to undisturbed time to engage in conversations that had been interrupted the evening he had cashed in his lottery ticket, and Claude had assaulted her near the Au Pied de Cochon restaurant. They had approximately thirty-five years of history to catch up on.

Monique hesitated for a few moments while she composed her question. "When you arrived in Paris, in Saint-Germain-des-Prés with your family, I was really happy. You were the first serious boyfriend I'd ever had. Eventually, you were the first boy I had ever kissed." A rosy blush grew on her cheeks. "One kiss and I was smitten. That was the evening before you moved back to Canada. I thought it was very romantic but I was so sad that you were leaving. For personal reasons, there were few people I called close back then. I have a few more now but still fewer than most of my friends. Today, they can be counted on the fingers of one hand. You would be first on the short list."

Andrew maintained eye contact with her as he sipped his wine. He said nothing but savoured the moment.

Monique continued, "I tried to contact you after you left Paris but for some reason, I couldn't. I was not obsessed with finding you but I just wanted to become pen pals and explore a long-distance relationship. I contacted other Canadian friends who had lived in Paris after they returned to Canada, but still could not locate you. I did find out that it had something to do with what your father and his associates did. I asked Papa for help. He said he was unable to find out where your father had been transferred. I remained curious for a long time. It wasn't until I graduated from the Sorbonne that I realized Papa rarely responded to my questions with the whole truth. If he attempted to do so, it was always wanting in detail. I accepted the fact that was just who he was."

Andrew remained silent for several moments. "If it is any consolation, I wrote you a letter but never posted it. I don't know why I didn't," he replied to her endearing admission of young infatuation. "That is not to say I forgot about you. Quite the opposite. I thought about you a great deal. Your voice was constantly in my memory yet far away. For whatever reason, I had several girlfriends thereafter, each short term, always comparing each one to you. In retrospect, there seemed to be safety in numbers. As a military family, we moved frequently. I learned to engage in conversations but nothing in depth. As a result, I made acquaintances easily. I enjoyed a multitude of experiences, none I would describe as tedious. Like you, I had few good friends, though, most vaguely familiar." He failed to mention that serious liaisons were a novelty. His first and only puppy love with Monique had set the bar high.

Monique gazed at him as she inclined her head. Nothing could better express her feelings of what might have been but was impossible due to circumstances beyond their control.

Andrew took a long time to reply. "The first time I watched the 1942 black and white film "Casablanca" with my mother, I vividly remember the parting scene at the airport in the fog. Humphrey Bogart said to Ingrid Bergman, 'We will always have Paris.'" He hesitated again as a warm smile filled his face. "Each time I watched that film, and that was often, I thought of you. If our paths were never to cross again, we would always have Paris. When Philippe introduced us and I recognized you both, I was elated." He tipped his wine glass to her. "*À nôtre relation qui mûrit, ma chère amie… ma chère Monique* – to our maturing relationship, my dear friend… my dear Monique."

She returned his gesture by touching her glass to his. "I too was overjoyed." She lingered in thought. *"Do I kiss him again, now? What would he think? How would he respond? Perhaps I should just change the mood."*

He thought, *"Do I kiss her again? What would she think? How would she respond? Perhaps I should change the mood."* He chose the latter. "So, tell me about your life after we were separated."

"After I graduated from high school, I attended la Sorbonne, the Université de Paris and initially graduated with a degree in Tourism and Linguistics, with German. It was useful when I reviewed my copy of the document. It revealed enough to motivate me to find you and read your copy. It was a puzzle that could only be fully deciphered with both copies together." *With both of us together,* she mused.

"I must admit I had forgotten about finding the document," he added. "Your email a few days ago jogged my memory about where I might have hidden it. It also caused me to remember all those times when we were young adventurous teenagers." He lingered on the thought. "They were too brief but wonderful times nonetheless." He paused again as he continued to reflect on those Parisian days and all the moments together decades ago.

She took a deep breath before continuing, "I met Claude at university and married him after I graduated. You know how that ended. He was an abusive bully and remained a tyrant throughout our relationship. He was spiteful in petty matters and cowardly in important ones. He rejoiced in his victim's shame – a *bête noire,* a pet peeve of his. The threads of suspicion in his Saint-Denis associations – crime, corruption and cover-up, were thinly veiled and soon became exposed. He seemed to be at the hub of the wheel from which despicable spokes radiated. As time passed, I learned to survive his cruelty by retreating into myself. I readily admit in retrospect that I was a fool and foolishness had its price."

Andrew replenished their glasses. It seemed to fill the awkward moment that both experienced.

Monique continued after a sip. Her smile returned as did her gleeful chuckle. "I admit that I was also motivated to kiss you again. I really had been smitten. It was more than infatuation, more like a puppy love, *un coup de foudre* – love at first sight."

Her admission triggered an unexpected heartfelt smile, a youthful *joie de vivre* he had forgotten about, misplaced by recollections of events in the intervening years. "We should talk more about those times," he replied while maintaining eye contact.

He tipped his wine glass to her again. "*À toi.*"

She reciprocated again. "*À toi.*"

He slowly leaned forward and gently kissed her as he had done all those years ago. The awkwardness of the moment merged into relaxed banter and jubilant laughter between two friends, older now, lamenting the moments lost while contemplating memories yet to be fused and displayed on the monitor of the mind.

His focus drifted to thoughts of previous trips to Paris he had taken with his wife, Lynette. His thoughts pirouetted in such fond recollections.

He chuckled to himself as a fleeting image entered his mind and departed just as quickly like a shooting star crossing the clear night sky. He wondered whether Monique had ever considered becoming a female *flâneur*, a *flâneuse*, an elegantly dressed chic lady of leisure, a connoisseur of Parisian culture, either as a solitary urban observer or in the company of himself as the *flâneur*, an exquisitely attired gentleman wanderer with the time and money. Probably that might not be an easy role for Monique, he reconsidered, given her unhappy relationship with Claude fraught with repeated incidents of domestic violence that left her with what she concluded was her only option, mere survival. Had she shared her ordeal with her best friend, Natalie, or perhaps with her family, Philippe, Gaston, or with Angelique?

He slowly leaned forward and gently kissed her again as he had done only moments before.

CHAPTER 14

At Andrew's request, Natalie met at Les Deux Magots. They were again greeted by the server who almost imperceptibly exchanged a nod with Natalie. On this occasion, she guided Andrew to the same corner table with a nuanced directing touch on his shoulder, a signal to their server that Andrew was a trusted confidant. She scooped innocuous real estate papers from her satchel and placed them in full view on the table for the benefit of anyone who might be interested in why they were meeting. At the end of the meeting she would express an open smile to signal the supposed successful conclusion of the business-related rendezvous, again for the benefit of any curious onlookers.

"*Thé vert,*" the server said quietly accompanied by a standard gesture he used when greeting all guests to this acclaimed café restaurant. The level of reception and service confirmed his acknowledgement of Natalie's tactile blessing similar to a priest's benedictum, or endorsement of a sorcerer for their apprentice. Both Natalie and the server were professionally schooled in the art of such covert communication.

Natalie opened the meeting with what had become a standard exchange of information provided to her by the surveyor of Andrew's new property. On this occasion, there was an element of tacit intelligence related to the spying activities of the original occupant on behalf of Emperor Napoléon Bonaparte. The common denominator was Andrew's house. The courtyard enclosed by the high stucco walls was now taking on the trappings of a Bastille-like bastion sheltering the secrets of the citadel within.

The carefree life of a *flâneur* that Andrew had fleetingly envisioned was being transformed into a dual-purpose *raison d'être*. The first persona would be the ambivalent figure of a recent retiree who would wander the tree-lined boulevards and parks with no perceived purpose apart from observing the Parisian culture he had grown to cherish. The second persona would be the part-time gatherer and recorder of that which he observed, what Beaudelaire called a "botanist of the sidewalk." Today would be the first lesson as a trainee gatherer of information and intelligence in the footsteps of his father, intrinsically linked to the Abreo family. He could more easily take on the trappings of the latter as he emerged from behind the ramparts of his Saint-Germain-des-Prés urban estate. Today, the walls held surveillance cameras in place of guards physically patrolling the imagined parapets.

Natalie lost no time reporting the latest details, increasingly more mysterious than mundane. "As the surveyor delved deeper into the archives related to your property and linked it to adjoined properties, it became apparent there was more than one access point to your courtyard through at least one other secret entrance. Nothing appears on any maps or sketches located in the surveyor's research yet mentions appear in otherwise innocuous papers. As the adjacent properties were sold, these hidden entrance points were covered in layers of stucco and tinted whitewash. If you didn't know the exact location, an inquisitive amateur sleuth would be none the wiser."

With widening eyes Andrew suggested, "Worth snooping around. Any indication where I should begin?"

"There is one reference to the back wall and the north-east corner where a chicken coop and a *dovecote* or *pigeonnier*, a bird house for doves and pigeons, once stood. From my experience, occupants from previous decades and centuries would have kept other small animals such as rabbits in pens next to the chicken coops to supplement their diet in the long winter months."

"I remember seeing a chicken coop and a rabbit hutch in the backyard of the house where I lived with my parents," Andrew noted. "The owner of the house collected the eggs every morning.

He entered the yard through a back gate near the coop. In the late fall, he dug up the ground under the pens and spread it on the garden which became increasingly prolific. Natural fertilizer was better and far less expensive than chemicals."

"You might want to check the ground around the north-east corner of your property. If the grass or weeds growing there seem richer, or the ground seems more trodden down by boots walking to or from the wall, then look more closely. It might point you in the direction of a concealed door in the wall."

Andrew merely nodded as he considered his options. He had ample time to explore now that he was a gentleman of leisure.

"Another note," Natalie suggested. "Fact. During the Nazi occupation of Paris, your house was occupied by a high-ranking member of the Nazi Gestapo. Based on rumour alone, the French Resistance, the *Maquis*, operating in Paris, are purported to have accessed the courtyard through some secret access point. Their purpose was to participate in the ancient craft of spying, to watch and record who came and went, and to covertly listen to conversations among the permanent Nazi occupants and their guests through electronic means."

"That would be consistent with tales of the original owner leaving and returning from missions on behalf of Napoleon Bonaparte through some secret passageway," Andrew responded.

"If it was pure rumour with no physical or recorded evidence, I would not have mentioned this to you. But *Maquis* sources, like Gaston Abreo, suggest otherwise by the mere absence of comments to the contrary. You may wish to follow up." Natalie's inviting gesture and subtle expression suggested further conversation with Gaston might be fruitful in providing provenance such as blueprints or formal documentation pertaining to his property.

"Have you been in contact with Monique recently?" Andrew asked Natalie. He thought she would be his best avenue to her father. "You know her habits best. I am not worried but as her landlord and unofficial guardian, I am mildly concerned about her absence. I've had no email or message, and given her turbulent divorce status it's worrying." Where is the mention that she has gone missing?

"Perhaps slightly more than mildly concerned," Natalie suggested as she raised her eyebrows. A silence filled the space between them. "The two of you appear to have grown closer."

He lingered a moment as he held her candid gaze. What should he say in response, if anything? A subtle, warm smile confirmed Natalie's astute observation.

"I have not, come to mention it. Let me try again." Natalie pursed her lips lightly as Monique's cellphone went to voicemail without a message. She shook her head in response to Andrew's inquisitive stare. "Let me try Philippe's personal phone." His cellphone also went to voicemail without any explanation.

"I'll call Novotel Paris Les Halles and ask for the manager," Andrew muttered in response. He introduced himself as a current guest. It reminded him that he had not yet cancelled his room reservation. The receptionist formally advised him that the hotel manager was not in his office. She offered to leave a message. She then forwarded his call to the assistant manager who also advised that Philippe was not available. His tone was uneasy. He hesitated before stating that Philippe had told him he was not to add any details to enquiries about his whereabouts.

"Did he leave a message for me?" Andrew pressed. He doubted that King Arthur would leave his kingdom without at least reporting some details to his trusted companion, the Mythical Merlin.

"One moment please," the phone went silent as Andrew was put on hold. A brief lull followed before he was reconnected.

"Can you confirm your room number, please?" the assistant manager asked politely in the same cautious tone.

"Yes, 707," Andrew replied promptly.

"Thank you. I can confirm that the hotel manager has left a message for you. I do apologize for the enhanced security, Monsieur Dupont. You are to call the following number..."

Andrew did not have to note the number. He remembered it as the only other number he had called since arriving in Paris. Philippe had given it to him when he returned from his aborted dinner date with Monique at Au Pied de Cochon. It was Natalie's number. Now he *was* worried, very worried, and Natalie could see the change in his complexion and body language. He cancelled his call to Novotel Paris Les Halles and stared at Natalie as he took a series of deep slow breaths.

She met his guarded look with an equally apprehensive expression. "And?" she challenged his blank frown.

Andrew repeated the message given to him by the assistant manager and the wary atmosphere around the release of the communiqué from Philippe.

Without saying a word, Natalie speed dialed from her cellphone. She stared vacantly, eyes searching everywhere yet focusing on nothing in particular. There was no answer. Her call was not forwarded to voicemail. Monique was now missing in action as was Philippe. Gaston appeared to have become *incommunicado* too. There was only one place they could be. She knew of it through personal experience but had not been there for years. Instructions were crystal clear. Only under the direst circumstances was she to go there and then only after she had followed a series of steps to ensure that no one was following her or could ever discover the location.

Her former life was no longer an illusion from her distant past. It had been convenient to summarize that earlier life in the context of working with interesting people, doing interesting things, in interesting places. People could conclude what they wanted from such an implicit non-descriptive response.

CHAPTER 15

Andrew did not recognize Natalie at Les Deux Magots as he settled in for his morning *petit-déjeuner*, this morning with croissant and cappuccino instead of *thé vert*. Her travelling attire suitably disguised her appearance.

Their preferred server placed the cup on the table where Andrew sat and passed along a verbal message in a low voice. "Your usual companion will not be joining you." The server left a small envelope under the saucer, tapping on it to ensure that Andrew was aware of it and, most significantly, its importance.

Andrew's cellphone vibrated with an incoming message. "Enjoy the change in beverage, a deviation from your usual *thé vert*. We will be absent for the next few days. I will be in contact throughout but not by cellphone. The same dog sitter for Langue will be in contact today to take care of him while you are away."

As he shrewdly scanned other patrons in the café, he did not recognize Natalie who he intuitively concluded was close by. He then opened the envelope. Enclosed was a ticket for a Eurail trip from Paris Gare de Nord to Graville Le Havre Gare, and a hotel reservation at the Novotel Le Havre Centre. He assumed that Philippe had suggested this accommodation because Andrew had always stayed at Novotel hotels when travelling in Europe with Lynette.

Natalie next sent a text to Daan at the European Union Intelligence Unit. Her e-communiqué read: "Need backup. Details to follow shortly."

⚐ ⚑

NATALIE OCCUPIED THE EURAIL FIRST-CLASS seat at the knight's chess position to the right of the aisle. There were fewer travellers in this preferred section of the coach. Hence, there were fewer prying eyes to scrutinize other passengers when paths might have crossed with mal intent. Andrew sat directly behind her. Two seats behind her, Alexandra and Paul settled in for the 197 km Eurail ride from Paris to Le Havre, located at the mouth of the estuary of the Seine River on the English Channel. The closer their train got to Le Havre the more guarded Natalie became. She reached inside her satchel for her prescription acid reflux medication which reminded her why she had left this line of work. In Le Havre, Natalie rented a vehicle, Alexandra and Paul another. Andrew hired a taxi to take him to Novotel Le Havre Centre, where he was given an envelope by the receptionist. The instructions were specific and succinct. He was to remain in his room in the hotel until he was contacted.

The fishing village of Honfleur on the opposite bank of the Seine was on the right as Natalie drove across the Pont de Normandie suspension bridge. Alexandra and Paul followed, keeping her under careful surveillance. They watched the traffic between them and Natalie for any suspicious vehicles as well as any vehicles following them. Initially, there did not appear to be any. However, just before leaving the bridge for Honfleur, a vehicle sped past them and cut into traffic leaving the bridge behind Natalie. It was not an uncommon manoeuvre for drivers less familiar with the region or caught off-guard because they were daydreaming, but curious, nonetheless.

Natalie, Alexandra and Paul parked in the designated area on the wharf next to the fishing boats. Adjacent to the car park was an area reserved for buses. The driver of the vehicle that had cut them off parked closest to the buses with a line of sight to the car park partially obscured. From there, Natalie walked to the Musée du Vieux Honfleur on the Quai Saint-Etienne. Adjoining the museum was the 16th century jail on rue de la Prison with the warden's house adjacent, accessed from a door behind the prison bars and a second from the winding lane. The unknown female driver followed Natalie at a discrete distance. Third in line were Alexandra and Paul, their curiosity piqued. They all entered the Musée du Vieux Honfleur.

Paul commented to Alexandra, "When the car cut into traffic leaving the bridge, the driver was not a blonde. She was a brunette."

Natalie's earphone crackled. "You may have someone following you. A blonde wearing a light blue jacket. Her hair may be a wig," Alexandra commented.

"Confirmed. I see her," Natalie replied.

"We will cut her off. Make your exit when you notice our intervention," Alexandra added.

Beside the door to the curator's office and recessed in an alcove was a non-descriptive door without a handle but with a secure double keypad, one for a combination panel, the second with a partially hidden fingerprint reader. CCTV surveillance cameras monitored all movements.

"Excuse me. Have you visited this museum before? Do you know where the anchor exhibit is located?" Paul asked the blonde as he stepped in front of her. His lean toned body overshadowed her diminutive physique thereby cutting off her ability to keep Natalie under surveillance.

"Enter now, quickly," Alexandra directed Natalie.

Natalie tapped the code into the keypad.

"No, I do not," the blonde replied with an abrupt terse tone. "I haven't been here before. Go back to reception and ask." She hastily stepped away from Paul and scanned the exhibit room. Not seeing what she wanted, she hurriedly left, following the arrows to the next display area.

Natalie entered while Alexandra and Paul remained wandering in the first display of the museum, innocuously taking note of the artifacts and all other visitors. No one seemed to be overly interested in Natalie or the partially hidden door through which she had disappeared. Natalie approached a second door to the left which gave access to a corridor and subsequently to a final entrance to what had been the warden's quarters centuries before but was now a lavishly furnished three-floor residence. The third floor was a refurbished gabled garret suite. CCTV surveillance cameras recorded her steps.

Gaston stood sentinel like Horatio at the gate as she approached, his expression stoic.

"I am very pleased to see you," Natalie declared as she shook his hand heartily, augmented with a warming smile. "How is Angelique?"

"And I am pleased to see you also but more surprised to greet you in person and so soon," he replied curiously. "Why are you here?"

"Is Monique here and Philippe?" Natalie followed up. He had not answered her first question regarding Angelique's wellbeing.

"Yes, they are upstairs," he confirmed. "In response to your first question, Angelique is okay. We are managing, though." His face morphed from pleasant astonishment on seeing his Parisian guest, to seriousness, remembering Angelique's experiences. He would never forget the SS Gestapo major who had tortured his Angelique even though he had seen that Nazi floating face down in the Seine on D-Day. The war was not over, nor would it ever be as long as Nazi Gestapo and especially French Carlingue Gestapo walked this earth. He would hunt them down and bring them to justice *his style*. Being in Honfleur once again, he could sense their presence.

Natalie held his hand a little longer as she shared his concern for his wife's heightened state of distress.

"But why do you ask about Monique and Philippe?" Gaston followed up.

"Monique seemed to disappear without notice. Her cellphone

was not forwarded to voicemail, nor was Philippe's. Even more troubling, neither was your phone."

Gaston hesitated before providing an explanation. "Your intuition is accurate as always. I will allow Monique to tell you what happened to her and why she contacted her brother. As for me and Angelique, a *Maquis* colleague told me that one of the last members of the French Carlingue Gestapo had let it be known among the Marseille crime mob that, as a final vendetta, he had placed a substantial price tag on Angelique's head. He knew that I would do everything in my power to safeguard my dear Angelique. I know of this French Gestapo member. He is a thug. My *Maquis* colleague strongly believes that one of the communists on the list that Monique and Andrew found, a former politician and later a politically appointed bureaucrat, is funding this vengeful crusade. He wants the list of names if not the entire document immediately, in addition to our heads on a silver platter. I guess I should be honoured to be in the same class as John the Baptist."

"How did this person find out that Monique and Andrew had the document?" Natalie needed more details.

"Apparently he has technical spies on his payroll whose sole purpose is to eavesdrop on e-traffic. When Monique and Andrew briefly exchanged emails regarding the document, that brief e-conversation raised red flags. Monique was known as my daughter. Andrew was an unknown. The ex-communist politician was aware that Monique was in the process of divorcing her husband. Claude, being a gutter snake, gave her up. The equivalent of thirty pieces of silver was an inexpensive exchange. I told Monique and Philippe what had happened as I was leaving Paris with Angelique for this safe haven. Although she continues to experience bad dreams, it is safer than being in Paris. She is protected here. During the war, this was where our *Maquis* cell hid downed Allied pilots before smuggling them back to England aboard fishing boats. Accordingly, I did not contact you because of the electronic monitoring of Monique's phone and messages. Monique and Philippe did not contact you or anyone else for the same reason. I was confident you would follow the old Hansel and Gretel breadcrumb trail to this location." He shrugged. "Sorry about that."

Natalie's earphone crackled again with a cautionary message from Alexandra. "The blonde has returned to the first display room but is now a brunette. She has backtracked, hoping to pick up your trail where she lost it in the first public display area. You need to leave from another door."

"Confirmed," Natalie replied.

Monique walked down the stairs where she joined her father and Natalie chatting quietly.

Acknowledging her, Gaston mentioned that he had explained why no one had told Natalie the reasoning behind their rapid exodus from the City of Light.

"Andrew is in Le Havre and concerned for your safety," Natalie said as she hugged her. "He is VERY concerned for your safety," she whispered. In a louder voice she said, "Obviously, the two of you cannot meet in person, given the circumstances and the need for heightened security. I will reassure him accordingly without identifying your location."

"Thank you," Monique acknowledged. "Please tell him that I will apologize in person when we next meet." She returned Natalie's warm hug and smiled. The essence of the communiqué was abundantly clear.

Gaston interjected, "I do not need to remind everyone but I will. No one is to use their standard cellphones or other electronic means of communication."

"In anticipation, I have brought an encrypted phone for emergency use," Natalie advised. "My phone is also encrypted. Note that Andrew's cellphone is not. He just has his normal phone with his Canadian service provider which we now know has been hacked. So, no direct communication with him. We are confident that his physical identity remains unknown nonetheless. Even if he wanders throughout the boulevards of Paris as a gentleman stroller, I am confident he will not be recognized. His recent purchase of the property in Saint-Germain-des-Prés is also unknown and of no consequence as long as it remains that way, even to Claude and his criminal cronies. Having said that, I will instruct him to limit going outside when I speak with him this evening."

Monique's guilt at not informing Andrew before she departed so quickly overwhelmed her. She had never had to consider Claude's feelings when they lived under the same roof. She repeated her remorse. "Please pass along my regrets for my unannounced departure from Paris," Monique asked. "As he can appreciate, since Philippe introduced us at Novotel Paris Les Halles, my life, our lives, have been a crazy kaleidoscope of changing patterns and unforeseen events seemingly out of our control. Interspersed have been all too brief periods of relative tranquillity when we could catch a breath. I do want to spend some quiet time with him just getting caught up on our lives since 1962 when he returned to Canada." She paused. "What about Langue?"

"Not to worry," Natalie reassured her. "One of my colleagues from the Police nationale is dog-sitting. She is regularly monitoring the CCTV surveillance tapes around Andrew's walled compound and in his house."

"One last inquiry," Natalie posed to Gaston. "During the Nazi occupation of Paris, it is rumoured that the head of the Gestapo lived in the house which Andrew has just purchased."

"That is correct," Gaston replied brusquely.

"Rumour also has it that a *Maquis* operator entered the compound through a secret door. Once inside, he planted microphones in the house and at key points in the compound where conversations took place."

"That is also correct. Unfortunately, that *Maquis* agent died under suspicious circumstances so I cannot comment further on details of the surveillance or what was overheard." Gaston hesitated as he glared at Natalie, unsure why she enquired into past exploits of the *Maquis*. "Why do you ask?"

"It might be related to the document that Monique and Andrew discovered. As you suggested, I contacted a colleague with the European Union Intelligence Unit. They are now taking the lead in this investigation due to the possible inter-EU and international implications. It's a hornet's nest to say the least."

Gaston nodded cautiously, acknowledging the explanation although still wary. Few people, even internal intelligence agents, delve into such old clandestine activities at that level of detail. Natalie had come highly recommended as the Police nationale liaison officer for the European Union Intelligence Unit. But there was a Judas traitor within the ranks of the *Maquis* who had betrayed Angelique to the French Carlingue Gestapo. On D-Day, he too was found floating face-down in the Seine alongside the SS Gestapo major. There were other turncoats on Gaston's personal list yet to be held accountable for their reprehensible war-time deeds. Being back in Honfleur and in the residence of the former jail wardens, Gaston focused his attention on their ultimate capture, trial *in absentia*, and summary execution. Gaston hesitated briefly but long enough to keep Natalie's attention.

"Is there something else I should be aware of?" she asked. She had spoken with Gaston often enough to know that he rarely if ever told the whole truth.

"You recently sold the walled-in property to Andrew."

Natalie held his silent stare not wanting to take the bait clearly intended to pique her curiosity.

"You might want to research the vocation of the previous owners and the circumstances surrounding their divorce proceedings. I cannot advise you further because I am not aware of all the details." With an abrupt nod, he turned away. Further details would be up to Natalie to uncover. His thoughts were elsewhere and not for disclosure.

"Am exiting via alternate means," Natalie's secure text to Alexandra read. "Appreciate your escort as I return to the car park. Any update on the blonde-brunette interloper?"

"No concern. My colleague has her under surveillance at a café. He will join us shortly. Unbeknown to her, the police have had her vehicle towed for parking in a bus zone." Alexandra replied.

"Convenient," Natalie replied.

"One additional titbit of news and do not mention this to Monique," Gaston instructed Natalie in a low voice as he walked with her to the hidden exit from the warden's house. "Police in Saint-Denis are investigating the death of Claude Laurent who was shot in the back of the head twice, organized-crime execution-style. A police source advised that one of Claude's associates with a long criminal record was not pleased with the amount of law enforcement attention he had been attracting. Death declared its intention in Claude's case. An unregistered semi-automatic handgun was found in his possession at the scene. It had been used in the killing of another person linked to the Paris crime syndicate. More than likely, police investigators will be present taking photographs of all who attend Claude's funeral service, if there is one."

Natalie doubted Monique would be receiving condolences on the passing of her abusive husband let alone genuine expressions of sympathy for her loss. Yet, there would be mixed emotions lying in wait for her as she processed the news of his violent death.

Grief distorts everything. In Monique's case, the grief was not for the passing of a spouse but for lost opportunities over the years for a happy, rewarding life. That was the tragic truth. Any funeral would not be a celebration of life but a celebration of his death and her freedom. She might fleetingly lament his passing with a fine bottle of Pinot Noir currently maturing in Andrew's wine cellar.

He would need to replenish his collection of French wines as the patriotic duty of a recent honorary Parisian. The consumption of French wines had been in decline since the early 1960s when he and Monique first met and first kissed in the midst of their passionate puppy-love.

Natalie would also have to discuss with Monique the sale of the house she had shared with Claude. It was a house that held no endearing memories, rather only pain.

CHAPTER 16

Andrew's room at Novotel Le Havre Centre became the briefing venue. Natalie gave him a big hug. "From Monique," she explained. "She is safe and will apologize and make amends to you in person as time and place permit."

"Thank you. If the opportunity arises, please tell her that I very much look forward to that occasion." His open smile summed up his acknowledgement and appreciation of the embrace.

"Have you ever been inside an old jail as a tourist or for any other reason?" Natalie asked cautiously.

"Can't say that I have," he replied hesitantly, uncertain of the intent of her enquiry or the implications of his response, be it positive or otherwise.

"Allow me to take you back in history to a time when your house was being constructed for Napoleon's resident spy to keep the Emperor's secrets secure. The Bastille was still standing but not holding the King's prisoners on the right bank of the Seine in what is today the 4e arrondissement. There appears to be a link between the present and the most recent past when your urban estate was occupied by others involved in security and intelligence gathering. Nothing much seems to have changed since the initial owner took possession in 1815. On a positive note, the details of its history are coming to light and not merely through coincidence."

Andrew was still perplexed by Natalie's discussion. Perhaps that was how emissaries of spies talked, he surmised – with truths, partial truths and make-believe truths disguised in riddles.

Natalie related the essence of her discussion with Gaston, particularly the assumed vocation of the previous owners. She would investigate their identity further if for no other reason than her knowledge as a recently credentialed real estate agent. "Let us step back to several owners before you. Most Western European nations were falling before the advances of Nazi Germany, especially France. Vague details might have been related to the mysterious death of the member of the *Maquis* who had stealthily entered the courtyard and house of the urban estate in Saint-Germain-des-Prés through an unknown door sometime during the Nazi occupation of Paris. Microphones had apparently been installed to record secret conversations, the details of which remain unknown to this day."

Andrew grimaced but said nothing for a moment. "I detect a few issues, possibly all related. One is the provenance of my property that the surveyor has been pursuing, more a matter of personal interest for me but perhaps something related to the arcane vocations of previous owners." A lull followed before he summed up his thought. "I conclude your previous vocation and that of others employed with the European Union Intelligence Unit best suits you for this line of work rather than me with my comparatively mundane work experience."

"You are correct. Your request for background information related to provenance was both reasonable and innocent enough, or so we initially thought. We had not considered the document you and Monique discovered all those years ago, and the *Maquis* exploits of Gaston and his fellow French Resistance fighters. I am keenly aware that knowing some but not all of the details at this juncture may result in more questions being asked, but fewer answers being provided. There is a silver lining to all of this, though, a tangential relationship."

Andrew took a long time to reflect before responding to her speculation. "I think that the lack of background information has an obvious explanation. It seems my house has always been a residence for spies." He pursed his lips in reflection as he slowly lowered his head. *I may have to replace my planned life as a flâneur with that of a sleuth,* he considered. He chuckled to himself under his breath.

"Hold that thought," Natalie responded as she raised her eyebrows. "The second issue is the most pressing, that being the contents of the document you and Monique discovered. There are others of different political persuasion who were aware of its existence but not its whereabouts. They desperately want to get their hands on your discovery to either suppress it or sell it to the highest bidder with a different agenda. These people will stop at nothing to achieve their objectives. It goes without saying that you and Monique are their primary targets. Particularly Monique for reasons I have already mentioned," she emphasized.

Natalie was not confident that Andrew was fully aware of his own predicament let alone the dire repercussions that could be unleashed in the geopolitical arena. Cold War version 1 could pale in comparison. On a personal level, the potentially fatal consequences were imminent. She believed he needed a stronger dose of reality.

"Is that why you asked me to accompany you to Le Havre and to remain secluded in my room at this hotel?"

"Yes, on the off-chance the three of us could meet in order to discuss the circumstances relating to the discovery of the document. I asked Daan Segers, the head of the European Union Intelligence Unit, to assign Alexandra and Paul to provide security for reasons that are now becoming more obvious. We were indeed followed. In brief, it is not safe for the three of us to be seen together. Monique will remain in hiding here in the Normandy region because she is being pursued by two entities. The first entity is the people wanting her copy of the document. Second, she is being sought because she is Gaston's daughter, a former member of the *Maquis.*" Natalie focused on Andrew's reaction, to judge his appreciation of the seriousness. "Thoughts?" she asked.

He reflected back to when he had arrived in Le Havre as an

innocent young boy with his family all those years ago. They had left Canada for France aboard the Cunard ocean liner, the *S.S. Saxonia*. From Le Havre, they travelled to Paris on a World War II vintage train without any of the modern comforts of modern rail coach cars. Circumstances today could not be more different. He was currently a resident of Paris, with an urban estate and all the comforts millions of francs could buy, but a prisoner in his own kingdom with a price on his head, unlike the fabled King Arthur.

Natalie barked forcefully at him. "Are you listening to me, Andrew? It is essential that you realize the *Maquis* is still active, still fighting for or against the Nazis. The same is true for the French Carlingue Gestapo which is still hunting Gaston and Angelique, Monique and Philippe in addition to his colleagues. There are fewer on both sides but it only takes one bullet from one gun. Allow me to re-emphasize, Andrew. There are those from that era who are pursuing Gaston and Angelique to settle an old vendetta related to actions taken by the French Resistance on D-Day. You have heard Gaston say that the war is not over. The war is not over for them, for Monique or you because of your growing relationship with her. Philippe will remain in hiding, at least for the time being, because of his relationship with his parents and his sister."

"I understand," Andrew acknowledged. Yet he seemed to be searching with wandering eyes for exactly what, he was unclear.

"Let me put it all in perspective," Natalie enunciated deliberately, continuing to glare at him for emphasis. "I was asked, no, directed, not to divulge to Monique what I am about to share with you. I pass this on to you in the strictest confidence and request that you keep it to yourself until otherwise advised." The tension she created with this declaration was palpable.

The foreboding announcement caused Andrew to open his eyes wide and stare directly at her, his focus sharpened.

With an audible intake of breath, she continued before he could add anything more. "Claude Laurent, Monique's husband, is dead, killed by the criminal gang he was associated with in Saint-Denis. It was two bullets to the back of the head, double tap execution-style. We suspect he was shot with his own gun. When I say these people are nasty, I mean sociopathic, without so much as a tinge of remorse. A contract had been put out on him by another gang from the Marseille district. You and Monique are named in another contract put out by associates of French communist sympathizers named in the document. Gaston and Angelique are being hunted by the French Carlingue Gestapo. You are all connected to a single event, D-Day." Natalie continued to glare at him. Her voice was curt. Her articulation was exact. "The war is not over. Do you fully understand, Andrew?"

"Yes, I understand and appreciate the consequences," he confirmed in an equally blunt way. "I am just trying to grasp what all this means and what part I will play in this drama which I have been thrown into with no training or any experience whatsoever. At best, I was barely exposed on the periphery of my father's world of cloak and dagger."

His expression took on an added gravity as he raised his hands and slowly drew his rigid fingers down over his face. The thunderous roaring in his ears blared like trumpets summoning all guards to mount the ramparts in preparation for mortal combat with enemies sensed but not yet seen. Where was Emperor Napoleon's *Grande Armée* when he needed it most? The security of his walled compound, CCTV surveillance cameras and motion detectors would have to do for now.

The return train trip from Graville Le Havre Gare to Paris Gare de Nord was uneventful. That was not to say his mind was relaxed. He found his thoughts focused on Monique's safety, in addition to Gaston and Angelique. In the company of her parents, he supposed she was marginally more secure than with him and Langue behind the walls and security surveillance system. One thought plagued him. If the *Maquis* was able to breach the bastions through some secret second door during the war, perhaps the French communists chasing after Monique and himself today could also enter if they became aware of the location. Finding that entrance point had to be his highest priority.

Before he could consider any factors, he might use in his search strategy, Natalie advised that she would change her strategy of not telling Monique about Claude's murder in order to spare her from further stress. The Police nationale had asked her to get permission from Monique to search the house she and Claude had lived in rather than requesting a search warrant.

She called to pass along the message in a more personal way. A text message was not the best means of explaining the circumstances of his death. She defended her rationale for not passing the information along as soon as she had received it.

Monique paused before responding. "Good riddance," she replied without so much as a tinge of remorse in her voice. "I appreciate your concern for my emotional wellbeing. We move on. We will celebrate in proper form after I return to Paris." She hung up promptly.

"A smile on your face," Gaston commented. "Good news?"

"Oui, Papa. The best. Claude has been killed by his own kind."

Gaston gave no indication that he had known before she did. He just gave her a warm fatherly hug.

"I have a request," read the subject line on Monique's cellphone. The text began: "The Police nationale have a request. Can you give them permission to search your house for weapons and any other contraband that Claude may have kept? Your recorded consent via a reply will be sufficient permission rather than having to be present when the search is carried out."

Monique's reply was terse and to the point. "Yes, permission granted. Thank you for not requiring me to be present when the search is carried out. There are too many bad memories associated with that place."

"I have just forwarded your reply. For your information, the police have begun searching the property as we e-speak."

"Thank you," Monique acknowledged.

Moments later, Monique's cellphone boogied across the table at a follow-up question from Natalie. "For my information only, why didn't you give permission for the police to search before?"

"Two reasons. First, they never asked me. Second, even if they had, I would not have given permission. Had I done so, I was confident Claude would have killed me, at best. At worst, he would have beaten me to pulp and left me for dead. I am not a professional psychologist but I know a sociopathic personality when I see one. Claude demonstrated those behaviours, if not psychopathic. Absolute fear was the reason I asked you to help me to escape this final time."

CHAPTER 17

Andrew sat on his veranda sipping a glass of what had become his favourite Côtes du Rhône Pinot Noir from his wine cellar. Distant memories of happiness with Lynette and the loneliness without her travelled through his mind. Langue lay on the floor beside him, his eyes open, his ears erect, monitoring his environment. Andrew carefully scanned the ten-foot-high security wall enclosing his backyard. All the while, he asked himself where he would build a second door. But for what purpose? To access the raised vegetable beds for ease of gardening? To covertly leave and re-enter the property as a requirement of the tradecraft? Two completely different end states requiring two entirely dissimilar criteria.

He concluded that if he were that member of the *Maquis* who had secretly entered the courtyard and house in order to plant electronic microphones to eavesdrop on Nazi Gestapo conversations, this entry point could not be in plain sight. He came up empty handed. Having first scanned and then walked the perimeter with Langue by his side while meticulously inspecting the structure, he concluded there was none. *Perhaps along the wall bordering the front half of the property*, he thought. He repeated the search pattern but had no better luck. A clue might reveal itself if he examined both the outside and inside of the house itself, the logic being that a door in the perimeter wall would be closest to the house in order to keep the dash time to a minimum. He harrumphed in exhausted frustration: *Nothing.*

He considered another option. Would this story of such an audacious *Maquis* infiltration be a purposeful rumour in order to cause the Nazis to redirect scarce resources chasing after a ghost? Such a deceptive exploit was a common tactic employed by all military

85

strategists. There did not appear to be a record of intelligence acquired via electronic eavesdropping. But not all intelligence surreptitiously obtained was chronicled. In fact, much was purposely not recorded so if found by the primary source it could not be traced back to the time, date and location of the leaked transmission. Any combination might identify the perpetrator and other conspirators. His frustration continued to mount.

He had spent the last several years of his bureaucratic career as a statistical analyst searching for solutions to problems that others had attempted to solve but could not. Perhaps his efforts thus far had been thwarted because there were no numbers to crunch, just qualitative descriptive criteria to consider. People tended to be fickle, not finite. Regardless, if this truly was a home for moles or clandestine operatives starting with Napoleon Bonaparte's resident spy, how would previous residents have approached this conundrum? A copy of the original blueprints would certainly help. *Perhaps that is why none exist*, he reluctantly concluded.

He needed sustenance beyond wine to nourish his exhausted brain. None came more highly recommended than the café brasserie for its superior French cuisine and Parisian ambiance, Les Deux Magots. It was there that he arranged to meet with Natalie. He gently patted Langue on the head. "Guard the house," he directed. Langue curled up on the Persian carpet beside the front door, his eyes closed but his ears alert.

As Andrew approached Les Deux Magots, he recognized the waiter who appeared to intentionally block his way as he was cleaning a table.

Without looking up, the waiter gestured slightly with his head and spoke quietly as if for Andrew's benefit only, "The coq au vin is not good this evening, monsieur. May I recommend the Brasserie Le Pré aux Clercs, just a ten-minute walk in the direction from which you have just come. Reservations have been made by your colleague for 7 p.m. under the name Daan Segers. Bon appétit, monsieur."

Andrew retraced his steps, still thinking about possible locations for the missing door in the wall.

"Do you have reservations, monsieur?" the concierge at the Brasserie Le Pré aux Clercs politely asked.

"Yes, under the name Daan Segers," Andrew replied as he scanned both the exterior and interior of the brasserie for Natalie. He did not notice her but she was a master of disguise.

"This way, monsieur," the concierge said politely as he motioned very slightly with his arm extended.

Andrew followed as the concierge wended his way through the maze of tables and patrons already seated and engaged in conversation. They passed through an alcove that merged into what appeared to be a private dining area out of sight of the main dining room. He was unable to identify either of the two seated guests. On second glance, he did remember both as colleagues of Daan Segers who had accompanied him. They had all arrived together at his house to examine the document that he and Monique had found. Alexandra and Paul rose from their seats.

"It is good to see you again," Alexandra said as she welcomed him with a pleasant smile and a firm handshake.

Paul greeted him, saying, "Regrettably, Natalie is unable to join us this evening but passes along her kindest regards. She extends best wishes from your mutual friend who co-discovered the document all those years ago. This friend of yours is well and once again regrets she is unable to join us for dinner along with her brother from Novotel Paris Les Halles. This brasserie is not Au Pied de Cochon but the food is exceptional nonetheless."

Andrew's anxiety had initially risen with the unfamiliar venue and Natalie's absence. Paul described Monique as the co-discoverer of the document. He also mentioned the name and circumstances of their cancelled dinner reservation at Au Pied de Cochon on the evening he deposited his lottery winnings into the bank account she had helped him open, so he relaxed as he would among reliable friends.

"We need to update you on the findings of our research regarding the document. But first I must provide you with the most secure means of communication," Alexandra explained. From her satchel she produced a cellphone and charger.

He examined it carefully but did not recognize the brand name. He admitted to himself that he was unfamiliar with European telecommunication products.

Alexandra continued with her preliminary instructions. "Do not use your Canadian cellphone from this moment forward. We must conclude that your Canadian service provider and your number have been hacked as a result of receiving texts from Monique regarding the document. Please turn on this cell phone and enter a password as instructed with the appropriate alphanumeric sequence. Then search for contacts. There you will find four coded names. The first is Natalie, the second is Monique, the third is myself, and the final one is my husband, Paul. All have the same model of cell phone with the same advanced levels of encrypted security."

Andrew followed the instructions. He then raised his head and looked at Alexandra and Paul. He smiled as he confirmed their identities in the contact list that did not name them individually. "Thank you," he replied. The carefree *flâneur* lifestyle seemed to be eluding him.

"I appreciate the level of stress you have probably experienced since arriving in Paris less than a fortnight ago, especially after winning the lottery," Paul noted with a tinge of compassion in his voice. "Unfortunately, what Alexandra is about to tell you will raise that stress level again. But rest assured, we will all be here to support you. Suffice it to say, if you are suspicious of anyone, contact us promptly."

Andrew took a series of slow, deep breaths in order to relax his tightening muscles and lower his heart rate. "Understood," he acknowledged hesitantly. His creased brow indicated his apprehension. "What have I, what have Monique and I got ourselves into?" he asked in trepidation. He locked eyes with Alexandra as a signal that she begin with her account of what the document revealed and, more importantly, the possible ramifications. If the news was as bad as he anticipated, given Alexandra's wary introduction, he would not be able to innocuously return to Canada to retire into an anonymous mundane existence, never mind enjoy Paris.

There was only one option, to remain in Paris and prepare to engage with whomever it was who desperately wanted to get their hands on the document. He would have to establish his emotional grounding. His centre of operations would be his semi-secret lair.

Only one public entrance and exit to his compound was a strength from a security perspective but it was also a weakness. Anyone could easily verify his presence or absence within the walls. He would search again in earnest for the fabled second door that the supposed member of the *Maquis* had used half a century ago, and Napoleon Bonaparte's resident spy may have used almost two centuries earlier. His dinner companions might be able to help him get electronic imaging devices to aid in the search. For now, he needed to know what the document had revealed.

"Your preliminary translation was correct." Alexandra began. "They were written in Old German in addition to Russian Cyrillic script because there were Moscow-trained German-speaking communists planted in the Wehrmacht as part of the Russian strategy. They anticipated that the Nazis would invade and occupy France. Moscow had spies in Hitler's war cabinet employed as cypher clerks. Thus, they knew which German Units would be used to invade France. These Russians became the backbone of the French Communist Party.

There were instructions about how French communist political candidates were to conduct their campaigns prior to and during the first post-World War II general election in 1946. Most damning were the names of these French communists including the assassins who had been trained by the Nazi and French Carlingue Gestapo. They were to be employed to kill non-communist French candidates who appeared to be leading in the ridings as the election drew closer to voting day. After the war, some of these ex-Gestapo members remained in France and merged into the general population. They were employed as bureaucrats by others who had previously slipped into influential positions as tactics in the broader pre-war strategy. I mention this because they trained other assassins, two of whom are stalking you and Monique in an effort to find your document."

Paul showed Andrew an e-pic of a numeric sequence. "Memorize this, then erase it. It is the password to the image file on your new cellphone."

He paused as Andrew focused on the sequence, committing it to memory. He then opened the file on his new cell phone. Two pictures appeared, one male and one female, both tall with typical blue-eyed blonde Arian features.

"These are the two assassins whom we believe are looking for you and Monique. They have photos of her. Fortunately for you, they do not have any pics of you. That is why you cannot be seen in public with her, for now. It's less of a problem with Natalie as she is your real estate agent and it would be normal for the two of you to get together. Just do not meet in public too often, and less as time passes for the simple reason that she is a known friend of Monique and her family. Now that you have moved out of Novotel Paris Les Halles into your own house, you have no reason to meet with Philippe, so do not do so. Likewise, do not visit Gaston and Angelique, despite the fact Gaston and your father were old friends from the war and again around 1960 when you lived in Paris with your family. In brief, you need to reinvent yourself."

Andrew tightened his lips as he frowned at these restrictions. "I understand fully but don't like the conditions," he lamented. "The Abreo family have become my new friends along with Natalie." He hesitated. He would think about them all but particularly Monique. From the frying pan into the fire. Claude was no longer around to subject her to physical and emotional spousal abuse. Instead, she was being hunted by a man and a woman who would stop at nothing, not even death, to get their hands on the document.

"These conditions won't last forever. We will let you know when you can publicly reacquaint yourself," Alexandra replied to his disgruntled response. "In the interim, play the part of the retired gentleman of leisure soaking up Parisian culture. It goes without saying, if you recognize either of the two assassins, do not go home but contact us immediately. We will direct you to a safe house. Understood?"

Andrew acknowledged this warning with an abrupt nod. She did not have to emphasize the importance of this final condition.

Paul added, "Because we do not believe these people have ever knowingly seen you, the probability of them purposely following you is infinitely small, more coincidental. Alexandra's caveat is purely precautionary."

Again, Andrew nodded straightaway to acknowledge the restrictions.

Paul continued to fix his attention on Andrew. "Again, we can appreciate the stress you have been under with the lottery win and now the increase in communication security but I sense that there may be something else on your mind?"

After a moment of reflection, he nodded. "I have been thinking about when I first lived in Paris with my parents, memories of when I first met Monique next door. Seeing her again after all these years and having her as a tenant in my new house. We are older now but, in some respects, nothing seems to have changed."

"Nothing seems to have changed." Alexandra reiterated his emotional response.

A beat of silence filled the space between them.

"We had grown close back then. It is as if time has not past." He hesitated once again. "We are now even closer."

"And how does that make you feel?" Alexandra probed.

"My wife, Lynette, has only been gone a few years. I think about her a great deal and sometimes wish she were here to help me with rational decisions, the momentous decisions such as purchasing my Parisian urban estate." He sat quietly in thought resting his chin on his steepled fingers.

"And Monique, how does she fit into your decisions?" Alexandra enquired, sensing that Monique's close presence was at the centre of his perceived conflict.

"Lately, she has been involved. If she is not at the centre of my concerns, then she is my primary concern, my only concern. She occupies the place Lynette once did. If that makes any sense."

Paul glanced over at Alexandra who responded with a discreet smile of permission to reveal details of their own history.

"Your background with Monique is similar in some respects to Alexandra's and mine," Paul commented. "We met as teenagers, experienced our first puppy-love, then were separated for reasons beyond our control. We met again on the eve of our respective retirements. We were both married at the time to partners we should not have married. To add to our stress and like the situation you and Monique find yourself in with the French communists, Alexandra's life was being threatened and mine by association. To make a long story short, we are now happily married. It is as if we had never been separated for all those years." They affectionately held hands as they exchanged glances and smiled warmly.

"You cannot expect to remain forever faithful, although some do," Alexandra commented. "By having strong emotions for Monique, thinking about her, wanting to be close to her, you are doing nothing to tarnish the memory of Lynette."

Andrew responded without responding. Instead, he allowed the space to be filled with a tranquil stillness as he gazed into his distant thoughts. His attention slowly migrated back to his current company as evidenced by the flickering of his eyes, the freshness of his complexion and his lightheartedness. "Thank you. I very much appreciate you sharing your story. It has helped me to put my circumstances into perspective. And thank you for not only acknowledging but validating the stress I have been dealing with. My lottery win has been both a gift and a curse."

"You are more than welcome," Alexandra answered with a heartfelt smile.

Paul reciprocated her feelings, bowing respectfully. "If there are no other issues, we should order dinner. I can recommend the Coq au Vin and Beef Bourguignon," he suggested. "They have a sommelier on staff who has a certification from the *Association de la Sommellerie Internationale.* He will suggest an excellent wine to pair with either entrée or another if you wish. That is one of the reasons we dine here when our work with the European Union Intelligence Unit brings us to Paris."

CHAPTER 18

Andrew looked down at his new cellphone as it vibrated with an incoming message from Natalie. The subject line read: "Provenance Update." The surveyor had additional information based on research he had conducted on the property. She wanted to meet in private with an emphasis on *in private* because of the sensitive nature of what she was about to divulge.

"Life is just full of surprises," he muttered under his breath. After his dinner meeting with Alexandra and Paul, just about any upbeat news would be welcome.

Andrew's reply was two single-syllable French words, *"Chez moi."* The incentive was equally enticing: Pinot Noir.

Langue met Natalie at the front door with an affable lick on her hand and a wagging tail. "Our surveyor has been busy reviewing various archived files, some indirectly referencing to your house and property. Of greater relevance are titbits of what some might refer to as intelligence revealed in confidential interviews with a select few people, some from your neighbourhood. Perhaps more telling is the trustworthy information passed along by others who are long-in-the-tooth with far-reaching memories of past events that some would rather not recall."

"You have my undivided attention," Andrew replied, as he poured two glasses of optimally aged premium fruit of the vine from his cellar.

"First, it is important that you have a comprehensive under-standing of my background and that of many of my associates whom I depend upon for credible information, including our sur-veyor who has a distinguished career in intelligence gathering. He has an undergraduate degree in construction engineering which comes in handy when researching matters relating to real estate.

Suffice it to say, he knows where and how to access details over-looked or denied to others." She hesitated for several moments as she sipped her wine before summing up her introduction. "You get what you pay for. He is one of my most trusted sources."

Andrew held her gaze with an expression of unspoken confidence. He was becoming accustomed to this style of interpersonal communication. Her announcement was confirmed with a blink only perceptible by the intended recipient.

Natalie provided him with a broad overview of her past under-cover work and subsequent appointment as the Police nationale liaison officer with the European Union Intelligence Unit. That was where she had met Daan Segers who, in turn, had introduced her to doctors Alexandra Belliveau and Paul Bernard. They were the top agents in the EUI Unit who had successfully neutralized the greatest threats to the European Union since its formation.

"I guessed as much," Andrew admitted. "You had to be more than a flat-footed *flic* rattling door knobs when working on night patrol," he laughed. He allowed himself that latitude when alone in her company.

"Your house and property have an untold but storied history, which seems to echo the irony of its provenance. It relates to the circumstances surrounding the contents of the document you and Monique found in addition to other geopolitical events."

"A subset of quantum mechanics suggests that everything is connected to everything," Andrew responded to her introduction. The grander the event, the more likely it will have a colourful chronicle, he surmised.

"It doesn't end there," she continued, "and I owe you an apology in some respects. I did search the property title and the deed extensively, as did the lawyers for the two sellers. The lawyers asked their two divorcing clients about it but they said they didn't know its history which reached back two centuries to the first French

Republic. No one, with the exception of our surveyor, is aware of what I am about to reveal. I say only the three of us because it has surfaced as a result of analysis of intelligence acquired on the periphery. Given your analytical background, you will appreciate how such a conclusion can be drawn."

Andrew tilted his head. To date, there had been nothing straightforward about Natalie or the provenance of his property. He had no reason to believe that what she was about to tell him would be any different.

"You may not have seen any activity in the adjacent property north-east of you in the direction of rue de Seine. That is because there is no one living there and there never has been." A lull followed on the heels of her unexpected disclosure. Andrew wasn't sure why she had taken the time to talk about the empty neighbouring lot. Perhaps it was a cultural innuendo related to French or just Parisian real estate sales.

Her next statement answered his question. "This vacant lot is part of your estate." A slightly longer pause filled the space between them as she took a sip of wine. "I will get you the digital access codes to the new electronic locks that are replacing the original manual key as we speak. The security surveillance cameras are also being upgraded. The access code will be your primary means of entry to the pedestrian door via the side lane. The gate to the driveway will be opened and closed electronically, similar to the steel gate to your urban estate."

"What?" Andrew exclaimed in astonishment as he poured himself another glass of Pinot Noir.

"*C'est vrai* – it is true," she confirmed. "We know that the original owner was a resident spy. Rumour has it he was fond of money and fonder still of *les Parisiennes*. Napoleon awarded him a handsome stipend to maintain the property and his lifestyle. Construction of the residence was completed about the time

Napoleon Bonaparte had appointed himself Emperor and developed the military strategy for his ultimate conquest of all of Europe at the head of his *Grande Armée.*"

"How large is this second lot? Bigger than the property my house is occupying?" Andrew enquired. If Natalie's surveyor was having difficulty verifying the square metres of his urban estate, two lots could double the challenge.

"I can best answer your question by providing you with more background information. The empty lot accommodated the current house and stables. Initially, there was no wall dividing the two. In the 1850s, the urban architect, Georges-Eugène Haussmann, was contracted by Napoleon III to conduct a massive urban renewal program to replace the slums and back lanes of Paris with wide tree-lined boulevards and expansive parks. Inhabitants were ordered to relocate all livestock, including stabled horses, outside the city limits. The initial owner of your property quickly complied with the directive and shut down just about all the stables."

"Where does that leave me?" Andrew asked as he took a deep breath. What do I legally own?" He looked worried.

"A timely question regarding the wall. With the invasion of France by Germany in 1870, the government in Paris was secretly informed that the Kaiser had his eyes not just on the region of Alsace-Lorraine but also the French capital. The informant was a diplomat for the French ambassador in Berlin. Thus, his intelligence was deemed credible. He was also the owner of your property at that time. More germane to the perceived threat of a German occupation, the ten-foot outer perimeter wall of your property was constructed with imposing iron gates opening to both the residence and the stables, according to the tenor of the times. An inner wall between the two properties was subsequently constructed. By 1900, part of the stables had been converted into a garage to accommodate motorized vehicles."

Still concerned about his lawful right to the urban estate, Andrew pressed Natalie for a definitive response. "Do I own my house?" he asked bluntly, leaving no room for misinterpretation.

"Short answer," she replied emphatically, "yes, you own your house absolutely and the land it sits on."

"Thank you," he replied with a smile of relief. "I sense there is more to this saga of my estate than is implied in your one syllable response, yes."

"Again, *yes*," she reconfirmed as she nodded abruptly."

"Yes, with a qualifier? I am not feeling warm and fuzzy," he stated.

"With the invasion of France again by Germany marking the start of the Great War, a telephone wire connecting the house to the stable-garage was laid over a renovated stronger trestle that highlighted the newly planted rose garden. The wiring was upgraded in the years between 1933 when Adolf Hitler was elected Chancellor of Germany and 1939, the start of World War II. Another diplomat in the French Embassy in Berlin, and subsequent owner and resident of your property between 1933 and 1939, predicted the invasion of Paris. On this occasion, a select few took the intelligence to be credible. The rest is history."

"I am stunned by this information," Andrew admitted as he stared wide-eyed at his real estate agent.

Natalie became acutely aware of his mounting impatience. She sensed that he could direct her to re-sell the enlarged urban estate if she did not address at least one of his concerns. If that became his non-negotiable stance, she doubted he would contract her to secure another house.

He glared at her in frustration. His dream of becoming a relaxed *flâneur* seemed to be slipping ever further through his fingers.

"Let me address your worry about a second door," she said with assurance, hoping to allay his anxiety. "The final part of the saga relates to the member of the *Maquis* who supposedly entered the property through a hidden door in the wall and planted microphones in the house in order to eavesdrop on the head of the Gestapo. True and false," she emphasized. "True, this member of the French Resistance did enter via a door in the wall but not the inner wall separating the house from the stable-garage lot. Rather, it was the far outer wall that opened to the lane, the door that is still there, the one in which we are installing the access code. The member of the *Maquis* did eavesdrop but via the telephone line that had been positioned atop the rose trestle that extended from the house to the stable-garage. Microphones had been installed on the eve of the Nazi occupation of Paris in 1940 by strategically thinking members of what would formally become the Paris *Maquis*."

Andrew emptied the final drops from the bottle into his glass. His head buzzed from the wine, the sheer volume of information, and the convoluted history. He was silent for a moment as he attempted to process all that Natalie had told him. He contemplated the magnitude of the consequences.

"Open another bottle," Natalie requested, more in the tone of a non-discretionary directive that needed to be followed without hesitation.

He complied without asking for clarification, going down the worn stone steps and into his wine cellar where he retrieved two bottles. One he opened straightaway replenishing Natalie's glass and his own. The second bottle he placed in an inconspicuous wine rack built into the kitchen counter.

One perceived challenge had been partially resolved, that being a second less-obvious entrance to his courtyard. With the new digital access code, he could now enter the old stable-garage lot via the side door off the lane that had not been accessed for longer than most neighbours could recall. All he needed to do would be to find the original door or have a second secure door built into the dividing wall between the two lots that would assure some security. He had an idea. He would first need to consult with Natalie's surveyor colleague.

Out of routine, Andrew scanned the monitors from the CCTV cameras before Natalie departed. No one seemed to be in the vicinity of the exterior gates to his house or those securing the entrance to the stable-garage. He would need to have additional CCTV cameras installed on both the exterior and interior perimeter wall of the lane, now his stable-garage lot.

Langue rose from his sentinel post on the Persian carpet adjacent to the front door. His eyes danced around as he pricked up his ears which moved like radar screens methodically scanning all compass directions. He then escorted Natalie to the front door, licked her hand and wagged his tail as if to communicate that all was clear. He sprinted to the front gate as she got in her car and drove off. Langue then returned to Andrew's side after the gates closed with a reassuring clunk and the click of the automatic locks.

"Good boy." Andrew patted him on the head. *The Police nationale may have been too quick to dismiss him as a potential police dog*, he reflected. He greets friends with an affable lick of his tongue and a wag of his tail. Perhaps he perceived police officers who played the part of bad guys to be tracked and cornered were actually good guys, so no need to be aggressive. We will have to see how he reacts to foes who enter his jurisdiction with what his senses perceive to be mal intent.

CHAPTER 19

A ndrew thought about what Natalie had told him regarding the provenance of the property, especially the stables being converted into a garage at the turn of the century. He also reflected on Napoleon III commissioning Georges-Eugène Haussmann to build boulevards and parks in the 1850s. Sometime thereafter, the one large lot had been subdivided and an interior wall separating the two had been constructed. *There had to have been a door between the two*, Andrew deduced. Else, those living in the house would have had to leave through the iron gate, walk several steps to the second iron gate and then re-enter the lot for the stables. More than likely this door would have been inside or outside the garage on the house lot.

"Walkies," he said to Langue who promptly rose from his sentinel post. Andrew locked the pedestrian door in the larger iron gate after he went out. He turned left and left again into the lane where he located the locked pedestrian door that entered the stable-garage lot. The new code that Natalie had given him opened the lock with ease. Once inside, he stopped to find his bearing and familiarize himself with the size of this second lot and the position of the buildings. He was confronted with a weed-tangled overgrown acreage that he concluded had not seen a scythe or sickle for decades. Langue obediently sat on the path beside his left leg as he had been taught, also scanning his new domain.

The converted stables occupied the property approximately one third of the way into the lot from the road. The fields in front and behind the building were still lush and rich with growth from the years of manure that had been piled up over the decades. It could be a prolific vegetable garden. In the far-left back corner in the rear of the lot stood a derelict garden shed.

He entered the stable building cautiously, unsure of what might confront him. An ominous hiss of silence made a shiver run down his spine. Carriage harnesses, saddles, bridles and other equestrian equipment hung on stable partitions and on the walls closest to the lane. Langue loitered around the first stable stall sniffing repeatedly. "What do you smell?" Andrew asked. "Just the scent of horses?"

He strolled on intending to become familiar with his surroundings. He eventually looked back at Langue who remained in the first stall, not apparently excited yet preoccupied with the smells. "Come," he beckoned to his companion. Reluctantly, Langue obeyed the command and walked toward Andrew.

As Andrew approached the far end of the building closest to his house, the space took on the trappings of a vehicle garage. Each section was like a separate time capsule spanning the evolution from the French Revolution and the first French Republic to the Nazi occupation, the third French Republic including the Haussmann transformation, the Franco-Prussian War, the arrival of the combustion motor car, World War I and ultimately World War II. With the hasty retreat of the Nazis from Paris in 1945, time seemed to stand still. All doors were closed, all gates locked, and all memories, good and bad, shuttered. An industrious entrepreneur could turn the building into a money-making museum. Sightseers would enter via the pedestrian door in the lane and leave through the larger iron gate onto the road, or *vice versa*. Such an enterprise was not Andrew's interpretation of secluded privacy in retirement.

He was confronted by a solid wall with no indication of a door between the two lots. He tapped on the wall with an iron bar he found on a ledge. He could not detect any sound that indicated a difference in the construction material of a door or later a wall over it.

Frustrated once again, he called for assistance. "Langue, come."

He obeyed his new master. "Search," Andrew directed as he pointed with his hand along the floor abutting the wall. Langue took deep breaths as if searching for the trail of a felon, but to no avail. He then repeated his search pattern before sitting and looking up at Andrew who praised him, "Good boy, Langue, good boy."

Andrew continued to feel frustration. It just seemed logical that there would have been a passage in the wall between the two lots. *If there wasn't one in the initial construction plans when the dividing wall had been erected, the rational Nazi master mind would have built one,* he argued with himself.

After a pause, he called to his four-legged sleuthing partner as he slapped his hand against his left thigh, "Langue, come."

The two left the building and walked into the back field along the dividing wall. Andrew continued to tap the wall with the bar while Langue sniffed as if wanting desperately to find whatever it was his master was seeking. Andrew's rising frustration was palpable. Langue believed his purpose in life was to please his master. He stopped at the locked door to the dilapidated garden shed and sniffed in earnest. With each deep breath, he whined a little more and then growled as Andrew approached.

"What have you found, boy?" Andrew asked.

He growled more loudly as Andrew inserted the bar between the weathered door frame and the rusted hasp attached to the door. With a sharp bark, he jumped on Andrew, knocking him to the ground. The tapping bar had unhinged the hasp and the door slowly swung open. The hinges squeaked as if under protest.

"What was that all about, boy?" Andrew asked from his prone position.

All the while his four-legged partner's whining increased in intensity. Not achieving the reaction he sought, Langue barked with greater intensity and growled even more loudly, exposing his teeth in protest at his master's disregard.

Andrew stared inside the garden shed. He shuddered in horror. He carefully crawled away from the open door. Langue followed, his growl becoming a whine. He licked Andrew's face as if apologizing for his aggressive behaviour.

"Good boy, Langue, good boy," Andrew exclaimed repeatedly as he patted his head and hugged him with a gush of gratitude.

Andrew reached into his pocket, removed his cell phone and speed dialed Natalie. "I'm in the stable-garage lot, at the back by the garden shed. Enter through the side door in the lane."

As he waited for her to arrive, he thought back to when he had lived in Paris all those years ago. Two of his school friends had been exploring old war relics north of the city. They had opened a door to a bunker. The booby-trapped hand grenade detonated. One friend had been killed by the explosion. The other had lost his hand. In school, a military explosives expert had delivered a lecture the week after the incident. Andrew distinctly recalled the teaching aid of the inert booby trap with the wire attached to a model door and the neutralized hand grenade. The photographs of the white sheet draped body and the white bandaged amputated stub of the missing limb were effective. They shocked him then and reminded him of the ongoing threat throughout the intervening years. With equal horror, he witnessed the same terrifying images just now, only it was not a model. Instead, it was a rusted wire attached to the inside of the door and a corroded hand grenade securely attached to the door frame.

"YOU ARE A GOOD BOY," he repeated while patting Langue's head and the side of his chest. He would give the Police nationale a failing grade for not noticing Langue's extraordinary tracking skills and explosives identification talents. He smiled to himself as he continued to pat his sleuthing partner as much as a reward for his heroism as a calming gesture for himself. The police department's loss was his gain. Monique would have to negotiate for ownership of his loyal companion. She could visit or she could become a permanent tenant. They would agree on joint ownership. Not negotiable was Langue's permanent abode.

Natalie called the bomb squad who searched both the garden shed and old stable-garage. Nothing was found. They concluded that the booby trap in the dilapidated garden shed had been left by the Gestapo. Fortunately for Andrew, the fuse had corroded and the wire rusted in the intervening years since the rapid retreat of the Nazis in 1945 with the arrival of the Free French Army led by General Charles de Gaulle along with Allied forces as they entered the city.

"You are lucky you were not severely injured or worse, killed," Natalie said sombrely. "As Gaston has repeatedly reminded everyone, World War II is still not over, even fifty plus years on."

Following the bomb squad's declaration of *all safe,* Andrew re-entered the stable-garage lot. He walked to the dilapidated garden shed, gingerly lifted the bent latch and slowly dragged the door toward him. His heart pounded as the memories of the explosives lecture in school all those years ago and the images of his recent re-experience with Langue by his side flooded his mind. It took a few firm tugs to fully open the door due to his trepidation. Inside the shed on the far wall was a door that opened to expose the shed on the house side, now left open by the bomb squad. He knew that it would take several trips from one garden shed to the other before he could expect to feel less anxious. Even then, he would re-live the anxiety each time. Although never was a very long time, he would never feel completely safe.

Langue was with him providing emotional support as they carefully walked through the adjoining door and into the sunlight of his backyard. He readily admitted that the near-fatal event was a result of his curiosity. Prudence would guide his decisions henceforth. He had previously stared in solitude at his garden and the shed while sipping a glass of Pinot Noir on his veranda. On this occasion, a recently uncorked bottle sat on the table beside his second glass of wine. There would be a third and more than likely a few more to follow. Today, he sipped his wine but with increased awareness of the gentle wafts of vanilla, dark red fruit aromas and earthy palate.

Case solved. He had a second route to exit and enter. He would just have to secure a new locking mechanism on a far more secure door with CCTV security cameras and motion detectors on both the interior and exterior of both sheds.

He patted Langue's head repeatedly. Again, Langue rested by his side, his eyes closed but his ears erect and scanning for potential threats.

"I still cannot believe that someone would have to walk to the back corner of both lots to pass through the access door in the garden sheds," Andrew muttered to Langue. *"There had to have been a door in closer proximity to the house, more likely near the garage on his house lot. The booby trap had to have been a decoy set in 1945 by the vindictive mind of the resident head of the SS Nazi Gestapo as a parting gift for subsequent occupants of the estate and as a reminder to citizens of Paris."* He mulled over that thought.

"What was the reason for constructing the inner dividing wall with just a single half-concealed door linking the garden sheds? It just doesn't make sense," he said to Langue. He hesitated. "Unless…."

CHAPTER 20

"Our third Magot advised that you may have attracted the attention of two individuals, one female and one male," Natalie's wary email to Andrew read. "The last few times you dropped by Les Deux Magots for a *petit-déjeuner,* the female was already seated while the male appeared to follow you into the café. Our friend dressed in his customary black and white server's attire did not initially recognize the male but once he sat with the female, our server made the connection. The suspicious female may be the person who had me under surveillance during our recent trip to the Normandy region, specifically Honfleur," Natalie speculated.

Andrew strolled into the kitchen. He needed a fresh cup of coffee or rather a few cups to focus his thought process. He had been thrown into the intrigue of geopolitics that had defined Europe since the French Revolution. This was not his idea of retirement by any stretch of the imagination. On all the business trips and vacation excursions he had taken to Europe with Lynette, France was their favourite and Paris their preferred destination. They had naïvely talked about retiring here, admittedly without really conducting thorough research. In retrospect, he now acknowledged it was more a fairy-tale. Lynette was not here now to balance his decisions. Winning the lottery was the catalyst that propelled him into what had become an uncontrolled kaleidoscope of events, some intriguing, others beyond his imagination. He could not press pause, delete, and exit. He could direct Natalie to sell his urban estate, give Langue back to Monique, and tell her she would have to find somewhere else to live. It would be her decision. He bore no responsibility. He could return to his home in Canada.

He slowly sipped his coffee. It did not have the aroma of a cappuccino brewed in the ambience of Les Deux Magots café and presented with Parisian elegance by his favourite server. He looked down at Langue who had followed him from his sentinel post by the front door and into the kitchen. His brown eyes said all that needed to be said. It was as if he had become the medium through which Lynette was speaking to him. She had often commented that she could hear him best when he was silent.

Every choice has consequences, he admitted. It was his choice to reply to Natalie. So, what is the plan?" he texted, intrigued.

"Tomorrow morning, walk your normal route to Les Deux Magots. Our server will seat you at your normal table. I have been in contact with Alexandra and Paul, our friends from the European Union Intelligence Unit who gave you a secure cell phone. Another of my colleagues will already be seated, as will I, but as one of my alternate personae. Order your standard *petit-déjeuner*. After eating, follow your normal routine, slowly strolling the streets of the Saint-Germain-des-Prés district, observing everything but focusing on nothing in particular. Instead, simply savour the sights and sounds and smells."

"Confirmed," Andrew replied. "Should I return home afterwards? I ask because Alexandra and Paul had instructed me to contact them if I suspected I was being followed which may be the case according to our friendly waiter. They would direct me to a safe house if need be."

"Be prepared for either option. If they direct you to another location, we will arrange for your regular dog sitter to take care of Langue. I will provide her with a key to your stable-garage lot via the lane door."

Andrew took a deep breath at the thought of there being more than one key in circulation. He had not yet installed security surveillance cameras and motion detectors on the exterior of the perimeter wall along the lane, in addition to the interior of the stable-garage lot from all angles.

He harrumphed and his forehead crinkled with apprehension. Life was becoming increasingly complicated with three known factors at play. The first was the perceived menace of unknown persons following him with possible mal intent as a result of his lottery win. The second was the actual threat from those hunting for the document he and Monique had found, identifying cronies of the French communists. The third was the peril associated with Gaston and his World War II service with the *Maquis*. There was a concerted desire for vengeance focused on Gaston by members of the Carlingue, the French Gestapo, and now himself through the vicarious association with his own father and Monique.

Andrew trusted Natalie as much as he could trust anyone, he supposed. His preference would be to possess all keys and codes. *A copy in Natalie's pocket was the second-best option under the circumstances*, he pondered, *as long as she did not make additional copies.* On second thought, it had been convenient when he faced-off against the booby-trapped hand grenade.

There was no turning back from the lottery win, the re-discovery of the document with Monique, and the revelation of circumstances related to his father's serendipitous meeting with Gaston in the weeks leading up to D-Day and again in 1960. This triad of apparently pre-destined events culminated in his belated plans to attend the celebration of the 50th anniversary of the D-Day invasion with Lynette. He had never consulted a clairvoyant or used a Ouija board to explain events or predict the future and he wasn't about to start now. But he couldn't deny the inter-relationship of all three events that seemed to be beyond mere coincidence.

His responding email to Natalie was to the point. "The enhanced surveillance system has to be a top priority. Like yesterday," he kidded but in all seriousness.

Her response was equally concise. "As your real estate agent, I am attending to it as we e-speak. Our friends with the European

Union Intelligence Unit technical services have assured me that it will be installed within twenty-four hours. I appreciate your concern. Rest assured; security does not come any better. I will ensure that you are home with Langue when it is connected to your existing monitoring system."

He thought about her response before acknowledging, "Thank you, I think." His hesitation prompted another follow-up message from Natalie, a bit of a distraction, she hoped, from his growing disquiet.

"For your information, your tenant will be returning from the Normandy region within a week. I am confident that both you and Langue will be pleased to re-establish a more normal routine, as normal as normal can be, given the circumstances. I will offer my services to deal with the disposition of the house that she co-owned with Claude. Sometime after she returns, the three of us will meet to talk about how and where you initially discovered the document around 1960, in addition to how best to deal with the consequences you now face as a result of rediscovering the document a few weeks ago."

"Not the peaceful existence and relaxed pace of a recent retiree that I had imagined," he mumbled. Langue looked up as if he clearly understood Andrew's concerns.

Andrew recalled a statement made by a retirement consultant hired by his previous employer's human resources department. This alleged expert strongly suggested that the greatest challenge many retirees face is having a purpose in life without a working calendar that once regulated their working weeks. Each day, according to this consultant, it was imperative to accomplish one task to keep from feeling aimless. Andrew chuckled at the naïve proposition, at least in his case. His calendar had fewer annotated appointments in the years leading up to his retirement than it had in the past few weeks. The image of the booby-trapped exterior door to the garden shed with the unexploded hand grenade flashed through his mind. Retirement life would get better, less busy.

Once again, he mulled over the thought: what was the reason for constructing the inner dividing wall with just a single partly concealed door linking both the garden sheds? It just didn't make sense. Unless. Again, he thought a moment before answering his own question. *There is a reason for every action, however odd it may seem.* He would mutter this proverb softly at work when challenged with an analytical dilemma that appeared unfathomable. It took on a different connotation today and would continue to do so from this moment forward.

He texted Natalie. "Can you find out the name of the senior ranking SS Nazi Gestapo officer who lived in this house during the war? Has he survived? If so, where is he living now?"

CHAPTER 21

"The female of the duo at Les Deux Magots whom the waiter thought might be following Andrew was not the woman who followed Natalie to Honfleur," Alexandra and Paul confirmed in a joint text to Natalie and Andrew. Curiously, they were now reasonably certain that Andrew was not a target of that suspected surveillance. Time to test the supposition.

Andrew's cell phone vibrated with an incoming text from Alexandra. "Leave the café, turn right on boulevard Saint-Germain, stop briefly in front of Café de Flore a short block away as if reading a message, turn around and retrace your steps, re-enter Les Deux Magots and sit down again at your table."

Andrew nodded subtly. Although he didn't understand the reason for this manoeuvre, he had faith in the sender. A few minutes later, he was seated again. His server had cleared his table in the interim and now refreshed his *petit-déjeuner.*

The suspect couple had not followed him, nor had they taken note of his exit or re-entry, or even reached for their cell phones to communicate with another party. That did not completely eliminate them from being suspicious. Natalie preferred to think in terms of probabilities. Hence, their probability was simply lower, at least for the time being.

If Natalie's server believed there was something questionable about the duo's conduct, there would be reason to give credence to his concern. Natalie's colleague stealthily photographed the couple and forwarded the e-pics to Alexandra and Paul to cross-reference against the EUI Unit database. Andrew's backup team were very careful, given their knowledge that senior members of the French Communist Party named in the re-discovered document had contracted individuals to abduct and interrogate Monique and Andrew and assassinate them, if need be.

❄ ❄

"EUREKA!" THE SUBJECT LINE READ on Alexandra's email sent to Natalie and Andrew. "Meet for Pinot Noir."

"You enquired about the name of the head of the Nazi Gestapo who had lived in your house during the latter years of the war," Alexandra opened the meeting. "His name is SS Oberstleutnant Hans Dietrich. He was reported to have been killed during the hasty Nazi retreat from Paris. However, his body was never found. Curious, given first-hand reports by pre-war neighbours seeing him briefly in the vicinity of his family home in Deisenhofen, south of Munich, in the fall of 1945. Oberstleutnant Dietrich's family was alleged to have been closely connected to Reichsführer Heinrich Himmler, the Nazi Schutzstaffel Chief who recommended him to become a member of the Nazi Gestapo. Without this personal endorsement, his application would probably have been rejected for reasons now purged from his official record. His file along with other SS officers had been recovered by the Allies from the Wewelsburg Castle where they had undergone basic training."

"Of greater interest and more immediate concern is a French connection," Paul followed up. "Dietrich's family owned property south of Metz purported to have been part of a larger estate once administered by Charlemagne in what is today the French province of Lorraine. I mention this because Oberstleutnant Hans Dietrich's son, Manfred Hans Dietrich, had applied to join the Hitler Youth on the eve of the German surrender on 7th May 1945. Manfred was eight years old at the time. Today, he is almost sixty years old, a retired businessman who lives in the old city of Metz on rue de Petit Champé, a picturesque ten-minute stroll from the German

Gates. Of greater significance, Manfred changed his name to Henri Joseph Dubois."

Paul gestured to Alexandra. "We have uncovered information that suggests Oberstleutnant Dietrich knew of the document Monique and Andrew found but was unaware of the names mentioned, although he had advance knowledge of Moscow's intent to create and fund the French Communist Party. He had planned to use it to blackmail the French communists. To cover his own tracks, Oberstleutnant Dietrich had established contact with the advance guard for the Allies and made a deal to become a counterintelligence informant, like other senior SS Nazis including Klaus Barbie, the Butcher of Lyon. Many of these former Nazi leaders had been appointed by General Patton to become Bürgermeisters in German towns and related civil departments. The purpose of their appointments was to control the German population in the immediate post-war period. All Allies, albeit some reluctantly, had agreed with this decree as a counter to the increase in Russian spies infiltrating Western Europe in the wake of Allied victories."

"Member of the French Communist Party?" Andrew reiterated.

Paul nodded.

That triggered a related thought in Andrew's inquisitive mind. "What if," he pondered out loud, "what if there never was an obvious door in the wall between the two properties? What if Oberstleutnant Hans Dietrich either knew or purposefully had the door between the two garden sheds constructed because he wanted to hide something to discourage access. After the war, he could return to retrieve the buried cache. Part of his strategy to increase his odds of survival had been to make a deal with the Allies to become a counterintelligence informant."

"You're good at this game," Alexandra commented. "You are not the first to question the circumstances related to the whereabouts of key senior Nazi officers who seemed to have mysteriously vanished without trace between the D-Day landings in June 1944 and the unconditional surrender of Germany in May 1945. However, you are the first to link the disappearance of Oberstleutnant Dietrich to the imprecise provenance of this property and related events known only to a select few associated with security and intelligence. How would you like a part-time job in your retirement?"

"Not really. It was *never* in my retirement plans. And certainly not after my lottery windfall," he retorted without so much as a moment to reflect on the possibility. "Having said that, the life of a *flâneur* rose to the top of my list and with it a plethora of possibilities after I deposited the cheque." *Never is a very long time, though*, he contemplated.

"Neither Alexandra nor I had considered the notion of working after we formally retired. It was then that Daan Segers invited us to join his merry band of colleagues as agents for the European Union Intelligence Unit." Paul shrugged his shoulders and tilted his head as an open invitation to discuss further details over Pinot Noir from regions other than the Côtes du Rhône, like the renowned Moselle around Metz in Lorraine. Ironically, this high AOC wine standard was almost eradicated by fierce fighting including artillery bombardment in both World Wars, now seemingly linked to Andrew's Parisian property through former mysterious tenants.

Alexandra gazed down at an incoming text. She raised her head moments later. Through slightly squinted eyes she uttered for all to contemplate: "The male and female from the Les Deux Magots have been identified." She paused as she stared at her colleagues one by one. "He is Manfred Hans Dietrich, the son of SS Oberstleutnant Hans Dietrich. The woman is his wife, Louise Dietrich. They registered as tourists at Hôtel Fougère on rue Bonaparte, two blocks from Les Deux Magots and two blocks from our current location." She lingered a moment longer. "Coincidence?" Another lull followed. "Millions of tourists visit Paris each year. It's not uncommon although curious. Coincidental? Perhaps less so under these circumstances. Purposeful?"

"A photographer would be wise to look for what is missing from the picture and then ask themselves why it is absent," Paul added.

"Hold that thought," Andrew commented. "Serve yourselves another glass of wine while I scan the images from the motion detector surveillance cameras."

One by one, they gathered around the monitors Andrew was scanning with glasses topped up, eyes squinting at frames of people walking by.

"THERE!" Alexandra exclaimed. She pointed at the figures on the monitor. She then showed them e-pics on her cellphone taken at Les Deux Magots and forwarded by her colleague.

"Yes," Natalie agreed while looking at e-copies on her own cell phone.

Andrew continued to watch the security monitors. "They have not stopped in front of the main gate or looked up as if confirming the identity of this property."

"Perhaps they do not have a detailed description or complete address, if in fact finding this property is their true intent," Paul speculated.

"Curious. They do not appear to be troubled by the presence of the surveillance cameras or the fact that my property is the only one on this block to have such an elaborate security system," Andrew noted. "This goes beyond coincidental." The others sensed a hint of trepidation is his voice. He was still cautious that elements from the Paris crime world were maneuvering on the periphery and continued to pose a threat.

"Good news," Natalie smiled in an effort to lighten Andrew's mood. "Monique just advised she will be returning this afternoon. I will meet her. Just before we arrive at the pedestrian entrance off the lane, I will text you, Andrew. You can show her the way to the garden shed door."

"Not too sure her arrival is good news, given what has transpired," Andrew replied. "Would she not be safer in Honfleur with her father?"

"No place is completely safe," Natalie replied. "Claude was the biggest threat to her. Now that he is dead, there is one less worry, albeit a significant worry. Gaston is better able to deal with the issues related to his *Maquis* associates and safeguard Angelique alone on turf he is most familiar with. In addition, the European Union Intelligence Unit has assigned resources to the Normandy region to assist as needed. Alexandra, Paul and I are better able to coordinate security for you and Monique in Paris related to just one known threat, the French Communist party linked to the document."

"Understood," Andrew acknowledged reluctantly. "I will enjoy her company as will our companion, Langue."

CHAPTER 22

"We know the names of the tenants from whom you purchased the property," Natalie confirmed with Andrew. This was her first major sale of a house and acreage with history reaching back to Napoleon Bonaparte and the First French Republic. She was learning as much as Andrew about the provenance of older urban estates in Paris.

Andrew's expression was more enquiring than relieved. With each titbit of information added to his provenance of the estate, his appetite for the whole truth increased. "For all the homes I bought in Canada, there had never been an issue of lack of accurate records. Accordingly, I assumed the full history beyond the current *vendeur*/seller was not a factor. In Paris, I cannot make that assumption. Either that or the cultural uniqueness and secretive profession of the previous occupants contributed to the mystery and, as such, was not to be questioned. Violating the accepted code could have unintended consequences. Perhaps my years of experience as a research analyst has left me thirsty for the details."

"And in my retirement real estate profession too," Natalie countered lightheartedly

Andrew said in jest, "Touché."

Monique was learning how her landlord navigated through the no-man's-land of his enquiring mind. It was a refreshing change from Claude's tedious criticism and endless excuses for not contributing to the household coffers. The thought reminded her that she needed to formally hire Natalie to sell her house. It held too many memories of abuse to consider keeping it even for rental income.

"On a more sombre note, our house surveyor has been hard at work," Natalie noted. "We have a better idea of who lived in the house during the war, and some but not all residents since 1815 when construction was completed. Surprisingly, a record of all tenants since the end of World War II remains an intriguing conundrum."

"Curiosity supposedly killed the cat," Andrew responded. "So much for my dreams of living the life of a neo-Parisian gentleman of leisure," he responded with a trace of frustration.

More important matters occupied his mind. They included the names of the French communists referred to in the document who were hunting for him and Monique, his suspicions about criminals pursuing him for his lottery windfall, and now SS Oberstleutnant, Hans Dietrich's son, Manfred and his wife Louise, captured on CCTV in front of his urban estate.

"The plot thickens," Natalie suggested. "We know of another member of the *Maquis* who briefly stayed in this house between 1944 when the Nazis retreated and 1946 when it was revealed this person had been a known associate of the French Carlingue Gestapo. He was found dead, drowned in the Seine. His assassin has never been identified." Natalie shrugged. It was a known fact the police did not thoroughly investigate deaths of suspected Nazi collaborators after the war. Most simply disappeared.

"There was no formal record of who lived in the house, if there was anyone between 1946 and 1958. It is believed that the most recent owner in the years leading up to the war, had been killed by the Nazis when they goose-stepped into the city. It was then that select municipal records relating to ownership of property second-ed by the Nazis had been mysteriously purged. Had Germany won the war, there would be no one and no official records to contest ownership. Possession would be nine-tenths of the law. Likewise, Nazi stolen treasure once owned by innumerable Jewish residents and other prominent dissidents so labelled by the Nazis, plus other victims of the Holocaust, would not have been accounted for. Thus, it would have remained the property of the Third Reich to dispose of as it saw fit."

Just the mention of deaths associated with the French Carlingue Gestapo caused Monique and especially Andrew to reflect on threats made against them as a direct result of the revelation of the names linked to French communists in the document he and Monique had re-discovered.

He knew that his father had been employed as a military attaché in the Canadian Embassy in a time when Canada had no official spies. More recently, he wondered whether his father's work had involved duties related to the *Maquis* and the French Carlingue Gestapo. From his recent conversation with Gaston, it became apparent that his father had direct contact with a select few members of the *Maquis* who had helped him escape to England to fight against the Nazis starting on D-Day. Andrew would be eternally grateful to Gaston for filling in some of the details that his father had not mentioned and his mother had only alluded to as he grew up. There had just been the repeated response by his father to his requests: "There are some things you just do not talk about," in addition to Gaston's constant wary warning to Monique and Philippe when they enquired: "The war is not over." The same brusque tone was used by both his father and Gaston. What was not said held partial clues to his current dilemma regarding the provenance of his urban estate. He needed to speak to Gaston again.

CHAPTER 23

"Do you mind if we join you?" Paul asked Manfred Dietrich who was seated at a table with his wife, Louise, in the Au Pied de Fouet Café Restaurant on rue St. Benoît in the 6e arrondissement, Saint-Germain-des-Prés. Before Manfred had a chance to reply, Paul and Alexandra sat down and leaned towards them in a pincer-like manoeuvre. Clearly, Paul's question was rhetorical. His next assertion was not. "May I refer to you as Henri Joseph Dubois or do you prefer Manfred Hans Dietrich?"

Manfred gazed at them seemingly unperturbed. His initial reaction was not to answer. Why should he? He quickly decided to change his tactics.

Before Manfred could respond with a preference, Alexandra followed up. "It is imperative that we talk about matters related to your father, Nazi SS Oberstleutnant Hans Dietrich."

Alexandra paused as she leaned toward him, glaring. She then stated in an accusatory tone, "You have been observed walking with resolve around the proximate region of Saint-Germain-des-Prés. Your stride was purposeful." She leaned even closer now within inches of his face. "Why are you here, Manfred Hans Dietrich, son of Nazi SS Oberstleutnant Hans Dietrich? What are you looking for? Why have you changed your name to Henri Joseph Dubois?"

Manfred was astonished. He stared repeatedly between Alexandra and Paul and back again. His breaths quickened as his heart rate increased. His complexion appeared to fluctuate between sallow and a reddish blush. Beads of perspiration dimpled his forehead.

Louise recoiled from the Blitzkrieg-like onslaught directed at her partner, not knowing if she would be next. A rasp grew in her throat as fury welled up like a tidal surge. She breathed slowly and silently in an effort to control the impulse and any response she knew could erupt.

For a fleeting moment, Manfred considered retaliating with equal or greater force. He modified that strategy with the mention of his father by Nazi rank and specific SS Gestapo affiliation in addition to his own change of name. The label with his full former name, Manfred Hans Dietrich, suggested that his interrogators had done their homework regarding his family's identity. How much they knew of his past he wasn't certain but it was enough to conclude his inquisitors were professional. He scanned patrons seated closest to their table to ascertain whether or not anyone had overheard the brief outburst. No one appeared to have been distracted.

For the first time, he was permitted to take control of the direction of the conversation which would give him a few moments to consider options. "Let us move to a more private table away from prying eyes," Manfred replied in a quiet yet exasperated voice.

"Lead the way," Paul directed. He grabbed hold of Manfred's shirt as he stood, a physical reminder that escaping was not an option.

Alexandra followed Louise closely as they went to an empty table in a far corner. Paul did the same with Manfred. As they approached, a resident cat resting in a dark alcove gazed at Louise as if to discern her true identity and intent, for the sake of anyone who cared to pay attention. Louise glared back in contempt but the narrowed eyes remained unperturbed. Each recognized the formidable coldness in the venomous glare of the other like a mongoose and a cobra. The cat was ready to pounce. Louise would do well to befriend Saint Gertrude of Nivelles, the patron saint of cats.

Once seated, Alexandra set the agenda for Manfred to follow. "Start at the beginning in your family home in Deisenhofen, south of Munich. Your father is alleged to have been closely connected to Reichsführer Heinrich Himmler, the Nazi Schutzstaffel Chief who recommended he become a member of the Nazi Gestapo, even though he wasn't fully qualified. You might not recall that familial connection because you would have been just a toddler at the time. In contrast, you will have remembered applying to enrol in the Hitler Youth in the spring of 1944."

Manfred reflected on the facts he could not deny. At best, he could attempt to sidestep the obvious. "You are correct, I was too young to recall my father attending the Wewelsberg Castle for training to become a member of the SS. I admit to applying to become a member of the Hitler Youth but it was at my father's insistence because he believed it would help his own career. There was a great deal of peer pressure also. If you were not a member, you would be bullied and ostracized at school. I was only eight years old at the time and did not know anything about Hitler's manifesto as outlined in *Mein Kampf*. This publication would have been central to training to become qualified as a member of the Hitler Youth. I, like most of my childhood friends and, in retrospect, virtually all Germans, did not know the war would end within weeks."

"Where is your father?" Alexandra pressed.

"He died a few years go."

"How did you learn this if you changed your name?"

"The lawyer who helped me change my name knew where to contact me, in Metz. He is the only person who knew this. The lawyer informed me that I was the sole executor and beneficiary of my father's estate. I read through his will." He failed to mention that among his father's papers was his personal diary. "It was a painful process to have access to just these few estate documents because there was virtually no mention of what he did during the war and in the years thereafter. I was conflicted because, although I did not want to know about his record as a Gestapo officer, I did want to know more about his life. He disappeared sometime after the war so I never had the opportunity to talk with him about this, father to son." He hesitated as he held his head low. "Who will atone for the sins of our fathers?"

In this brief preliminary summary, Manfred had already started to contradict himself. "Where are the estate documents now?" Alexandra asked. There could be other information of less consequence to Manfred but pertinent to the EUI Unit investigation, if she could access them.

"I brought them with me to Paris. I will surrender them to you on condition I am not identified as the source." What he would not divulge was the fact he had vetted the papers of any incriminating evidence.

With a straight face, he continued his rehearsed admission likewise vetted of any self-incriminating admissions of guilt. "I want no association with the Nazi Party or my father in order to be at peace with my soul. That was why I moved to Metz after the war, changed my name, learned to speak French without any trace of a German accent, and completed a graduate degree in Business Administration."

Alexandra's face was a mask. If need be, she and Paul would escort Manfred back to his hotel room with the sole purpose of taking possession of the papers.

"We agree to your condition that you will not be identified as the source of the papers," Paul confirmed. In the realm of intelligence gathering, there were truths, partial truths and make-believe truths. Manfred had to be truly naïve not to be aware of that reality.

"Why did you come to Paris if it was so painful?" Alexandra asked.

Manfred reiterated with emphasis, "Louise and I agreed to come to Paris to deal with our individual ghosts. We walked around Saint-Germain-des-Prés where she had grown up and my father had lived and worked as the end of the war approached. The family that rescued Louise when her parents were arrested by the Nazis and subsequently shipped to Auschwitz have since died. We asked the neighbours but they said nothing. We sensed they did not want to remember more so did not recall – selective memory, I suspect. I know all too well the pain of memories and never-ending nightmares." His face contorted as he drew his eyebrows together, squinting, and tightened his lips.

"This is the first and will be the last time for both of us to visit Paris. It has been an agonizing prospect but an undeniably necessary pilgrimage. I hope you understand."

Alexandra and Paul exchanged glances while they nodded in acknowledgement of his description of events. They knew it was not the truth, the whole truth and nothing but the truth.

Manfred reiterated his purpose for coming to Paris, "I have come now to Paris for the first time to see where my father had lived and worked, then I intended to destroy all his estate records."

"And your wife?" Paul asked.

Manfred elaborated on his previous explanation. "Louise is French and the daughter of Jewish parents who were rounded up here in Paris and temporarily held in the Vélodrome d'Hivre. On the eve of the round up, Louise was hidden by a neighbour in Saint-Germain-des-Prés. Louise's parents were transported to Metz where they were briefly held in a transit camp, Fort Queuleu, before being shipped in rail cars to Auschwitz concentration camp. Like so many others, they became names without accompanying narratives, edited out of the family chronicles."

Manfred's shoulders drooped. "For all I know, they could have been sent to their death by my father." He hesitated again as he stared down, silent, then made eye contact again. "No. I need to correct that statement. My father did send them to their deaths. He alluded to this in his private papers. He then admitted to merely obeying orders of his superior, SS Obersturmführer Helmut Knochen, head of German Security Police in France. I need to acknowledge the direct link to this barbarism. That was why I read through my father's papers, to try and find any detailed evidence." Manfred spoke sadly. "There were no names of victims, just regions where the round-up occurred, primarily the 3e arrondissement the Marais, and 6e arrondissement Saint-Germain-des-Prés."

How vast the thievery was that robbed Parisians of their possessions and freedom, of their Old Masters. How devastating their sense of loss of both art and family, the former transported to private collections in Germany and the latter to concentration camps. You can lock up the wolves but you cannot silence the haunting howls.

"Does Louise know about your relationship with your father?" Alexandra followed up as she gazed intently at Louise, seeking her reaction which so far remained bland. Her expression hinted at something but offered no substance.

Manfred dwelt on the question, his head lowered. "She does now." His voice trembled. "The news almost destroyed our marriage. Because I never spoke of my father, only mentioned that he had been killed in the war. She believed me. She had no reason not to. Then I showed her my father's papers. We are hopeful that the war will now be over for us. I am certain that we are not alone, that there are others who are living with ghosts," Manfred muttered with a wishful expression. "Forever is a very long time. I can never forgive my father for what he did to so many people and I never will." He looked at Louise as he reached for her hand. "But I can move on in peace."

For the first time, Louise spoke, seeming polite but little more. "We can move on in peace." She sounded dubious.

Both Alexandra and Paul monitored Manfred and Louise for facial reactions to this revelation. There were none. For Manfred, at least, the first indication of remorse had long since passed, if one had ever existed.

After another break during which nothing was said, Manfred elaborated slowly as if for the first time. Guilt seemed to punctuate every word he uttered. "Ever since I was old enough to understand, I have felt terribly guilty being one of the Führer's children as we are referred to, the offspring of SS officers and Hitler's other henchmen. Through no choice of our own but only by virtue of birth, we have been condemned to bear the guilt of the horrendous deeds of our fathers. Some of my German childhood friends have committed suicide because they were unable to reconcile the sins of their fathers."

Alexandra and Paul continued to monitor their physical and emotional responses. The more Manfred said, the more fabricated his explanation appeared to be, certainly contradictory.

"I continue to struggle with my demons." Manfred's voice trembled. He paused as he attempted to control his emotions. "I have wanted to meet the family members and other victims of my father's brutality, to apologize. I do not know where to start, so I have not." As if unsure of how his communication was being interpreted, Manfred reiterated with greater emphasis, "This unfinished quest has kept me from ending my life."

Manfred seemed to be terrified yet calm. But terrified of what? Being discovered, of being fraudulent? Of feeling sorrow but relief, but for what? He was apprehensive but assured, as he expressed his sentiments quietly. The man and the emotion appeared strangely connected yet distant. Not two distinct personalities but two emotional dispositions that seemed to conflict were inconsistent with the persona he presented.

Both Alexandra and Paul remained neutral in their reactions to what he was saying and the feelings he was presenting.

Manfred stared at his interrogators with crocodile tears running down his cheeks. "How do you say that you are sorry for deeds you did not commit yet somehow feel responsible for?" he asked, his voice quivering. "How do you plan for this moment? I have wanted to make amends for a long time but never knew how. I have sought advice from my psychologist. It was easy enough for him to make suggestions but he isn't here now. I'm at a loss for words although I have rehearsed this moment more times than I can remember. All I can say is that I am so sorry. I feel so guilty for being one of Hitler's surrogate offspring."

He glanced at Louise. However, his rehearsed theatrics did not convince his interrogators. Alexandra and Paul remained silent in their responses and neutral in their reactions.

Manfred nodded. He reluctantly explained that he had grown up in Munich where he was schooled in neo-Nazi doctrine, the archconservative politics of the Christian Social Union of Bavaria, the CSU, with its quasi-clandestine neo-Nazi cells. In his personal diary his father had insisted he be a strong, active member of the post-war Fourth Reich headquartered in Munich. Yet Manfred had no intention of doing so in his reinvented French persona.

"Thank you for relating all this to us," Alexandra stated as she extended her hand in a gesture of appreciation for the opportunity to listen to what Manfred had to say and for what Louise did not have to say.

"You are welcome," Manfred replied, striking an almost lyrical note that seemed out of context. It would be incumbent on them to snare him, he mused with a sense of fabricated confidence.

Louise merely responded with a wafer-thin hint of a smile.

The four walked to his hotel where Manfred handed over the incomplete package of estate papers.

Once they departed, Alexandra and Paul exchanged glances.

"Actors and not particularly convincing ones at that," Paul replied to Alexandra's questioning gaze. "Manfred seemed to have said a lot of words but passed along much less information."

Alexandra remained silent for a moment while a grimace played on her lips. "I agree completely. What bothers me most, though, is his explanation of why he chose to live in Metz in order to become French or at least appear to be French. Metz was central to the German psyche pre- and post-1870 and the Franco-Prussian War. One only has to read the inscription on the Porte Serpenoise in order to glean a sense of the French response to the German claim to Alsace-Lorraine, as part of the former German empire. As much as Manfred tried, he could not hide his stereotypical Germanic traits."

"No doubt in my mind we will question them again, either here in Paris or in Metz," Paul stated emphatically.

"*Absolument,*" Alexandra confirmed. "The purpose of his trip to Paris is not as he described. He has an interest in Andrew's property, the house or the stable-garage lot with the garden shed that had been booby trapped, more than likely on the orders of his father, SS Nazi Oberstleutnant Hans Dietrich."

"I am unsure if Manfred and his wife pose an immediate threat to the current occupants or are in cahoots with others, the French communists perhaps. I am not confident that he provided all the answers to the questions you posed, certainly not all that you needed or he was prepared to offer. I doubt very much he has natural gravity rooted in inherent integrity."

"One of the meek who will not inherit the earth," Alexandra added with a sarcastic chuckle. "On a more serious note from a psychological perspective, when a man is sad, he is susceptible. Manfred did not demonstrate vulnerability. I can only conclude that he was not sad when he spoke of the deep regret he felt for his father's actions."

As a forensic psychologist, Alexandra had learned early in her career that there was safety in speculation or asking for feedback. "Thoughts, partner?"

"We need to advise Andrew, Monique and Natalie soonest," Paul replied without hesitation.

Alexandra nodded pensively in agreement. "The list of people searching for Monique and Andrew now includes affiliates of SS Oberstleutnant Hans Dietrich, the last high-ranking Gestapo officer who lived in Andrew's urban estate in the latter years of the war. Top on the affiliates list is his son, Manfred, and his daughter-in-law, Louise, whose presence is a veiled façade. Seduction and sexual intrigue go hand-in-hand with treachery. I am not confident that Manfred knows the full extent of that potential."

"There is far more to the meek Louise than she presents. A honey trap with alternative motives if I ever witnessed one," Paul admitted.

CHAPTER 24

"Under what circumstances did the two of you find the document with the names of the French communists?" Natalie asked Andrew and Monique. "I appreciate that it has been approximately thirty-five years. Think carefully. It is very important you do not omit any details. If you are not completely sure, say so and suggest possible options and why. The smallest of details could make a difference."

"We were exploring the basement of the house I lived in with my parents," Andrew began. "In the basement, there was a small storage room with a locked door. I discovered a ring of keys just behind the top shelf of the wine rack, the kind you might use to open an ancient jail cell door or a centuries-old cathedral. One key opened the door to the mysterious storage room. Inside on the right was an old wooden cabinet. On the middle shelf was the document underneath a set of olive wood rosary beads with an equally rubbed wooden crucifix attached. On the top shelf of the cabinet were remnants of what once were complete rolls of wallpaper. I recognized some from walls on rooms upstairs."

"Any in particular that stood out?" Natalie asked.

He reflected for a moment. "I can't recall exactly. Perhaps the bedrooms," he replied as his eyes darted around before returning to Natalie's stare.

"Anything?"

He answered by not answering. Instead, shaking his head back and forth.

"Continue," Natalie instructed with an encouraging gesture.

"I don't know what significance the rosary beads played, but they were the first to catch my attention. If I recall correctly, Monique reached in for the document and examined it first."

Monique nodded tentatively in agreement. "We didn't know what it was. I think we showed it to my brother, Philippe. He couldn't add any suggestions. Some words in the document were hand-written in French but didn't mean anything to us when taken out of context, which we were unaware of. Other text was in a foreign language, perhaps more than one language. So, Andrew and I divided it up, each taking every second page. I took my pages home and put them in my bookshelf among other cherished papers and memorable books. That is where they remained for thirty-five years."

Andrew added, "I hid my pages in a hollowed-out cavity behind the 14th cobblestone from the left above the wine rack. The cobblestone was wobbly so came out easily with a little bit of prying with a screwdriver and some coaxing. I put my pages in a tin box. It stayed there in its hiding place until I retrieved it the other day, with your help."

Natalie hesitated in deep deliberation, reflecting on the account of events Andrew and Monique had provided thus far.

"Think carefully. Can you remember if the document was enclosed in an envelope or some other folder? Allow me to reiterate, sometimes the smallest detail can make or break a case."

Monique and Andrew gazed at each other for several moments, each scanning their memories for specifics. Monique replied first. "I am pretty sure it was in a large light brown envelope discoloured in places with water stains. I can recall removing it. The room was dank. The envelope was damp and, as a result, it tore a bit on a side seam when I pulled the document out. I must have thrown the envelope out probably because of the musty smell."

Andrew nodded hesitantly in agreement with Monique's description. He then added, "I don't know if it is of any significance, but there was a large safe in the room standing against the wall opposite the wooden cabinet. I was never able to open it, certainly not for a want of trying and much frustration. I searched the walls and the furnishings for any etching of a combination. I found none. Each time I left the room, I relocked the door and placed the keys back where I found them on the makeshift hook behind the top shelf of the wine rack."

As an afterthought, Monique summed up her recollection of events in response to Natalie's enquiry. "We were just teenagers back then, doing what kids do. Why do you ask?"

Natalie replied, "Instead of waiting for the French communists identified in the document to make the first move to come after the two of you, I am thinking we should take the initiative. We might be able to set a trap to capture those who are after you, or at a minimum identify them by surveillance," she explained. "I previously mentioned that we could not identify the names of the occupants of your urban estate, Andrew, between 1946 and 1958. That negated the opportunity to find out who might have left the document in the wooden cabinet in the locked room you described."

"I wouldn't want the elderly lady who currently lives in the house I lived in with my parents to be identified, if for no other reason than to protect her. If these people named in the document are as ruthless as you make them out to be, we cannot expose her," Andrew cautioned. "In addition, she could implicate you and through you, me, the two of us as co-conspirators."

"I wouldn't do that for the reasons you just mentioned," Natalie confirmed. "We shouldn't have to if my strategy to spring the trap works. Instead, we would identify a vacant address with a dilapidated building or abandoned business that had been in existence since the war. There are old structures of that era in the Saint-Denis area. I used a few when serving with the Police nationale. With all due respect to the good citizens of Saint-Denis, it has an unsavory reputation which is ideal for our plan."

Monique smirked at the mention of Saint-Denis. "That was

where my ex, Claude, was murdered by some of his Mafia associates." With a nod, she summed up her indifferent reaction, "Enough said."

Natalie merely shrugged and tilted her head in response to Monique's reference to Claude. "We just have to create a plausible cover story. I will run the plan by Alexandra and Paul who can present it to Daan Segers at the European Union Intelligence Unit. If it is a go, Daan can secure funding from Yolina Lambert at the EU Commission in Brussels."

"One more question," Natalie asked Andrew. "Who have you talked to regarding the stable-garage lot? Apart from myself and Monique, who else knows about the side door off the lane to the lot?"

"I have told no one," he insisted, slowly shaking his head.

"Good. I recommend we keep it that way," Natalie suggested strongly, "especially any of the neighbours. If you think about anything else, let me know as soon as possible."

As an afterthought Andrew added, "The members of the bomb squad who removed the booby-trapped hand grenade would be aware."

"Right," Natalie confirmed. "I will take care of that detail."

Monique called Gaston. He admitted to knowing about the murder of the *Maquis* member who had stayed briefly in Andrew's urban estate sometime between 1945 and 1946. He said he was aware of the fate of this *Maquis* collaborator but insisted he was not personally involved in his drowning. In this period, Gaston was still living in Caudebec en-Caux with Angelique who remained in hiding from both the Nazi Gestapo and the French Carlingue Gestapo. That arrangement allowed him to remain close to her as she slowly recovered from her torture at the hands of the SS Nazi Gestapo major.

By the time the war ended in May 1945 and for several months thereafter, Gaston continued to be engaged in clandestine post-war operations with the *Maquis*. Work as a bargeman provided a cover for him to return to Honfleur on a routine basis. Thereafter, he and Angelique married and moved to Saint-Germain-des-Prés in the 6e arrondissement of Paris. Their growing family never seemed to want for francs, food or other means to live in relative comfort.

When growing up, Gaston had told Monique virtually nothing about the war, his role with the *Maquis* or in what business he had become employed thereafter. What he did say, Monique surmised, was far from the whole truth and nothing but the truth. Her mother commented on nothing that Monique could recall, not even the details of her torture and subsequent nightmares that never seemed to abate. Her brother, Philippe, recalled nothing of consequence either. If she or Philippe pressed the issue with their parents, her father would harrumph with displeasure and reprimand them severely. There were simply some things you did not discuss.

Being a co-discoverer of the document that named the French communists and being a tenant in Andrew's house with its shrouded provenance reinforced her father's repeated caveat that the war was not over. Monique acknowledged her father's sage advice.

Perhaps this common link of the document could bring her and Andrew closer together, she inwardly hoped. She had made it abundantly clear there was no lingering sentiments for Claude beyond outright contempt. She had also clearly expressed her puppy-love for Andrew after their first kiss when they were teenagers. Youthful emotions like those from a first kiss can be spontaneous but rarely are they forgotten. She now surmised a subsequent kiss, years later, seemed more complicated somehow.

In contrast, Andrew had said little about Lynette, only that she had died from injuries sustained in a car accident a few years ago. He had expressed sincere concern for Monique's safety and wellbeing on the eve of Claude's release from custody and her speedy escape from her own house with Langue in tow.

Now, forced time together under these menacing circumstances could be opportune for them to talk in more detail about their lives in the intervening years. That had been the purpose of their planned dinner at the Au Pied de Cochon restaurant before it had to be postponed at the last minute following Claude's violent assault.

In every adversity there are the seeds of its opposite, she reflected, one of which would be peace and tranquillity gained from sitting silently on the back veranda sipping wine with Andrew. They were face-to-face and very close. Separation and time away from Claude, although brief, had brought her proximity and the need to cherish and savour each peaceful moment like a bottle of aged Pinot Noir.

She recalled that Andrew had always been laidback, his disposition quiet without the onus for chitchat. They were past that, the unwritten rules and rituals of the courting game. Hence, there were no awkward emotions lying in wait. She reached down and affectionately patted Langue whom she envisioned would be curled up on the floor between them, eyes seemingly closed but ears constantly alert.

Sitting this close to her, Andrew became faintly aware of her breathing and dreamy look as she caught his occasional gaze. She held his smile, searching for some sign of hope for a renewed relationship. The first sips of wine began to draw them closer together. He longed for the emotions he had experienced with the first kiss of puppy-love, *un coup de foudre* – love at first sight, despite its torments. He surmised that love, even puppy-love, is on loan and can be recalled at any time like a library book.

At this moment, he found her to be not just beautiful but mysterious. Like a lady one would recognize in the amorous 18th century world of Marie de France and Madame de Pompadour where courtesy and gallantry did not need to be translated. He let the thought hang while he took a slow sip of wine.

She couldn't remember since she had last felt this safe and serene, void of any fear or need of alertness.

A sensation of emptiness occupied Andrew's thoughts, distant memories of happiness with Lynette and current memories of aloneness without her.

A palpable solitude of silence filled the air as they sat together on the veranda, each apart in their own space yet never more together. A curious awareness calmed them.

CHAPTER 25

"We have approval from Yolina Lambert at the European Union Intelligence HQ in Brussels to lure the French communists into a snare, specifically those who have been contracted to retrieve the document at whatever the cost. The initial location will be a derelict garage in Saint-Denis close to the Tramway T8. Alexandra and Paul will be our contacts with Daan and any assistance the EUI Unit may provide," Natalie announced with a hint of gratification in her voice. As a *modus operandi,* she much preferred to be on the offensive, planning, organizing and coordinating operations. Staking out the locations and waiting in boredom *ad nauseum* was the least appealing task.

Natalie then produced a plastic wrapper from her satchel and removed the contents – a duplicate of the document technicians at the European Union Intelligence Unit had painstakingly created. She handed it to Monique without saying anything. Tapping into different senses had been an effective intelligence-gathering technique like forensic hypnosis for acquiring and validating memories from the distant past.

Monique wrinkled her nose instantly at the musty odour. "Phew! That is what it smelled like and felt like when I first handled it. No doubt! And looked like," she added, holding the document at arm's length.

Natalie smiled at Monique's reaction. "Our technicians are very proficient at replicating the scent, sight, tactile sensation of artifacts decades old, occasionally centuries. The techies are still working on an envelope like the one you described. As I previously mentioned, the smallest of details can lure the rogues into tripping the trap, or send them running away, aiming a hail of bullets at us as cover."

Andrew reflected on Natalie's choice of words – *our techni-cians*. *Our* as in a possessive expression. *Was she a full-time mem-ber of the European Union Intelligence Unit and a real estate agent conveniently part-time?* he wondered. Selling select properties like his house with questionable provenance had its advantages. And her surveyor colleague with the engineering degree – was he also a member of the EUI Unit or a paid professional with convenient skills under the guise of a licenced real estate organization? What about the waiter at Les Deux Magots? He would have to conduct his own research without the aid of his real estate agent and her colleagues.

"So, how do we bait the trap and communicate its where-abouts?" Monique asked.

"Your ex, Claude, has provided the link. The Police nationale have a mole inside the Marseilles Mafia, currently operating in the Saint-Denis area. This informant associates with the same unsavoury thugs who murdered Claude but with a tad more integrity. We have let it be known through him that Claude had dis-covered the hidden whereabouts of the document. He was in the process of making a backroom deal to sell it to the highest bidder. Unfortunately for Claude, he backstabbed the wrong contact. Our informant has spread the word that he now knows where Claude had stashed the document – in the vicinity of the Tramway T8 station in Saint-Denis. There is honour among thieves and this informant has a reputation for not double-crossing brothers in the Marseilles Mafia, at least not to get caught with his fingers in the cookie jar, so to speak. The French communists are not the Mafia and, as such, not direct colleagues," Natalie grinned. "C'est la guerre – that's war."

"And contingency plans?" Andrew asked. "If I was the leader of the French communists and suspected a ruse, I would send an envoy to retrieve the document with instructions to play dumb if duped into a trap. I would certainly not dispatch the higher-paid contracted assassins. At a minimum, I would set up my own surveillance at that location."

"We have that in hand," Natalie replied. "It will be a triple drop to be completed in quick succession. All three will have European Union Intelligence Unit eyes and boots on the ground, in addition to electronic surveillance. The cache at the first drop will have a partial photocopy of the document listing a few names. This will validate its authenticity. The cache will also have instructions as to where to proceed immediately to the second drop. If the pick-up courier does not arrive within the stated timeframe, the process will be shut down. The second location will be a duplicate of the first. It will provide instructions where and how to leave the payment, which will be different from the other drop locations where the fabricated copy of the entire document will be left. This dual drop will allow us to identify any additional culprit."

"Am I correct in concluding that you are not interested in any criminal conviction through the courts of any French communists involved in the conspiracy to murder Charles de Gaulle or other non-communist candidates in the post-World War II election?" Andrew asked.

"Correct," Natalie replied. "Some are dead, and a posthumous prosecution would not be pursued by the government of the day after all these years because there would not be any political gain. Why? For the simple reason there are some serving politicians who have been voted in with the aid of unscrupulous folks operating in the shadows. We know about most of them living in France. Still others live in other jurisdictions within the European Union. Hence, it would be to our advantage to quietly approach these politicians and their colleagues with a copy of the document listing their names. They are of greater use to us as snitches in our supposed democratic system and as espionage agents in the ongoing Cold War against those in Moscow who benefit from such never-ending conflict. If the Russians want to eliminate them, so be it. It would be their choice. It is to our advantage to exploit that threat in order to motivate these felonious folks to disclose more current intelligence. C'est la vie," she suggested calmly. "It takes a thief to catch a thief."

"May I suggest that you would not have engaged in such stealthy activities to this extent in your previous profession?" Andrew responded with a sheepish grin, a wolf in sheep's clothing so to speak.

"I am not a police officer anymore. Instead, I am a licenced real estate agent helping my personal clients."

"And I am a newly-minted *flâneur*, a connoisseur and observer of life, who will leisurely stroll the streets of Paris while sensing the myriad of innuendoes of its fascinating culture, especially its cuisine and fruits of the vine, some of which fill my own wine cellar."

Gaston was correct, the wounds of World War II continued to fester, Andrew acknowledged to himself. The end of the war had too many loose ends that spawned the continued conflict, in addition to new elements which had hatched into manifestations of the Cold War. Canada and many other Allied nations had not had to tolerate foreign armies on their soil and pay homage to those who had made the ultimate sacrifice on national battlegrounds for years, like the Normandy beaches. In contrast, France and particularly Paris had suffered from the reverberations of German jack-boots goose-stepping on French culture.

Growing up as the son of a World War II RAF fighter pilot and, more recently, a dependent of a military attaché, had left Andrew too far removed. He was now a resident of a city that had once been occupied, and the owner of an urban estate that had once accommodated Nazi Gestapo officers who, in turn, had hunted for his father as a downed Allied airman. The stark reality of that war was now acutely evident.

He needed to speak with Gaston again, and soon, if for no other reason than to tie off loose ends that were now preoccupying him, some like red herrings, due to no fault of his own. Provenance or coincidence or unintended results? Resolution seemed to be linked to the mysterious history of his urban estate with its own loose ends that appeared to have alluded him. If, in fact, they had.

Had previous residents whose spying vocations appeared similar been beset with such a dilemma? Or had their questionable history been an attribute in the world of espionage and intelligence in which they worked and lived. There had been truths, partial truths and make-believe truths, including those related to SS Oberstleutnant Hans Dietrich. Perhaps they were aware that others had glimpsed a fragment of their own untold stories, their *noms de guerre* – war names, without accompanying narratives.

Andrew had never been a suspicious person. As of late, though, he had begun to suspect others he had previously never met, questioning actions of acquaintances, and second-guessing the motivation of friends. Any could be wolves in sheep's clothing in their own right, perhaps not necessarily working against him but not wholly supporting him either.

He reflected on the Russian proverb his father had recited on numerous occasions, *doveryay no proveryay* – trust but verify. He smiled inwardly at the calming wisdom of his mentor.

CHAPTER 26

"Gaston," Andrew said, "I would like to chat soonest as I have several matters to clarify, some of which reach back a few decades to when I first lived in Paris with my father. I have told neither Natalie nor Monique that I am speaking with you. I would prefer to keep this communiqué between us, at least for now."

"And I prefer not to discuss your concerns on the phone. We need to keep voice traffic to a minimum," Gaston replied tersely. "As good as technology is, it is not one hundred percent secure. Can you take the TGV train from Paris to Le Havre? Make reservations at the same hotel you were at on the previous trip when you visited. I will leave a message with the receptionist."

"*Oui*," Andrew confirmed in an equally cautious response. He ended the call straightaway, thus minimizing any opportunity for eavesdroppers to track him and his whereabouts or Gaston and his location.

The note handed to Andrew as he checked into Novotel Le Havre Centre was concise. The hotel manager appeared from his office and confirmed the meeting time with Gaston. Andrew proceeded to the manager's office at the designated time. The décor and furnishings were surprisingly much like Philippe's office in Novotel Paris Les Halles in Paris including a small round meeting table.

Gaston appeared from a second door to the right of the desk. "It is good to see you, young Andrew," he said with a sincere smile. "I am not surprised you have a few questions. I can guess some matters but will not presume to know all. So, ask away. Any queries I do not have the answer to, I will do my very best to find out. As a general strategy, I would encourage you to look for intimations that are out of the ordinary."

"Thank you," Andrew replied. "Most seem to relate to Natalie, the urban estate I now own and previous residents including a SS Nazi Gestapo officer, Oberstleutnant Hans Dietrich, who occupied the house during the latter years of the war. In addition, I need to know a few things regarding his son, Manfred, and his alleged Jewish wife, Louise. Finally, how Monique is connected. A common link to all appears to be the *Maquis*."

Andrew tried to deduce Gaston's emotional reaction to the topics he had just posed. There was none. His face was blank. Perhaps Gaston had correctly anticipated all the questions. He merely nodded and awaited Andrew's first query.

"Natalie," Andrew said slowly. "She was introduced to me as Monique's best friend from when we all lived in Saint-Germain-des-Prés, although I do not remember her. Most recently, she has become my real estate agent conveniently referred to me by Monique and her brother, Philippe." He paused, not wanting to inadvertently guide Gaston's response.

Gaston began, "Natalie served with the Police nationale. Her potential was recognized by her superiors early in her career. As a result, she was quickly promoted within her organization. She was recommended to the European Union Intelligence Unit as the representative of the Police nationale. All this you know. What you may not know is the fact she was asked to retire from the Police nationale with an attractive severance package and become a real estate agent which became a convenient cover story for her work as an agent with the EUI Unit. That is where she worked with Alexandra and Paul whom you have met. I was consulted by Daan Segers, Director of the EUI Unit, on these appointments. General Segers and I go back many years to when he served in the Belgian military as their Senior Intelligence Officer. Coincidently, I was working covertly with the *Maquis* after the war ended. We will talk about that at another time."

"You mentioned that you and my father knew somehow that I would return to Paris."

"That is correct. Call it a premonition on my part and career guidance on your father's part. I knew that you had come to Paris several times before with your late wife." Gaston began. "You are your father's son in more ways than one. You may not have realized it but your father subtly encouraged you to vacation in Europe and especially in Paris. His encouragement came in the form of financial incentives and reminders of all the good times you shared. He remained in contact with me regarding your travels. As a result, you were kept under observation because you exhibited similar traits to your father that would make you a successful intelligence gatherer in some capacity." Gaston smiled slightly.

Andrew pondered in quiet reflection as he gazed at Gaston with mixed emotions, inquisitiveness and a degree of astonishment but not resentment. What Gaston had just described was correct. His father had sown the seeds of travel to return to the City of Light in addition to compensating him for his travel expenses. He never told Andrew how he had influenced him but left clues like Hansel and Gretel breadcrumbs. These encouraged Andrew to follow up as circumstances permitted, including most recently with his youthful puppy love, Monique. He knew that Andrew had been smitten by her Parisienne personality.

"I passed on these details to Natalie but not Monique," Gaston explained. "That brings us to the topic of your current gated property."

Andrew leaned towards Gaston, listening more intensely. His urban estate or gated property as Gaston described it, held secrets that both intrigued him and left him feeling frustrated about the details of its provenance.

"Everything about your house is as explained to you by Natalie. It was built by Napoleon Bonaparte for his spy and remained the property of the French government, including the vacant stable-garage lot until the late 1950s. Records of provenance were purposely vetted for obvious reasons, to keep the identity of resident spies hidden." He hesitated, then intimated with a curt nod, "Some people are born secretive."

"And my lottery win?" Andrew asked. That could not have been manipulated. It had to have happened by chance.

"You won the lottery by chance. That windfall allowed Natalie to be introduced to you as a real estate agent. Everything was above board."

"And the couple who sold the house to me?" Andrew asked.

"The venders who sold it to you were government agents. They did own it and had planned to retire there. Fortunately for you, their marital bliss eroded into marital discord, thus altering their plans. Natalie conveniently used it to hide Monique from Claude's abusive tirades. The rest you know about, including the booby-trapped grenade which the Nazi SS planted as a departing gift. Sinister but not suspicious. The *Maquis* in Paris planted the listening device in the days leading up to the Nazi occupation. I do not know and have not been able to discover how they entered the compound after the Gestapo occupation. The few *Maquis* who knew have taken that information to their graves. Good luck to you if you want to pursue that. I will add that there are rumours circulating that SS Oberstleutnant Hans Dietrich hid undisclosed stolen treasure somewhere on your property. He took some with him when he departed hastily as the Free French Army under General Charles de Gaulle entered the city in August 1944."

The orderly Teutonic mind had become its own worst enemy when it came to the timely and orderly withdrawal of the Nazis from Paris. It was instead a hasty disorganized retreat for the most part.

"Like your father, young Andrew, you have an inquisitive mind," Gaston noted after considering the depth and breadth of Andrew's questions. "It will keep you in good stead. I encourage you to validate both your sources and the legitimacy of the information that has been passed along."

Andrew nodded ever so slightly in acknowledgement. His father had encouraged him to do the same on numerous occasions as he grew up.

"When you lived here all those years ago, your father and I met many times to talk about security and intelligence issues related to those early days of the Cold War that we were both engaged in. They were confidential matters that we kept between us because we did not trust many of our colleagues who had not proven themselves under fire. Former spies from the Axis powers, not surprisingly the Nazis, in addition to agents from Allied Forces like the Russians had infiltrated our ranks. Other supposed Allies joined the ranks of spies spying on spies. All entered the world of intelligence gathering as the war was ending. It is for that reason that your father had cautioned you not to talk about what had gone on, and I reminded my children, Monique and Philippe, that the war was not over. It is still not over. Since returning to Honfleur, old nemeses from the latter days of the *Maquis* activities around the time of the D-Day invasion have reared their ugly heads. I am confident that we will fight one last skirmish." He paused. "It is inevitable."

Andrew maintained eye contact with Gaston, saying nothing yet confirming his understanding of the full intent of what Gaston had related. He understood the gravity of his verbal communiqué.

"You and Monique have become intertwined on the periphery of the Cold War with the discovery of the document. It goes without saying that you need to be wary of the consequences of gaining this intelligence. Like the names in the document, there are some who would stop at nothing to learn what I am about to pass on. The burden is onerous, so share with Monique as you see fit. Again, I caution you to be guarded if anyone approaches you with a message supposedly from me. If so, ask for the code word *RAF*. Immediately contact Alexandra and Paul if you become suspicious."

"I will," he confirmed.

"For your information, Alexandra and Paul are currently following up on what SS Oberstleutnant Hans Dietrich's son, Manfred, said in their initial interview with him. There were too many inconsistencies, the most glaring being Manfred's wife's claim to her Jewish heritage and her parents' home in Saint-Germain-des-Prés district. There would have been greater truth in their story had she said their home was in the 3e arrondissement, the Marais, the Jewish quarter of Paris, not that there were not Jewish people living in other districts of the city. There were, including Saint-Germain-des-Prés. Her story just seemed to be too opportune, being so close to your property and the wartime residence of SS Oberstleutnant Hans Dietrich. Ask yourself the question, Andrew, would it be convenient for French traitors to covertly enter and exit the property via some hidden door in order to exchange information or be trained as informants for the Nazis?" Gaston raised his eyebrows. "Or were they purposely smuggled into the compound?" The intent of his question was abundantly clear.

CHAPTER 27

Alexandra and Paul boarded the TGV train at the Paris Gare de l'Est enroute to the Metz Gare de Nord, a trip of 280 km on a track with few curves. Scanning the scenery above the berms from the first-class seats on the upper deck seemed to shorten the hour and a half trip.

They would validate Manfred's declaration that he and his alleged wife, Louise, had entrenched French familial ties to the Alsace-Lorraine region. Such claims had been avowed by French residents of Metz yet challenged by German inhabitants since the Franco-Prussian War and the subsequent German annexation of the region. Manfred's insistence on being French, not German, appeared to mock the former Kaiser's historic assertion, perhaps with some justification.

Upon arrival, Alexandra and Paul proceeded to a safe house in Place Saint Louis. Through lead-lined stained-glass windows and Alsatian lace curtains in the turreted garret suite, they had a 270-degree view of the comings and goings in the square. Those who frequented the plaza in the cool of the summer evenings to sip Perrier or their favourite fruit of the vine were thankful the pigeons and doves no longer used the pigeonnier or dovecote that adorned the top of the turret under its shale roof tiles.

"Wardrobe change," Paul commented. "*Je t'adore* – I adore you whichever outfit you choose." He smiled in admiration of her allure. He always had since they first met as teenagers in Metz all those years ago, only to be separated by their parents because of their respective professions. Alexandra's mother had been an agent with the Director General External Security since the end of the war. Paul's father had been employed as a police officer for a similar length of time. Both parents were now deceased.

Alexandra smiled in response. She recalled a proclamation made by the acclaimed French fashion designer, Coco Chanel, whose mantra was: *dress shabbily, they remember the dress; dress exquisitely, they remember the person.* Accordingly, she would alter her attire so as not to be easily remembered by Manfred and Louise after their interview in Paris, should they cross paths in Metz.

After modifying their appearance, they strolled across Place Saint Louis in the old district of Metz, stopping briefly in front of an antique shop on Enceinte Fournrue as if window shopping. She smiled, alert to her surroundings. The backgammon board on display in the window had been rotated on the rotary display wheel, indicating he had arrived. They entered the adjacent shopping arcade from the Hôtel des Fleurs and took the escalator down to the arcade. Out of habit, she tapped in the code and pressed her thumb on the recessed fingerprint reader.

"Good morning, boss," Alexandra exclaimed buoyantly as she held out her hand to Daan Segers, the director of the European Union Intelligence Unit. Paul followed suit. Daan exuded the usual cultivated elegance that had come to define the character of this man of mystery. Alexandra noted the hair on his temples included half-a-dozen shades of grey since they had last talked face-to-face.

"I would like to introduce you to a recently recruited EUI Unit agent, Emma Bauer," Daan said. "Emma is on loan from the German Federal Criminal Police Office, the BKA. She holds a doctorate in linguistics specializing in eastern and western European languages. She uses the *nom de guerre*, Yana, a name that is culturally Slavic in origin and Hebrew in derivation. It has been a convenient *nom de guerre* when investigating war crimes against victims of genocide perpetrated by the Nazis during World War II. It is appropriate under these circumstances with Manfred and his father. Being born and educated in Munich, Yana will be able to recognize any subtle Bavarian accents or other Germanic cultural innuendoes which Manfred may exhibit unintentionally but might not be perceived by those who are not local."

"We look forward to working with you, Yana," Paul affirmed. "Given Manfred's claim that his in-laws were victims of his father's Nazi directives to round up Jews in Paris, the question of the relationship needs to be clarified. The unanswered question remains: Were Manfred's in-laws victims of, or informants for, his father, SS Oberstleutnant Hans Dietrich?"

Alexandra and Paul's cell phones vibrated simultaneously. The message from Andrew was clear. "Persons believed to be employed by the French communists identified in the document attempted to abduct Monique. Langue successfully defended her. One perpetrator is in custody, the second fled the scene."

"We are enroute to your location. Will advise ETA soonest," Alexandra replied without hesitation.

Paul showed Daan Andrew's message and Alexandra's reply.

"Keep me updated," Daan directed. "Before you go, please brief Yana on the results of your interview with Manfred and Louise, particularly your intuitive assessments of their authenticity."

"Will do," Alexandra confirmed.

"For your information," Daan added, "I have been in contact with Commandant Sophia Tessier of the Police Municipal de Metz because we will be working within her jurisdiction."

Daan shifted his attention to Yana. "You can start to track down Manfred and Louise. When you are conducting your investigation in Metz, I will work with you. Although some agents do work on their own, my preference is to work in pairs for security reasons and to help in sharing ideas."

A subsequent message from Andrew read, "Monique is safe and enroute to the family retreat with my real estate agent. Will update you with more details upon your arrival in Paris."

⊰ ⊱

"WHEN ARE WE RETURNING TO Paris?" Her voice was abrupt. Her tone had a tinge of impatience and frustration but Louise knew enough not to press him. Experience had taught her that if she did, Manfred would become increasingly distant and stop responding to her questions in a timely manner, if at all. That would further irritate her. If left alone, he would respond in the fullness of time. She just had to be patient and wait for his reply. She was uncertain whether or not he trusted her or had just not formulated an answer. Either were viable behaviours, she knew. In the time she had known him, and more recently as a married couple, their relationship had become strained.

Among Manfred's personal papers, Louise had found an envelope addressed to Henri Joseph Dubois, Manfred's French alias. The handwriting was in Gothic, Old German style. Enclosed was a map in pencil with lines that resembled streets but without names, and what appeared to be buildings and other stand-alone structures but without addresses. Perhaps the names were purposefully left blank. Whoever created the map seemed to have a detailed working knowledge of all the architectural features. However, conspicuous in its absence was any reference to the arrondissement. Traditionally, cartographers listed north at the top of any map but there was no compass direction on this amateur sketch. Thus, it was impossible to orient the map to streets she and Manfred had strolled along in Saint-Germain-des-Prés and other districts in Paris on both the left and right banks of the Seine encircling the Île de la Cité.

At one point in their most recent exploration of the 6e arrondissement, Manfred had stopped abruptly, turned the map round and mumbled faintly that they had arrived. The south-east extension of the diagram had been marked with a black dot within the parameters of what he concluded could be an oblong building.

A high stuccoed wall prevented visual confirmation, though. He could only assume that what was drawn on the map was an accurate depiction of what was hidden from sight. He recalled the directions his father had passed along to him about how to access the secret site. He folded the map and carefully slid it back into the inside breast pocket of his jacket without explaining to Louise why *they had arrived.*

Louise merely nodded and smiled but at what she wasn't sure, perhaps confident that she was closer to achieving her long-awaited goal. There was neither a street name nor an address on any of the building façades which could only be accessed through imposing wrought-iron gates. She made a mental note of the side streets at the first intersection they came to. It was the 6e arrondissement and Saint-Germain-des-Prés district. She would return on her own, if need be.

CHAPTER 28

Langue met Alexandra and Paul at the front gate and escorted them along the cobblestone path to the imposing front door where he licked their hands, his tail wagging like a metronome. Andrew greeted them warmly with his customary handshake. "I am pleased to see you both, very pleased in fact. Come in. It's a little early for wine but the coffee is brewing."

"Good boy," Andrew said as he looked down and patted Langue on the head. Once inside the house, Langue adopted his usual sentinel post on the Persian carpet by the front door. He kept his head high, ears and eyes scanning like radar, his senses on full alert.

"Monique left me a note this morning before I got up saying she had cabin fever, cocooned behind high walls and locked doors. She said she was going for a stroll in the neighbourhood with Langue. I was anxious, very anxious about her decision, although I understood her need to get outside. I admit that being behind these walls, I have felt a bit like prisoner 24601 Jean Valjean, the hero in Victor Hugo's 19th century novel, *Les Misérables*."

"At least she took Langue with her," Alexandra exclaimed.

Andrew nodded in response.

"As they approached rue de Seine, she stopped to savour the scent of freshly baked bread and croissants from a neighbourhood boulangerie. Then a dark blue Citroën SUV pulled up alongside them. The passenger jumped out and tried to grab her but Langue stopped him in his tracks. The dog jumped up and knocked the attacker to the ground. Luckily a patrol car rounded the corner just at the right time. One officer got out of the patrol car to arrest the man and help Monique. The driver of the Citroën SUV sped away leaving his partner in crime to deal with Langue and the police. The driver of the patrol car turned in pursuit of the SUV. All the while,

Langue held the man to the ground snarling ferociously with teeth bared. The driver of the Citroën abandoned his vehicle immediately after turning left onto rue de Seine and escaped on foot into the pandemonium created by the late-morning pedestrian traffic. He remains at large despite the admirable efforts of the police to cordon off the area."

"How did you find out?" Paul enquired.

"Monique asked the arresting officer to call Nicole who called me. The man who grabbed her remains in custody but is saying nothing at this time, not even requesting a lawyer, as if innocent of any wrongdoing. No doubt he has been taken into custody before because he is familiar with the routine."

Alexandra and Paul glanced at each other with expressions of delight at her rescue and shock at the brazen attempt to abduct her. More worrying was the possibility of a situation where she had not been saved by Langue's intervention.

"According to Natalie, we have one perpetrator in custody and available for questioning," Andrew said.

Paul replied, "I understand the perpetrator has remained tight-lipped beyond identifying himself as Jean-Pierre Leduc of no fixed address. He was not carrying any identification papers or cell phone. Thus, his identity cannot be confirmed."

"What about the blue Citroën SUV?" Alexandra asked.

"It had been rented under a false name and address," Andrew confirmed. "The driver and the passenger had been wearing gloves, so no prints could be lifted. A professional job all the way round. Natalie said the police could only charge him with common assault, although he claims the dog attacked him first and he was only defending himself."

Alexandra admitted reluctantly, "More than likely, any magistrate would release him on bail in the absence of any conclusive evidence, if charges were laid. The police may have to release him after he has been photographed and fingerprinted."

Paul added, "Perhaps more important is the supposition that they, whoever *they* are, had Monique in their sights. This begs the question – Do they know your identity, Andrew, in addition to this house? If they drove up behind Monique, they probably knew the general neighbourhood that Monique frequents."

"Or they had a photograph of her and recognized her by sheer luck. But how? The only people who know Monique and the fact she has been staying here are Natalie, you, Daan, Paul and me," Alexandra reflected out loud.

"Despite the fact the abductor has admitted to nothing, we should interview him," Paul suggested. "Before we engage with him, we need to have Monique review the EUI Unit e-photo file in order to establish a positive identity of the driver, if she is able."

"And how are you?" Alexandra asked Andrew, sensing his relief as if a cork had been removed from a bottle of champagne in his cellar.

"Better now that Monique is safe. Thanks for asking. As I read her note, my intuition suggested something menacing." With that disclosure, the furrows on his brow became more prominent. "To be completely honest, my heart skipped a beat. We will have a tête-a-tête regarding house rules when we next meet, alone," he mumbled. He exhaled a breath of relief. His concern for her well-being was palpable, not only to Alexandra and Paul but to himself.

Paul focused on Andrew. "In your email to us, you mentioned that Monique and Natalie were in transit to Honfleur and Gaston's safe house near the old jail. Do you know where they are at this moment?"

"Not sure," he admitted reluctantly.

As Paul continued to gaze at Andrew, he wondered how he was adjusting to his new post-lottery windfall life compared to his previous anonymous tourist lifestyle, worlds parallel in some respects but opposite in others. He reflected on the transition he and Alexandra had experienced before and after their retirement and decision to become members of the European Union Intelligence Unit at Daan's behest. *Our lives are the meaning we give them*, he contemplated.

"If she promises not to leave the confines of your urban estate, even with Langue, can she come home?" read Natalie's text message to Andrew.

"Of course. Where is she?" Andrew replied anxiously.

"With me at my place. I let it be known that we were enroute to the Normandy region in the event there was an e-communications or other leak."

Within the half hour, Andrew was staring at Monique as Langue licked her hand repeatedly. She did not have to comment but stood beside Natalie with her head bowed meekly like a truant school girl called into the principal's office.

"If you saw a photograph, could you identify the driver of the SUV?" Paul asked.

"Probably not. The windows were tinted. Plus, my attention was all on the man grabbing me and Langue knocking him down. Other people had come to rescue me by then. The SUV sped off with the police car in hot pursuit once it turned around."

Monique transferred her attention to Andrew. "I promise never to do that again," she apologized sincerely. "Never."

He returned her remorseful stare and gave her a hug. For her benefit only, he whispered with his lips on her ear, "You damn near gave me a heart attack. Where would you find such upscale accommodation at such an acceptable rental rate and with such a pet-friendly contract with no damage deposit, if I had died from cardiac arrest?"

The humour went over her head as she answered in an equally

low murmur, "I know, I know, I know. I need to start including you in my decisions. Please appreciate I never had to do that with Claude. The less I had to say to him, the less he would lash out at me, and the lower my stress level would be. That was my life back then." The seriousness of her situation seemed to go over his head.

A pause followed her honest explanation. Her breathing calmed. A renewed sense of security warmed her. She lingered before whispering, "How can I make it up to you?" She tightened her embrace.

CHAPTER 29

Yana sat at the table next to Manfred in Place Saint Louis. Daan occupied the table behind him with his back to him, close enough to overhear the conversation yet far enough away so as not to draw his attention.

"*Bonne journée,*" Yana said in a barely audible whisper but still loudly enough to attract his attention. Her voice was soft and mysteriously enticing which few males could have ignored regardless of their culture. She had practised that sensuous delivery until perfected.

It was the softness that was compelling, inviting Manfred to look up from the book he was reading. "Salut," he replied, almost unexpectedly. His rapid response surprised him. Rarely did he engage with people he did not know. When he looked at her, his slightly irritated expression became a gracious smile that lit up his face. *Paris could not claim sole tenure to all the most beautiful women in France*, he deduced. The murmur of other voices and background noise seemed to fade as he concentrated on the source of the greeting.

"Are you from this older district of Metz?" Yana asked. Her velvet voice mesmerized him, compelling him to maintain eye contact and respond without hesitation.

"I have lived here for several decades. I am almost a citizen," he jested. "Can I help you with directions?"

"Do you know the location of the German Gates? Am I far?" She enquired politely in the same soft voice that made him lean toward her in order to hear better.

"You are approximately fifteen minutes away. Walk east along rue des Allemands," he replied cordially. "It will appear directly in front of you with its centuries-old gate framed between two imposing towers. You literally cannot miss it because rue des Allemands leads directly to the turreted front gate of Porte des Allemands."

"*Vielen Dank* – thank you very much," Yana responded with a cordial smile. She was in her element drawing him into her web.

Manfred paused, unsure why she responded in German. He tilted his head as his friendly gaze morphed into a glare. He suspected her greeting had not been genuine, for whatever reason. Despite that, she had been pleasant company. He felt conflicted as if awoken from a tranquil daydream by flashbacks of the violent nightmares that had plagued him since early childhood.

"*Je suis désolé* – I am sorry. Please forgive me. I sensed a German lilt in your accent." She maintained her gracious smile throughout the explanation. "I did not mean to offend you by speaking in German. I noticed that you were reading a book on the Franco-Prussian War. I appreciate that cultural roots reach deep in this region of Alsace-Lorraine. *S'il te plaît, pardonne-moi* – please forgive me," she begged cordially, breaking eye contact which she sensed he desperately wanted to maintain. After a moment's pause she looked up, re-establishing eye contact.

"That is perfectly understandable," Manfred replied as he acknowledged her sincere apology. "Metz has been influenced by descendants of both modern-day French and Germanic cultures since the time of Charlemagne in the first century. I have a book on the German Gates and another on Charlemagne if you would like to read them."

"How kind of you to offer but I must be off. Thank you again for the directions to the German Gates," Yana remarked. "I hope to see you again and perhaps engage in conversations that matter about Charlemagne's Metz and the German Gates." She rose from her table, faintly touched him on his arm and walked in the direction of rue des Allemands.

Daan remained seated behind Manfred. *Damn, she is good*, he mused as he chuckled to himself. *No man and few women could pull that off with such fineness and with such professionalism.* He would commend her as soon as the opportunity presented itself.

"Who was that you were talking to?" Louise barked at Manfred in a sharp accusatory tone as she approached his table from the covered walkway intersecting with rue de la Tête d'Or. She sat down beside him abruptly, bumping into the table top. What did she want?" she snarled.

"Just a tourist asking directions to the German Gates," he replied equally brusquely.

She changed topics in a huff. "When will we return to Paris to identify the hiding place?" Louise asked. "You have the map and the alleged location that your father identified."

"Soon," he mumbled under his breath as abruptly as Louise had posed her question. *Longer than you would like*, he thought to himself. He retrieved the book from the table, opened it to the page marker and began to read where he had left off before being interrupted by the lady with the voice of an angel.

He reflected on the brief yet pleasurable conversation he had just had, particularly her enticing voice. He found her to be not just beautiful but mysterious. The pleasing manner of this mystery lady was in complete contrast to Louise's grating way, which he found increasingly irritating. He looked forward to chatting about the Franco-Prussian War and Charlemagne's Metz if he saw her again. In fact, he would frequent the plaza in the hope of meeting her again. He regretted not asking for her name and for not offering his. Her gracious approach had taken him by complete surprise.

"We need to go home now," Louise snapped. Her sharp dictate made Manfred flinch. Worse, it jolted him out of his escapist dream of a *rendezvous intime* – an intimate encounter with the mysterious lady. He would not forgive Louise for such an indiscretion. He drew his fingers lightly over his arm where the enchantress had touched him moments before. He concentrated on the mood she had created in hopes of committing everything to memory, never to be forgotten.

He reluctantly followed Louise away from Place Saint Louis and the pleasant encounter. They walked toward rue des Allemands and their home on rue de Petit Champé. Manfred hoped he might see the enigmatic lady who had so captivated him.

Daan followed a minute behind and met up with Yana as they approached rue des Allemands. They stopped momentarily and stared inquisitively at one another as they scanned the routes their targets might have taken. He took the opportunity to compliment her. "You are good. No, you are excellent. You had him mesmerized – he was like putty in your hands."

"That is what you are paying me for, boss," she jested with a flirtatious smile. "Now, let's track them down. I don't want to lose our targets on our first case working together. That would be embarrassing."

Louise glanced at Manfred with blank eyes. At the entrance to a vacant courtyard, she shoved him inside as she thrust a stiletto knife into his back.

He stared back with a confused expression, bemused, his complexion now pallid. *"Ich hade dich einst geliebt* – I once loved you," he whispered feebly.

"Tschüss – bye," she replied unashamed. "I warned you not to talk in such an unfaithful manner." She betrayed him in a way only a woman masquerading as a jealous intimate partner could, wearing an expression of callous determination.

Yana stared ahead, catching a glimpse of Louise as she ran out of the courtyard and into the street in the direction of her house on rue de Petit Champé. Daan and Yana sprinted to the courtyard. The piercing sound of two-tone police sirens approached.

Yana glanced in the vacant courtyard at the motionless body of Manfred lying on his back. His book about the Franco-Prussian War was wedged under his arm. She bent over as he reached up to her and gasped, "She stabbed me, she has the map, I hid my father's…German Gates." Blood gurgled from his throat into his mouth.

"Who stabbed you?" Yana pressed sensing that his life was rapidly fading. She might have only one chance. She smiled hoping to encourage him to focus on her long enough to provide the essential information she desperately sought.

"Louise," he whispered ever more feebly as he struggled to get another breath through the excruciating pain. "You are beautiful."

Yana kept her hand on his arm where she had touched him when he sat at the table in Place Saint Louis. She stared into his dying eyes as he took a final breath, smiling calmly up at her. He seemed to say, "Merci."

The police siren went silent at the entrance to the courtyard. Two patrol officers got out with pistols drawn and pointed at Yana who was still kneeling beside Manfred's body. Bright crimson blood flowed from his stab wound into the crevasses between the cobblestones.

"Do not move," one officer yelled at Yana who promptly complied with his direct order, not even turning to look up at him.

From a partially open window of a first-floor flat inside the courtyard a woman yelled at the police with a washerwoman's penetrating voice, "I was the one who called. It was another woman who stabbed him, not this one you are pointing your guns at."

Daan remained at the entrance to the courtyard. He had just ended his call to Commandant Tessier at the Metz Municipal police headquarters.

The second police officer glared at Daan as he acknowledged a call on his portable radio. "Who are you?" He directed his question at Daan in a gruff voice.

"Daan Segers, Director of the European Union Intelligence Unit. This lady kneeling beside the man on the ground is my partner, also an agent with the EUI Unit."

The second officer motioned to his partner who continued to hold his pistol on Yana. "Commandant Tessier has confirmed the identities of both. The Commandant is enroute to this location and will be taking over the investigation. We are to protect the scene."

The woman in the flat continued to yell at the police that the female they had in custody was not the person who stabbed the man.

In the background, other two-tone police sirens approached with lights flashing, followed by an ambulance.

Before the patrol officers could ask any other questions, Daan said, "We believe that the perpetrator is the man's wife, Louise Dubois. She may be going on foot to her home on rue de Petit Champé. She is in her early sixties, average height, dark brown shoulder-length hair, wearing a blue jacket and slacks. I recommend you ask Commandant Tessier for permission to advise all other units of her description and dispatch a second patrol car to rue de Petit Champé."

"Daan, good to see you but not under good circumstances," Commandant Tessier said as she got out of her car. "You can holster your pistols," she ordered the patrol officers. "Daan, can you brief me and my officers on the circumstances?"

Daan nodded hesitantly. "What I am about to share is a classified secret," he spoke quietly so that his intended audience could hear him but not loudly enough that the crowd of onlookers could hear. "The deceased is Henri Joseph Dubois of rue de Petit Champé. He was born Manfred Hans Dietrich, son of SS Oberstleutnant Hans

Dietrich, formerly head of the Nazi Gestapo in the 6e arrondissement of Paris."

Commandant Tessier met Daan's look wide-eyed. She glared
at her two patrol officers. "You say nothing to anyone. That is an
order! Am I perfectly clear?"

Both officers nodded abruptly. There was no room for debate
regarding the urgency.

"Yes, Commandant," they answered respectfully as they stood
to attention.

"How can we help, Daan?" she asked.

"We would like to search his house, but we appreciate that we
might find evidence relating to this murder."

"Not a problem. I will supervise your search personally. I will
have these two officers who overheard your briefing accompany
us to take charge of any evidence in Manfred's house related to
this case."

Whether they liked it or not, the two officers on the scene were
now involved in the European Union Intelligence Unit investigation. *The fewer the police officers involved with the European
Union Intelligence Unit the better*, Commandant Tessier thought.

She directed that two other officers remain in the courtyard to
secure the scene, pending the arrival of a senior investigator, a
coroner and identification services. "We can now proceed to rue de
Petit Champé. Daan and Yana will accompany me," she advised.

As they drove up to the house, nothing appeared untoward.
Commandant Tessier, Daan and Yana remained on rue de Petit
Champé close to their vehicle for protection. The two uniformed
patrol officers approached Manfred's house cautiously with pistols
drawn. The front door was ajar. They announced in loud voices
"police" as they crossed the threshold and several times thereafter
as they entered each room. There was no reply. Confident the house
was safe, they called back to Commandant Tessier, "All clear."

"You can enter and begin your search," she told Daan and Yana who cautiously followed her inside, scanning the rooms for any untoward sounds or movement. They had no reason to question the findings of the two patrol officers but a second set of eyes on the scene was always helpful.

Like the outside of the house, nothing seemed out of place, including dishes, as if ready for a real estate showing to potential buyers. The furnishings and décor were more spartan than extravagant. The one bed had been made without so much as a wrinkle. Books in the two-metre square bookshelf were in order obsessively by size left to right. A closer examination revealed that most of the books were related to the history of the Prussian state, a few published in the 19th century. A small vegetable garden that could only be accessed through a door from the kitchen was tidy, fastidiously so. Plants were aligned and pruned with regimental precision.

After a meticulous search, Daan and Yana exchanged puzzled glances.

"Curious," Yana said slowly.

"I agree, very curious," Daan replied, mirroring her reaction.

"Anything?" Commandant Tessier enquired.

"Surprisingly, nothing," Daan responded with a perplexed expression.

After a moment, Yana added, "Too tidy. Something is not right. What is Manfred trying to tell us? I didn't get this impression of him when we spoke in Place Saint Louis."

Commandant Tessier turned to the two uniformed patrol officers. "Your thoughts?" Additional eyes and reflections from seasoned officers were always welcome under her command.

They shook their heads slowly with astonished expressions that reflected Yana's summation. Something was out of place by virtue of the fact that there was nothing that looked out of place.

"Think what Manfred said to you in his final breath. Clearly, you had made a favourable impression on him. Anything that might be a clue?" Daan prompted Yana.

"He said that his wife, Louise, had stabbed him. At Place Saint Louis, he said something about a book he had on the German Gates and Charlemagne, suggesting that I could read them."

Daan raised his eyebrows slightly as he held Yana's gaze, saying nothing that might interfere with her thoughts.

He then looked at Commandant Tessier. "Thank you for allowing us to search Manfred's house."

"You are welcome," she replied, and shrugged. "Nothing might mean something. The absence of evidence often suggests the presence of other clues not previously considered."

As they started to leave the house, Yana stopped abruptly and put her finger on her lips. She turned and strode back to the bookshelf where she pointed to one title, *Mein Kampf*, located between a book on the German Gates and another on Charlemagne. Their regimented order had a symbiotic connection with Manfred's Bavarian mind, inexplicable to Louise.

"*Mein Kampf* – My Struggles. Adolf Hitler's book. I read *Mein Kampf* at the Ludwig Maximilian University of Munich as part of my studies on German language and culture. It was doubtful Hitler ever completed grammar school, yet he supposedly wrote this book and had it published for all loyal Germans to read." She stared at the inscribed title on the spine as she slowly pulled it from the bookshelf and opened it. "But this is not Hitler's book." She opened the cover of the relatively new binding. *Liebes Tagebuch* – Dear Diary had been handwritten on the title page in Old German. Underneath, SS Oberstleutnant Hans Dietrich had written his name, rank and the inscription 'Mein Kampf – My Struggles.' It was his diary, his account of his struggles as the head of the Gestapo in the 6e arrondissement, Saint-Germane-des-Prés, Paris.

"Eureka!" Yana exclaimed. "He told me where to look. He must have realized that he might not get another opportunity."

All eyes turned to her.

Daan reassured her quietly. "If it is any consolation, he took his last breath a happier calmer soul knowing that you were with him. I commend you again on your professionalism in gathering the requisite intelligence without having to formally interview him when there was no opportunity to do so. As Commandant Tessier astutely suggested, absence of evidence can mean presence of clues not previously considered. You are damn good."

Yana smiled, acknowledging his compliment, yet sadly so, as she was reminded again of the ugliness of death itself. The silence between them grew heavy for a moment under the circumstances. She reflected on what would be appropriate to say in response and what to leave unsaid. "Thank you," she replied gently.

CHAPTER 30

"Update on Manfred and Louise," Daan's text to Alexandra and Paul read. "Manfred was fatally stabbed by Louise who is at large with a warrant issued by the Metz Municipal police. We believe Louise is enroute to Saint-Germain-des-Prés. Further details to follow shortly by other secure means."

Daan followed up his text message with a phone call. He provided a comprehensive account of the murder and the results of the search of Manfred's house. His final instructions were explicit. Alexandra and Paul were to warn Andrew and increase security. Alone, Daan did not believe that Andrew or Monique were intended targets but they could become casualties if they got in the way of Louise getting her hands on a cache of money and other valuables that SS Oberstleutnant Hans Dietrich had allegedly hidden somewhere on Andrew's urban estate. Louise had killed in cold blood once so she was likely to repeat the offence.

"What did the diary say?" Alexandra asked anxiously. She wanted to know any details related to their interview with Manfred and Louise, seeking any points contradictory to what he had said on that occasion.

"There were numerous references in his father's diary to ongoing close ties with Manfred throughout the war and during the postwar period when Manfred claimed that he had had no contact with his father. On the contrary, Manfred hid his father in his own house when he attended university. Although there were no directions to the cache of stolen property, the diary did refer to conversations they had in which his father told Manfred not to attempt to access anything for several years, perhaps decades after the war. A wise decision. By then, any rightful owners, if they had survived the concentration camps, would give up their pursuit, or if they did pursue claims, there would be less tangible evidence. His father did not mention any details if his diary fell into the wrong hands. From these references, we can conclude that SS Oberstleutnant Dietrich did collaborate with others to steal cash, gold and works of art from the 17th, 18th and 19th centuries. Oberstleutnant Dietrich did take with him considerable cash and treasures that could easily be converted to cash when he hurriedly left Paris under the veil of night as General De Gaulle and the Free French Army began to liberate the City of Light. Lights that were being turned back on in celebration. This kept him solvent in the post-war years. There were a few references to a Swiss bank in Davos which suggests he may have deposited cash and gold over the period of his tenure as head of the Gestapo in Saint-Germain-des-Prés. The extent of these deposits would have to be confirmed."

"Paul and I suspected Manfred was not telling us the whole truth when we interviewed him," Alexandra confirmed.

Daan added, "You were certainly correct in your assessment of the truth regarding his claim to a robust French heritage and denial of any meaningful German connection. Yana noted a convincing Bavarian undertone in Manfred's accent. Everything about the furnishings and décor in his house echoed a German heritage. Manfred had a collection of books published in Germany that related to the Kaiser and German claims to the region of Alsace-Lorraine that reached beyond the 19th century and the Franco-Prussian War."

"And Louise," Alexandra added.

"Yana did not have an opportunity to speak with Louise. Thus, she can neither confirm nor deny her heritage. Yana suggested that Louise's sole interest in Manfred appeared to be his father's hidden cache. I would tend to agree. For that reason, you need to ensure that Andrew and Natalie, and Monique, if she plans to stay on in Andrew's urban estate, are informed and ready to avoid confrontation with Louise. Metz municipal police have not been able to find

THE 14TH COBBLESTONE **171**

Louise since the stabbing in the courtyard. Thus, there is a high probability that she may be in Paris as we speak," Daan concluded.

"Ironic, the tables are now turned," Alexandra noted. "When Claude was after Monique, Andrew was the one who had to remain vigilant."

The news of Manfred's murder had caused Andrew to again re-think his plans to become a carefree *boulevardier* in the City of Light. He contemplated his options in earnest. Would he have to abandon the plans of living the Parisian lifestyle of leisure that Lynette and he had talked about? If Natalie sold his urban estate privately, he would not need to establish a comprehensive provenance of the house and property including the stable-garage lot. That might relieve some stress but create more as he would have to buy another house. But where could he go? The French communists would still be chasing after him and Monique, and Langue through association. The trio was taking on the trappings of an informal family configuration that he had not anticipated in his interpretation of a free and easy lifestyle. In addition, there was the great unknown, the criminal element he perceived might be pursuing him because of his lotto windfall.

My Catholic sensibility suggested otherwise. Perhaps that was just a figment of my imagination, Andrew thought.

He missed Lynette and the calm guidance she had always brought to their marriage. A smile came to his lips as he stared down at the Canadian Mountie Dudley-Do-Right watch he always wore. Lynette had given it to him on the last Christmas they shared before her death. It was a reminder to maintain his sense of humour in times of stress. She was with him now.

Andrew considered the possibilities. He wasn't going anywhere. The only threat to his dream of becoming a Parisian gentleman of leisure was Louise. He was confident that he could deal with Louise by avoiding her. He thought it was highly improbable the tree-lined boulevards and parks of Paris would be hiding SS Oberstleutnant Dietrich's cache of stolen property.

He kept reminding himself that he was not pursuing an abstract Buddha-like meditative existence, but instead a simple gentleman stroller role. When not strolling the broad boulevards and parks constructed by Haussmann, he would be sitting and listening to the cooing of the pigeons as they pecked for crumbs of baguettes and croissants scattered by kind-hearted patrons. Over countless hours, these generous mostly elderly souls had encouraged their feathered friends to join them for *petit-déjeuner* and *déjeuners de l'après-midi* as they sat outside at white cloth-covered tables in the shade of traditional red Parisian awnings over the sidewalk cafés.

CHAPTER 31

"I have relatively good news and somewhat bad news regarding the man who grabbed you, Monique," Natalie began.

"Relatively good news and somewhat bad news. Not sure if I like those parameters," Monique muttered as she slowly inhaled. "Please start on a positive note with the *relatively* good news. It will help me to put the *somewhat* bad into perspective." She smiled wryly.

"The good news is the man who attempted to force you into the SUV is no longer a threat to you. Or anyone else."

"I sense a caveat in your tone," Monique said sceptically.

Natalie qualified her announcement. "His body was found floating in the Seine with two bullet holes in the back of his head, double tap execution style. A common *modus operandi* it seems among the local criminal gangs for sending a warning to other colleagues to say nothing but, more importantly, be perceived as remaining loyal to the code of silence. The first criteria, he met. He remained tight-lipped throughout his interrogation, even with Alexandra and Paul when they reminded him that his days might be numbered when he was released because his employer and colleagues might conclude he had blabbed. He failed to meet the second criteria. To his credit, he did not identify the driver of the SUV who is still at large. In the final analysis, there was insufficient evidence to charge him. That is the not-so-bad news."

"I don't know whether to dance gleefully under the trellis in the rose garden or open another bottle of Andrew's favourite Pinot Noir," she joked.

Natalie continued, "I say not-so-bad news because the photo of the deceased is on the European Union Intelligence Unit database. It came up positive for several *noms de guerre*. A frequent associate of his is another criminal freelancer, also with several names. We suspect this second person may have been the driver of the SUV. Both have reputations for being professional enforcers. We suspect the driver murdered his partner for fear he might have negotiated with the police for his release by revealing his identity. Suspected dissenters have a bad habit of disappearing."

"*Vive gladio mori gladio* – if you live by the sword, you die by the sword," Andrew muttered, relieved there was one less felon to contend with. "Some might interpret it as unorthodox but others would describe it as bad karma."

"Additional good news," Natalie went on, "the suspected driver has outstanding warrants for his arrest. So, now the word is out that he is on the police *most-wanted* list. That should send him into hiding for a while."

Monique took another sip from her crystal wine glass which Andrew had generously topped up along with his own. "And Louise, any word on her whereabouts?" Monique asked.

"Nothing since Metz. She may have gone to ground there. More than likely, though, she is here in Paris closing in on SS Oberstleutnant Dietrich's cache. That was her goal all along, to hang out with Manfred in order to gain access to his father's map. We still don't know if they were ever married. No doubt she has associates. I say that because it is highly unlikely she would kill Manfred on the spur of the moment without having an escape plan. That would suggest at least one accomplice."

"You have been uncharacteristically quiet, Andrew," Natalie added. "What are you thinking?"

Silence defined the moment. Even Langue looked up inquisitively. "Two thoughts," he murmured." *Actually, two and a half*, he thought to himself. "First, it dawned on me, like the Oracle of Delphi, that if the names of the French communists and corrupt politicians and bureaucrats identified in the document were revealed, no one would chase after us to prevent the information from being released. It would take the wind out of their sails." He paused thoughtfully. "The truth could be more prosaic, a straight-forward simple solution," he conjectured. "With that full disclo-sure, I could live the life of a *flâneur*, undisturbed." He glanced over at his tenant as she gazed back over the brim of her wine glass. "Monique could join me strolling the boulevards and parks of Paris without constantly looking over her shoulder for criminals ready to pounce out of SUVs with abduction on their scheming minds."

"And the second thought?" Natalie probed. She had an idea what it might be. It had been a low priority on her to-do list since her meeting with Gaston in the safehouse in the seaside fishing village of Honfleur.

Andrew began in the same confident tone as he had with his first thought. "Gaston suggested that I or we contact the previous owners of my estate to find out if they could add anything to our pursuit of information about provenance, especially considering their suspected underground vocation."

Natalie nodded. "Provenance, possibly, yes. Also, they might be able to shed light on another previous resident, SS Nazi Oberstleutnant Hans Dietrich and perhaps a few of the Gestapo's antics. And what they know about the cache of stolen property. I will do my best to contact them through their real estate lawyers."

"Thank you," Andrew acknowledged. He felt calmer having some input into the direction the research could take. Natalie's engineering and real estate contact had been able to provide some details. But it was a trickle rather than a flood, and not the elusive gold mine of details.

"I'm sensing something else," Natalie prompted.

Andrew hesitated again. *Two and a half thoughts*. The remain-ing half.

"That would just leave one threat, the unknown criminal element stalking me in order to get their grubby hands on the lotto windfall." *This unknown is infringing upon my flâneur lifestyle plans*, he ruminated.

"I appreciate your worries," Natalie acknowledged. "You are not alone. Many winners experience these problems. To my knowledge, no previous recipients in France, at least, have been harassed or physically accosted, only subject to the somewhat random pleas for charity and investments into dubious commercial schemes that plague any rich person. I cannot speak with confidence about other jurisdictions in the European Union. If no one has appeared on the radar screen thus far, I suggest the probability is very low, even lower given the level of security and surveillance that you have with your urban estate. One final factor – neither Alexandra nor Paul have suggested any concerns."

"Add in Langue," Monique said with a confident smile. "Remember he is a trained police dog."

Natalie interjected, "Andrew, you also have a tenant who has experience of watching out for suspicious activities, like stalking husbands."

Monique gazed at him solemnly as she thought she would like to change the part-time tenant status to full-time. They would have to chat over wine on the veranda about what that might entail.

Andrew contemplated the logical reasoning of both ladies in his life as well as Alexandra and Paul, all of whom he had come to trust. As distant as Gaston had been at times due to his own mysterious *Maquis* background, Andrew was confident that Gaston would advise him of any substantial threats, if for no other reason than his long-term relationship with his father. In addition, he would certainly muster all resources to protect Monique. Andrew breathed slowly and deeply. Confidence was not a black and white phenomenon but varying shades of grey that had to be factored in. *La nuit tout les chats son gris* – at night all cats are grey.

He had worked in the world of statistical analysis which suggested that any person can only be ninety-nine-point-nine-eight percent confident of any raw data and results. That had been good enough for him throughout his career and would be sufficient now in retirement in order to have an elegant, leisurely existence in Paris. What there was for a gentleman of leisure to learn could be nuanced, he supposed.

CHAPTER 32

L angue began barking loudly as he rushed anxiously between the front and back of the house before positioning himself at the back door.

"What's bothering you, boy?" Andrew asked as he walked quickly to the back door. *Strange*, he thought. *He has always adopted his sentinel position on the Persian carpet by the front entrance.*

Without warning, the surveillance system sounded intermittent beeps. It indicated the security cameras at the lane door on the east side of the stable-garage had been tampered with.

"Monique, can you see what has upset Langue? This is the first time he has acted like this. I will check the monitors."

Monique responded to Langue's repeated yelping which he had never done before even when Claude was threatening her. She opened the back door to scan the backyard for any unusual activities. Before she could hold him, he bolted into the backyard and to the garden shed in the far corner. She sprinted in his direction calling him to come back but he took no notice. He navigated through the tools in the shed and out of the door on the stable-garage side before she reached him. By the time she got out, he had reached the pedestrian door leading to the lane. He yelped loudly and collapsed, whining. She took a few long strides to reach him. He looked up at her as if confused. He had done what he was trained to do, to protect his property but was now injured on the ground.

Andrew hurriedly scanned the bank of security monitors. The new cameras covered the pedestrian lane, the east side of the stable-garage and the interior of the building closest to the first stall with the harnesses and saddles. None was showing any images.

Instead, they flashed black and white. The only surveillance system functioning was an original camera mounted high on the exterior wall onto the lane. He quickly replayed the last image from that camera which showed what appeared to be a male and female wearing hats pulled low over their faces as they entered the stable-garage through the lane door. Moments later, only the male left, his identity still obscured. He ran a few paces before turning left towards the rue de Seine, out of range of any cameras. The door from the lane remained ajar.

"URGENT Security violation. Bastions to the inner compound breached," read the text in caps from Andrew to Natalie.

"On my way. Have forwarded your text to Alexandra and Paul."

Monique stumbled into the house through the back door, staggering under the weight of carrying Langue. "He has been badly injured," she cried out in panic. Blood was dripping from an open wound to his forehead above his left eye. Andrew gaped in horror. He grabbed a tea towel and applied pressure over the wound as Monique sank to the floor with Langue in her arms. All the while, the security alarm system continued to pierce the air. In the excitement, he had forgotten how to disable it.

"I'll be right back," he told Monique, attempting to sound calm. Moments later there was silence, although the disabled monitors continued to flash as did the pulsating security alarm strobe lights in the hallways.

While Monique remained in the house comforting Langue, Natalie, Alexandra and Paul followed Andrew to the lane door that remained ajar. He closed and locked it before entering the east side door to the stable-garage. Floorboards in the first stall had been removed. Andrew stared in the cavernous space at the body of a female, the same one who had been caught on the surveillance camera a few days before walking alongside Manfred. It was obvious from the contorted position of her head that Louise's neck had been broken with considerable violence. Yet her face appeared eerily calm as if she had not perceived her death was close.

Her lifeless body had been dumped into the dank cavity among what appeared to be a disarray of bric-a-brac debris including expensive broken picture frames. Small empty boxes and lids were strewn about the floor.

A mixture of revulsion and horror consumed him as he took a deep breath and let it out slowly. Such violence was no longer a departure from the norm. Sadly, it had become the norm. The gruesome scene kept them together, scanning the interior.

Andrew stood momentarily frozen in his tracks. A tremor of alarm, as he had never experienced before, never imagined in his wildest dreams, overwhelmed the core of his being. He could not grasp the callous depravity and brutality of such a murder. A certain macabre aftertaste associated with death seemed to paralyze his emotions.

His father had related accounts of unimaginable viciousness between armies at war and of soldiers slaughtering innocent civilians from the skies and face-to-face in concentration camps. Tears flowed down his face as the ghosts from those mass graves overwhelmed him. He and Lynette had heard the silent screams and cries of the dead when they visited Dachau concentration camp. After Dachau, he and Lynette believed this death camp had to have been an anomaly. But after witnessing the horrors of Auschwitz, reality set in, scarring their memories permanently.

Any aspirations of becoming a leisurely gentleman strolling Paris were resolutely purged from his mind in that instant. He was even too dazed to consider a glass of wine. It would have been tainted by the circumstances.

Within minutes, police cars entered the stable-garage leaving tread marks like the Nazi vehicles operated by the SS Gestapo that had been there for decades. The thought of what these police officers had to investigate left him numbed.

Natalie, Alexandra, Paul and Andrew returned to the house to review the surveillance footage over and over. They left the crime scene to the senior investigator. Andrew recalled Langue lingering in the first stall sniffing repeatedly when they first entered the building in search of a door between the two lots. He needed to learn to listen to his four-footed companion who was trying to warn him of danger.

The corpse held one final surprise. As the coroner turned the body over, the flash from the police identification services camera highlighted a pistol wedged under the body. The slide on the frame of the French 9mm semi-automatic PAMAS pistol appeared at a contorted angle, mirroring the position of the victim's head relative to the lifeless torso.

Like the mass graves in Auschwitz where SS Oberstleutnant Hans Dietrich had purportedly deported Jews from Paris, Andrew perceived the vacant stall where Louise's body lay as hallowed ground. Regardless of the role she had played in her own demise, her death was tangentially linked to the war which Gaston repeatedly reminded them was not over. Andrew was the landlord and was now responsible. For what, he was not certain. He knew that, by law governing real estate, he could not simply sell the lot without having to declare a murder had taken place there. He also knew that he would have to cleanse the soil of the evidence of violence if he was going to enjoy what the stable-garage had to offer. The carefree life as a *flâneur* seemed increasingly unlikely.

Natalie thought to herself that in a clandestine world of espionage and counter-espionage in which truths, partial truths and make-believe truths dance, black and white truths are beset by countless shades of grey. There is supposedly victimless white-collar crime and then there are almost innumerable means of murdering another living creature. Natalie only vaguely appreciated what Andrew was experiencing.

"Whoever it was who gained access to the lot with Louise must have had advanced knowledge of electronic surveillance systems or worked for an organization that employed highly skilled IT technicians," Natalie suggested to Alexandra and Paul.

Paul nodded in agreement. "My son, Jean Bernard, is the head of the European Union Anti-Terrorist Cyber Unit, recently on secondment from the Police nationale. If anyone can shed light on this intrusion, it is Jean."

"Need your technical assistance," Paul's text to his son read.

"On my way, ETA soonest," Jean replied. His father rarely contacted him with work-related requests. When he did, it was technically complex.

"How is he?" Andrew asked Monique who had stayed with Langue in her arms throughout the ordeal. He was thankful for the loving care she gave Langue and grateful she had not been exposed to the violence of the murder.

"The bleeding has slowed. Animals are like people when it comes to trauma to the head. Torrents of blood tend to flow immediately after impact. The stained tea towel is evidence of that. He probably suffered a mild concussion." She would call the veterinarian emergency line.

Langue raised his head enough to give Andrew a shaky lick on his hand. He whimpered with gratitude. Andrew recalled his thoughts regarding ownership after Langue had saved him from the booby-trapped hand grenade. Monique could have visiting rights. Seeing Monique's tender care today, he resigned himself to the fact that negotiating care and stewardship would be more a matter of joint custody. Langue had bonded with Monique and Andrew. Both would need to be present to care for him. That was now readily apparent and non-negotiable.

Langue raised his head again as Jean arrived but only rose to sit momentarily to great him with a weak confirming lick.

After being briefed on the security breach, Jean reset the alarmed monitoring systems. He then inspected the exterior and interior surveillance cameras around the lane door and the first stall inside the stable-garage.

"Initial thoughts?" Paul asked his son.

"Professional job. No doubt in my mind whoever it was had advanced technical know-how. They knew what they were doing, how to get in and out in the shortest time and without being identified. Feasibly, inside knowledge."

Natalie nodded. Jean had confirmed her own assessment.

Jean elaborated, "Sadly, the criminal underworld has overtaken the capabilities of most cyber law enforcement organizations. In the global community, China and Russia in addition to a host of rogue players operating out of India and several undisclosed African dictatorships have unofficially declared war. The battle space is global cyber, including but not limited to cyber-war, cyber-terrorism, and cyber-crime. The consequences make any known counter virus seem impotent. We, in the Western World are in a constant mode of just trying to catch up. I mention this because what we are facing may very well fall under this shroud of cyber insurgency directed from beyond the physical borders of France and very likely outside the European Union."

"Do we need to upgrade the security strategy?" Andrew asked, worried that his current system was inadequate. He would certainly instal a secure manual door-locking system with surveillance cameras and motion detectors between the two garden sheds.

"Your electronic security system is as good as they come and it's functioning properly," Jean reassured him with a smile. "Having said that, I am not aware of any electronic security system that is completely impenetrable. We need to shortlist those who have the technical ability to by-pass the system. Two possibilities come to mind, one more troublesome than the other. Whoever it was has left their electronic footprint. I just have to follow it back to its source. Given the history of this house, I have an idea. If correct, we may be facing roadblocks, not insurmountable but certainly challenging."

"I think we should forewarn Daan immediately if this first option is what I think it is," Paul commented. "He will need to advise Yolina Lambert at the EU Commission in Brussels."

Alexandra nodded.

"This first possibility is the preferred state, technologically, even with possible roadblocks," Jean suggested with reservation. "The alternate scenario involves the Dark Web which is where cyber criminals tend to conduct their business. It attracts very nasty people. Some of their cyber cells create software that can break into the databases of virtually all major corporations, financial institutions and governments sufficient to cripple them, certainly to corrupt operations. It is not a crime to write the software. As a result, these people do not use the software themselves. So, if caught, they cannot be prosecuted. Instead, they sell it via the Dark Web to players in a growing criminal cyber community." He hesitated as he took a deep breath. "Welcome to the e-world of Bonnie and Clyde," he smiled sombrely. "In the short term, I am not hopeful that whoever breached your electronic bastions will meet the same end as the American outlaws who terrorized the Midwest in the Dirty Thirties."

Jean hesitated as a prelude to his final assessment of what they could be facing. "Bad news, the two scenarios are not mutually exclusive in the case of your security system being breached, Andrew, like other cyber incursions we are working on. There is a strong probability that both scenarios may be operating concurrently which divides our counter-intelligence cyber resources. Good news, counter-cyber police resources in the European Union and many in Interpol are working together because the cyber world knows no borders."

After the police had left, Alexandra put on her forensic psychologist hat. She smiled at Andrew as she posed her standard debriefing question, "How are you doing?"

"Improved since seeing Louise's body through the hole in the floorboards of the stall." A shiver ran the length of his spine causing him to jerk uncontrollably in response to a flashback of Louise's lifeless image. This was the second time in as many weeks that he had been shaken to the core of his being, the first being the near fatal experience of the booby-trapped hand grenade in the gardening shed.

Andrew looked at Monique, who remained seated on the floor soothingly patting Langue. She returned his look of deep concern for both her and Langue with a reassuring smile.

His composure reflected his quieter breathing which was reassuring to Alexandra. "We can chat more later," she assured him.

A reed-thin smile showed his sincere appreciation of her heartfelt concern for his wellbeing and her willingness to assist. He was hopeful that speaking with her would help him rest this evening, ideally without the nightmares associated with the images of the hand grenade wired to the shed door. Mixed with his nightmares were memories of joyful experiences he and Lynette had shared and those they had planned on adding to their diaries of further European travels.

With the suddenness of a lightning bolt, his face showed the realization of the conflict of thoughts. The repulsive truth struck him as he mused in frustration: *I won the largest lottery to date. With it, I am able to purchase virtually anything I want with the stroke of a pen, including this urban estate. Yet I am unable to purchase what I want most, a zone of peace and serenity.* He sighed but faced the reality as he muttered the final desperate call by King Richard III from Shakespeare's play of the same name: *A horse, a horse, my kingdom for a horse.*

CHAPTER 33

Natalie confirmed with Andrew that she had heard back from both real estate lawyers. "The couple, Luc and Estella Moreau, are legally separated now although still associated with the same enigmatic employer. Estella is no longer living in Paris. Luc Moreau has agreed to meet with us briefly although he acknowledged that he travelled a great deal with his work when he lived here. As a result, he had spent little time relaxing in the house, strolling among the rose bushes in the gardens or ambling along the streets throughout the bustling neighbourhood of Saint-Germain-des-Prés. Thus, he might not be a great source of information," Natalie explained with a hint of reservation in her voice. She lingered a moment longer as she gazed into the distance seeking anything of potential consequence. Still, she sensed there would be something to be gained from what he might have to pass along.

"And the direction we want to take?" Andrew asked. "I will follow your lead unless I sense an opening when I should follow up with a question."

"Given recent events and Louise's violent death, our conversation with Luc Moreau may take us nowhere or, perhaps, to places we had not considered thus far in our quest for confirmation of provenance. We will not mention the document you and Monique unearthed. Instead, we will focus on provenance and anything that might provoke a useful response."

Andrew was content to play a supporting role in this theatre production as it unfolded. From rubbing shoulders with published authors and other literary friends of his mother, such as those he had met at Les Deux Magots café all those years ago, he had learned to be an attentive listener. Often, he purposefully eavesdropped for morsels of information that might fall like crumbs from croissants dropped by patrons seated at the sidewalk tables later to be digested by birds astutely perched on the periphery.

"Enter," Andrew replied over the intercom at the request from the front gate. "You know the way." At the front door, Andrew awkwardly shook Luc Moreau's hand. Andrew assumed that Luc might be experiencing similar emotions although he did not exhibit any as he stood at the entrance. Yet some darkness, some secret that had nothing to do with the provenance seemed to emanate from him.

Langue snarled at Luc from his post on the Persian carpet as Luc entered. Luc glared down at the canine sentry. He then motioned for Andrew and Natalie to follow him into the living room as if he were the host and knew the way, which he did. He seemed comfortable, despite Langue's objection to him being in the house.

"Wine, from a private cellar," Andrew offered his guest.

"No, thank you," Luc replied gruffly through a forced smile. He took a moment to regain his composure. "It belonged to my ex. She is an accredited sommelier with the *Association de la Sommellerie Internationale* and a member of the French Sommelier Guild. It was a part-time interest that took her out of the house more often than not. Her choice of wine isn't to my taste, so to speak." His statement of fact was blunt, his voice resuming its nearly normal tenor. "I prefer other vintages."

Andrew acknowledged the rejection of his hospitality with a noticeable blink. Was the 'other vintages' remark a reference to having other sexual inclinations?

"Now, how can I help you?" Luc asked briskly, clearly upset with himself for having mentioned his estranged spouse. His demeanour morphed into that of a man of mystery with an unassuming French name, extraordinarily ordinary.

Natalie began the interrogation. "What can you tell us about the provenance of the property? We can find no formal records in the Paris municipal planning department."

Luc shook his head. "As I mentioned to my real estate lawyer who told me you were interested in finding out something, I know virtually nothing. I say virtually nothing because I never asked for any background details when I purchased the estate over and above the suggestion that the first owner in 1814 was a resident spy for Napoleon Bonaparte. That fact is hearsay to the best of my knowledge. In retrospect, perhaps I should have undertaken some research. I certainly had enough resources at my disposal to do so. During the process of buying the property, I was told by someone, I can't remember their name, that the Nazi Gestapo had occupied the house during World War II. That fact is accurate, I can assure you. You may have learned about this more recent occupant by now."

"What about the vacant lot to the east adjacent to this property?" Natalie asked on the heels of her first question. She wanted to maintain control of the interview.

"Only recently, I learned from my lawyer that it was part of the property. Prior to this conversation, I knew nothing and never took the time to enquire. Sorry." He shrugged nonchalantly.

"So, anything about the stables and the garage and any activities associated with these buildings?" Natalie continued.

Luc shrugged again. He enjoyed the art and stratagem of verbal fencing with the lunge, parry and riposte of the foil, epée and saber. She asked open-ended questions; he would provide close-ended replies. "Nothing. Regret. Cannot help you." *Touché,* he uttered silently. He was a master at this game having been schooled by the experts in techniques of interrogation and informal banter.

"Are you aware of any door in the wall between the stable-garage and this house lot, or the garden sheds in either lot?" Andrew interjected without hesitation. He too had learned the art and science of interviewing. He regained control of the informal meeting with his less intimidating query. After all, he was just the new owner of the urban estate, naïve in the ways of Parisian culture or French architectural design.

Luc shrugged once more. "Nothing. I was aware of the garden shed in the backyard of this house but no other shed in the adjacent lot as I didn't go there. In retrospect," he repeated, "I should have made more in-depth enquiries regarding all your questions. I deeply regret not being able to help you. Please appreciate that my work often took me away."

"What did you do for work if I may ask?" Natalie probed.

He stared intently at her as he took some time to formulate his answer. "I worked with interesting people, doing interesting things in interesting places. You are probably aware of my employer, given your previous association with the Police nationale and more recently with the European Union Intelligence Unit."

It was Natalie's turn to smile smugly as she changed tactics. "Perhaps we have both gathered information regarding the French communist interests as of late. Would you care to share?"

After another moment of deliberation, he calmly stated, "I can neither confirm nor deny any knowledge." He admitted to himself that there were few secrets between secret keepers. Thus, it was safer to establish a neutral non-committal stance.

Natalie and Luc looked at each other acknowledging the knowledge shared between some agencies of enigmatic codes and cyphers, and recognition gestures. Luc considered Andrew an unknown outsider, saying little yet increasingly inquisitive about his background. He doubted Andrew was a complete novice though in this modern yet medieval jousting contest. To his knowledge, all previous occupants of the urban estate had been seasoned professionals in this arcane tradecraft of security and intelligence, and as willing participants in the perpetual game of cat and mouse.

Luc transferred his attention to Natalie while carefully

appraising her colleague's apparently officious presence. "There is interest from this current government regarding property lost including documentation of some sort. I am not aware that anyone knows about the location of this documentation. You would be wise to be very careful if you know, Natalie. There are nasty people out there, debt collectors who will stop at nothing to fulfil the terms of their contracts. Word has it that the body of one of their kind was recently recovered from the Seine. Another person is missing, perhaps in hiding or also floating in the Seine yet to be discovered."

Natalie smiled at the opaqueness of the innuendo. "Thank you for your advice. I will bear that in mind."

Luc continued with his somewhat vague comments. "I understand that someone is looking into activities related to Nazi Gestapo activities during the latter years of the war, some perhaps related to this house. Again, be careful of threats not necessarily of harm but pressure from within that could terminate or stifle an otherwise promising career."

"Again, thank you for the advice," Natalie replied neutrally. She felt like the protagonist in an Agatha Christie mystery novel, even though the Orient Express had long since ceased to travel the rails from Paris to Istanbul in such luxury as only an accomplished author of that era could record with pen and paper.

Luc took control of the meeting at this juncture. "Nothing more to be said, Natalie. I must be off. Andrew, thank you for the opportunity to visit my previous house. I extend my best wishes to you. And enjoy my wife's wine. I am confident it will be of superb vintage."

"One last question, if I may," Natalie interjected. "Well, not so much a question about provenance as a query of personal interest." She gave a cautious smile which did little to mitigate Luc's growing misgivings. He had already outstayed his comfort levels. The more unrehearsed responses he provided the greater the chance he would be caught out on details. The mantra of the craft was there were truths, partial truths and make-believe truths. The more you revealed, the more you would have to remember what you had said and not said. It was always best to remain vague and brief.

Luc's eyes became opaque like blinds being drawn against the midday Sahara sun. He answered without answering, instead appearing inquisitive in response to her query.

"What model of pistol do you use?" Natalie asked. His training as an operative in the internal intelligence apparatus would have included familiarity with several makes and models of domestic and foreign weapons including those used by snipers in preparation for innumerable hours on the range, honing skills. Life as an agent for the Directorate General Internal Security was not limited to surveillance of suspects from overpriced tourist cafés and brasseries along the Champs Élysées.

"A Beretta 92F," he enunciated quietly.

It was Natalie's turn to be quiet. She just held his gaze for several moments before replying, "I thought DGSI agents had been issued the PAMAS G1 9mm pistol."

"As you probably heard, the slide tended to malfunction after a period of use. Like a game of musical chairs, no one wants to be caught out when the melody stops. Bad for morale," he jested. "I returned mine to the armourer for the consistently reliable Beretta 92F as did several other agents I knew. Why do you ask?" The silence that filled the space between them grew in intensity.

"Just personal interest." Natalie responded. The image on the monitor of her mind returned to the photograph taken by the Police national identification services photographer of Louise Dietrich's contorted body and the equally awkward positioning of the PAMAS G1 pistol wedged underneath her. It was later revealed the slide appeared to have malfunctioned, reflecting Luc's assessment of its reliability.

At the front door, Luc gave both Natalie and Andrew a firm yet hollow handshake and nodded at Langue who again growled at him menacingly. One last time, he gazed at his reflection in the antique hall mirror. He was startled at its apparent normalcy. For some reason he could not fathom his reaction. Perhaps he had lived more than one life yet had not understood any of them. *Could that be why Estella had applied for a divorce?* he reflected. He thought about Andrew's minimal involvement at the meeting. He did not like unknowns.

Andrew monitored Luc's air of confidence as he sauntered to the ironclad gate. The clanging of the door closing behind him followed by the thud of the automatic locking device did nothing to mitigate Andrew's comfort about his enigmatic guest. Out of habit, he watched Luc vanish from sight on the CCTV monitors before confirming that the gate had indeed bolted. Luc would have known the security system exceptionally well. Andrew was confident that he might be able to tamper with the locking mechanism. He was thankful and disappointed to hear what Luc had to say or in fact chose not to divulge. Luc's reticence in answering Natalie's questions stuck in his craw as did his reluctance to identify the true nature of his vocation that Natalie seemed to know. Understandable, perhaps, in this game of cat and mouse.

Andrew accepted the fact that he did not possess the experience that Natalie had gathered in her policing career. Nor was he so naïve that he believed there was something to be gained from chasing after windmills like Don Quixote. Nonetheless, he regarded Luc with some wariness. He also preferred more certainties and fewer unknowns.

Luc walked away from Andrew's urban estate knowing that he was being watched by the surveillance cameras he had installed. *"Na zdorovie – На здоровье –* To your health," he mumbled. He was careful not to show any overt expressions, instead, just the sullen sadness that most Russians tend to exhibit. Long ago, he had resigned himself to the fact that motives could be complicated. Thus, he dedicated himself to a single cause, gaining a deep understanding of the dangers associated with *Homo Sovieticus,* the Soviet communist psyche.

Natalie did not believe for one minute that Luc would have admitted to any involvement in Louise's death. She was correct in that regard. However, there was the slight possibility he might let something slip. Denial could be construed as evidence to the contrary. To date, she had no knowledge of his employer apart from being associated with either intelligence gathering or counter-intelligence insurgency. At the end of the meeting, she still wasn't sure. There were two possibilities, though.

First was the *Direction Générale de la Sécurité Intérieure* – the DG of Interior Security, France's special intelligence service under the authority of the Ministry of Interior, equivalent to the British MI5. Second was the *Direction Générale de la Sécurité Extérieure* – DG External Security, France's foreign intelligence service, under the authority of the Armed Forces, equivalent to the British MI6.

Whichever organization was involved, the political masters did not want knowledge about cash and art stolen from French citizens of Jewish faith by the Nazi Gestapo made known to the public. Despite the fact that SS Oberstleutnant Hans Dietrich had mastered the art of concealing stolen artifacts, they feared there would be a hoard of Holocaust victims beating on the doors of the respective ministries laying claim to their stolen property. That would have begged the questions: How long had France known and why had they kept it a secret? Perhaps more troublesome, what of the other caches known to exist yet not revealed, and for how long had the French government held this information? Difficult truths, long ignored. Louise, now deceased, would not be able to respond to the allegations that she was involved possibly as a KGB agent dispatched by Moscow and affiliated with the French Communist Party. Her Moscow mandate would more than likely have been to disrupt the orderly operation of the democratically elected French government.

This was the roadblock that Jean had mentioned. The level of frustration was palpable but not the worst-case scenario, the Dark Web. *It appears we have entered the realm of French internal security at the highest levels*, Natalie thought to herself.

If there was something, her intuition suggested there could be connections associated with Nazi Gestapo activities during and after the war and with the names listed in the document. In addition, there seemed to be a link to the French Communist Party and its association with Moscow.

The mysterious male and Louise could have known each other or knew of each other as collaborators. More than likely, he would have known that SS Oberstleutnant Hans Dietrich had stolen monies and other valuable treasures and hidden them somewhere. Louise knew the location approximately but did not have the electronic where-with-all to gain access to the cache. It became apparent as her partner in crime violently broke her neck and dumped her lifeless body. She must have been marginally more trusting and more naïve.

CHAPTER 34

Alexandra's cell phone boogied across the table with the vibration of an incoming message from Daan. "Arriving in Paris this afternoon with Yana. We need to meet face-to-face in our office." Paul received the same message. The tone of the text indicated wariness which left Alexandra and Paul uneasy. They had worked with Daan on enough cases to grasp the gravity of such a direct request.

"You're looking bothered," Paul told Daan as they took their seats around the table in the EUI Unit office.

"What we are about to tell you is for your ears only. It is not to be shared with Andrew. Natalie will already have some knowledge of some of the details."

Alexandra and Paul glanced at each other before returning their attention to Daan and Yana.

"Understood," they confirmed.

"Yana has been doing some digging into Louise's background as a follow-up to Manfred's murder and the subsequent search of his house on rue de Petit Champé in Metz." Daan's dour expression had not changed. He looked at Yana. "Please reveal what you have found out about Louise."

"Louise and Manfred were legally married. That is now confirmed. Louise has two aliases. The first is Louise Arnault but Arnault was not her maiden name. She is a serving member of the French Communist Party. Becoming a member was a prerequisite of admission to the inner sanctum of the organization."

Alexandra and Paul held Yana's sober stare. They looked at Daan and back again at Yana. Nothing about Manfred and Louise's marital status seemed to warrant the need for a personal visit by Daan and Yana. There had to be something more.

"That is not the worst news," Daan responded as he nodded at Yana to continue with her briefing.

"Louise is also known as Yulia Tarasova, a KGB agent working here in France. We strongly suspect she is the liaison between Moscow and the French Communist Party," Yana added with trepidation.

Alexandra and Paul held their breath as they stared at their colleagues.

"I now understand why you appear bothered, Daan," Paul acknowledged.

Daan continued, "Fingerprints came back from ident who attended the crime scene where Louise's body was recovered. Luc Moreau's prints were also present, verified not just from his French DGSI file but also linked to a top-secret KGB dossier and that of Yulia Tarasova a.k.a. Louise Arnault a.k.a. Louise Dietrich. When Natalie interviewed Luc, he denied any knowledge of the stable-garage and certainly ever being in the building itself."

Alexandra interjected, "Natalie was not convinced Luc had told her the truth. Given his employer, she was not surprised."

Daan added, "I have sent Natalie a text instructing her to cease all enquiries into Louise's death and mention nothing to Andrew. The Direction Générale de la Sécurité Intérieure, Luc's employer, has taken over the investigation. Because of Louise's link to the KGB, the Direction Générale de la Sécurité Extérieure is also involved. Note that we do not know Luc Moreau's status – whether he is also an active KGB agent or a double agent for France or Russia."

"What about Andrew and Monique?" Alexandra asked, conscious of their safety and wellbeing.

"We don't know if the French communists are still hunting for the document Andrew and Monique unearthed which listed the names of the conspirators in the plot to assassinate Charles de

Gaulle in the 1946 postwar election and infiltrate the French bureaucracy. Until otherwise advised, we have to assume that they are still chasing Andrew and Monique. The good news is that we can safely assume the French communists are not aware that Andrew and Monique are behind the walls of the urban estate. They have been able to identify Monique, most likely as Gaston's daughter, as evidenced by her attempted abduction, but not Andrew. An unknown and possibly serious factor is Luc's status. If he is a loyal French agent of the DGSI, Andrew and Monique are safe. If he is a KGB agent, they are now known targets in a known hideout."

"Nothing has happened to them so far. Can we assume the former?" Paul asked.

"I have asked DGSI for an answer," Daan replied, "but I have not yet heard back one way or another. Perhaps they are preoccupied with seeking suspected traitors in their own ranks."

"Such is the realm of agents and double agents, of espionage and counter-espionage," Alexandra reluctantly concluded. "Lenin and his loyal followers wanted order without modernization. To achieve this, they would create disorder among all whom they perceived to be their enemies – initially the Nazis then the capitalists – tribalism at its worst. I agree with your assessment, Daan. They may have turned inward to seek and eradicate perceived enemies and threats in their own ranks."

Yana added, "One last point of less consequence – Commandant Tessier from the Metz municipal police has been advised of Louise's death. She has closed their file and surrendered the arrest warrant to the court."

"You will both continue to take the lead on this file regarding the names of French communists in the document in addition to the protection of Andrew and Monique from further abduction attempts," Daan confirmed. "Yana and I will be working out of our

Paris office and are prepared to provide support. Rest assured, I will call in additional resources if need be."

Daan failed to mention that Commandant Tessier had received a call from the junior patrol officer present at the courtyard where Manfred had been murdered and at the house when Daan and Yana conducted the search. He requested the officer be attached to the EUI Unit, even temporarily, if the opportunity arose because he was so impressed with how the search was conducted and how Yana located the diary. Daan advised Commandant Tessier he would bear the request in mind if Commandant Tessier recommended the patrol officer because he was always seeking new talent that demonstrated initiative. A lengthy security clearance would have to be undertaken. Daan was always reluctant to accept applications from anyone. He was the one who contacted agents like Paul and Alexandra and then only after distinguished careers in other professions. Otherwise, he was suspicious.

CHAPTER 35

"*Bonjour mon ami*, hello my friend," Théo Cartier said. His weasel-like impertinence and querulous voice were complimentary but endeared him to few. Neither his disposition nor his demeanour had changed for as long as Gaston had known him or cared to remember.

Gaston's blood pressure rose as he turned and fixed the grey-haired former member of the Communist *Maquis* cell with a disdainful glare. His plain insincerity made Gaston suspicious of his every action when they first met, working as young boys on the Seine barges. Nothing had changed. Gaston had not laid eyes on him since finalizing the plans to rescue Angelique from the grip of the Nazi Gestapo in the early morning hours of the D-Day invasion. Théo was supposed to have been part of that ambush mission but never showed up. That wasn't the first time he had been AWOL for an operation. He also had the reputation of being a peddler of worthless intelligence – information as useless as bric-a-brac from second-hand pawn shops or flea markets that once occupied the Marais district of Paris and other municipalities.

Théo had been a member of the *Francs-Tireurs et partisans,* a resistance organization created in northern Normandy in the summer of 1941 by the Communist Party. They mostly worked out of Le Havre, but also across the Seine estuary to Honfleur, ambushing German soldiers and collaborators in addition to feeding information to the French Carlingue Gestapo.

Maquis cells had a common purpose, to defeat the Nazis, but were fervently independent like Swiss Cantons, occasionally working at cross-purposes. The motivation of the Communist *Maquis* was not mercenary, but ideological with an obligation for unquestioning obedience to the communist dogma. On numerous occasions, Théo had tried to recruit Gaston but without success. Gaston was a loyal patriot of the tricolour, with its roots deeply entrenched in the French Revolution and *La Marseillaise*. For many reasons, the least of which was his failure to show up to help rescue Angelique, Gaston did not trust him then. He trusted him even less now.

Gaston initially chose not to return Théo's amiable yet hollow greeting. He confronted him as if they were rivals intolerant of each other's presence, which was closer to the truth. He remained intent upon having nothing to do with ex-communist *Maquis*. The venomous glare he gave Théo reinforced that resolve.

After a pause during which Gaston silently took several slow breaths, he nodded reluctantly at Théo. "It has been a while, for sure," he acknowledged, *but not long enough,* he thought to himself.

Gaston had remained conflicted since returning to Honfleur from Paris with Angelique. *The war is not over*, he had reminded himself more times than he could remember. It had defined his life with Angelique since 1945, and influenced the way Monique and Philippe perceived their reality. In the past few days, he realized that he had no control over people like Théo. He only had control over how he reacted to them. He could continue to fight or move on in peace. Perhaps it was time to leave history to the historians.

"One of our equals has returned…" Théo lingered for a moment on that ambiguous declaration before continuing, "from back when the Gestapo major captured and started to torture Angelique and the others. This mutual associate knows who betrayed us. He would like to meet in order to pass along this information personally."

Gaston's reaction to Théo's remark was suspicion if nothing else. Angelique had identified one of the confederates who had been executed along with the Gestapo major on D-Day by members of Gaston's *Maquis* cell. But there was one other who had betrayed their colleagues and escaped a watery end. Gaston continued to stare blankly at Théo, unsure why he would make such an unsolicited disclosure. Théo was cagey in his communiqué but that had always been his nature as long as Gaston could remember.

"Do you recall the wharf where we tied up the barges, close to the Nazi pillbox where the *Boche* inspected our cargo?"

Gaston's expression remained neutral and uncommitted. He wasn't going to encourage Théo one way or the other.

Théo continued with what Gaston interpreted as empty rhetoric with meager bread crumbs of truth. "He has asked me to pass along an invitation to meet with him on the wharf tonight just after sunset. He would have contacted you himself but is concerned that he is being stalked possibly by Fourth Reich agents, themselves seeking revenge for deaths of Nazis on D-Day which he was involved in. If you cannot make the rendezvous tonight, he will understand. Perhaps another time can be arranged."

"His name?" Gaston asked cautiously, still uncertain of Théo's honesty. The war is not over he reminded himself once again.

Théo recognized the lingering hesitation in Gaston's response. Not wanting to appear overbearing, Théo added, "As we all did back then, he continues to use his *nom de guerre*, Anschluss. He is older than we are and wants to pass along this information to you before he dies, ideally by natural causes." Théo lingered on that explanation before continuing, "I was left with the impression that he does not believe he will walk this earth much longer."

Gaston nodded slightly as he considered what Théo had said and, more importantly, his demeanour. He remembered the nom de guerre and the trustworthy reputation associated with it as clearly as if it was yesterday. Anschluss was the term used to describe Hitler's annexation of Austria. In addition, it referred to members of the Austrian communist resistance headquartered in Paris and Brussels. There was also a questionable connection to the French

Carlingue *Maquis* that Gaston could not recall clearly. That vague recollection caused a chill to run down his spine. Such errors in judgement could result in untimely deaths.

Daylight ebbed and the veil of night fell, disguising the old paths Gaston had taken from the wharf to Angelique's loving embrace all those years ago. He left the warden's house through the concealed gate. Moments later, Angelique followed, still able to distinguish his silhouette.

Gaston approached the wharf cautiously stopping every few steps to scan the river and the bank with the overgrown hedges camouflaging the Nazi pillbox. He knelt several times listening for sounds that would be out of place or sounds that should be normal but suspended, including the flurry of birds and the nocturnal activities of water creatures. His eyes first focused on Théo hiding among the reeds and cattails in the brackish waters around the wharf, then on another figure beside him. If Anschluss was in such poor health that he needed to send Théo as a messenger, would his feeble condition allow him to stand in frigid waters? Was this person standing beside Théo really Anschluss or a turncoat collaborator?

As that thought crossed his mind, Gaston warily took his first step onto the wooden wharf rotting from decades of exposure to the elements and neglect. The second figure lunged forward like a coiled viper from its watery lair amongst the bulrushes beside Théo. He reached up immediately and grabbed Gaston by the ankle. Both toppled into the brackish water. The second figure surfaced immediately. Gaston did not.

Angelique aimed the German Lugar pistol with its silencer. "Poetic justice," she mumbled, "to kill a Nazi collaborator with a Nazi weapon of choice." The first bullet crushed his throat. The second smashed his jaw. He grabbed his face as hot blood gushed through his fingers. He slowly sank below the surface as Gaston silently rose a few meters away. "Swim to the wharf," Angelique called out to her beloved partner.

Théo slipped as he attempted to climb from his hiding place and push Angelique off the wharf.

"Behind you," Gaston yelled at Angelique. Images from nightmares of her hectic rescue and Théo's suspicious absence from that *Maquis* mission flashed on the monitor of his mind.

Angelique turned around. Théo stared at the gun momentarily, not at her. She aimed carefully at the second target and deliberately squeezed the trigger twice, again a double tap. The muffled thump of the bullets hitting the body was absorbed by the damp mist hovering over the marsh and estuary and the dew that had coated the bulrushes and cattails standing as silent witnesses to the thwarted conspiracy. Théo transferred his fading glare to Angelique as he awkwardly toppled off the wharf into the Seine. Angelique reached over the quay to help Gaston climb up a dilapidated ladder.

Gaston and Angelique scowled into the dead eyes of Théo and the second body floating face up. Both seemed to stare up from the shallow depths of the Seine, yet from a different world, like Athenian actors in a Greek tragedy.

"*Vae victis* – woe to the vanquished. Those defeated in battle are entirely at the mercy of their conquerors," Gaston declared with contempt. He felt no mercy for the hands that had tortured his Angelique, nor would he ever. "They exist only in memories and such memories cannot be purged, just appeased," he mumbled to himself.

"The war needs to be over for us, *mon cher* Gaston," Angelique whispered in a tired voice as she stood beside him, her arm around his waist. With all her force, she threw the Lugar pistol from her gloved hand into the Honfleur estuary.

"Yes, you are correct. The war is not over but it needs to be over for us. Others must take the torch and carry the fight forward." He transferred his gaze to the pillbox that was scarcely perceptible in the filtered moonlight that shone through the high clouds. The fortifications of the war were constant reminders, ignored by those who had not experienced its horrors of battle, yet never to be forgotten by others whose nightmares would be constant reminders.

She gazed up at Gaston. "You are shivering from your untimely swim in the Seine. We need to get you back to the warden's house and into a hot bath."

They made their way back along the path to their hidden safe house. Suspicious of the darkened doorways, they did not know if they were chasing collaborators or memories of comrades, spies or shadows of ghosts. That was the curse of the condemned. The end of the war held too many loose ends that spawned the next conflict, which had rapidly become cold.

"The change will only come with their deaths," Gaston exclaimed solemnly to Angelique. There was too much hate and vitriol lingering in the memories of betrayal. Truth, loyalty, and good faith had been forever tainted. He had no tolerance of human foibles like deception and dishonesty. He interpreted them as weakness.

With the death of Théo and his anonymous colleague, there were two fewer traitors who could be bought with a purse containing a paltry thirty pieces of silver. They would join the Gestapo major and the other malicious Nazis forever condemned on the morning of D-Day to their watery grave in the Honfleur estuary while the toll of the vacant Nazi pillbox rang silent and no black flags fluttered again.

CHAPTER 36

Time fogs the memory. As such, the images of war become recollections interpreted through the prism of each participant as they recorded their thoughts at the time. They were not necessarily events that had occurred. Those individual memories were often perceived as if through the distorted lens of a kaleidoscope which morphed constantly with each turn.

Gaston and Angelique returned to Paris with Monique, believing there were no serious threats to any of them. That did not mean they could throw caution to the wind. On the contrary, it just meant that they could collaborate with colleagues, old and new. Andrew would be the first.

"I apologize for not being wholly truthful with you," Gaston lamented as he nodded at Andrew. "Like your father, I reminded you to keep what I said to yourself because the war is not over. And it is still not over. We have to adjust to how we deal with events from the past but not to the point that we become paralyzed with paranoia. On the contrary, we reinforce strengths by sharing information. I do so now, in respect for your father and the bonds we developed."

Andrew took some time to acknowledge Gaston's change in strategy. He muttered, "Yes, my father constantly reminded me not to talk about what he had shared with me. On his death bed, he warned me that in his world of security and intelligence, secrecy was seductive and the scent of treachery lingered forever. Patriotism and betrayal were strange bedfellows. It took me a long time to appreciate what he was saying. Having met you after all these years, I now understand the implications in his sage advice. For that, I will be forever grateful to you both."

"We constantly need to imagine the unimaginable," Gaston said solemnly. "I will start by telling you the whole truth about secrets held by the *Maquis* as I recall them. Central to my motivation is to protect my Monique because I believe your relationship will continue to grow stronger and that association will bring with it additional dangers."

An elusive smile crossed Andrew's face which was all that Gaston needed in confirmation. He was correct in his assessment that their relationship which had been spawned decades before was now becoming a reality.

"Allow me to start with the present and then move back into the past with events involving the *Maquis*. You are wise enough to understand the interrelationship of all the events. First, you should research the vocation of the previous owners of your urban estate, Luc and Estella Moreau. Investigate Luc Moreau and his involvement in the death of Louise Dietrich as it relates to his employer, the Director General of Internal Security, France's special intelligence service. DG Internal Security is also connected to Louise's death and not just on the periphery. My informant in this matter is an old *Maquis* member I have kept in contact with." He chuckled, "We are all getting on in years."

"As you are digging into Luc Moreau's background, consider the following. The Nazis had plans to build an underground munitions factory where Metro Line 11 was being built. In May 1944, the expansion was halted for several reasons the least of which was the rapidly dwindling resources of the Third Reich coffers. They were not being replenished as quickly as they wanted, despite the massive scale of the theft of gold from all conquered countries. Some of SS Oberstleutnant Dietrich's stolen treasures were allegedly buried there before construction was halted. The sources of that intelligence have died so it cannot be verified. Luc Moreau was pursuing the truth of the information held by his employer in that file as it related to Louise Dietrich, the master of deception or in her case, the mistress. I pass that on to you for what it is worth."

"My father said on several occasions that not all pricks come from the same source. Wood produces splinters whereas rose bushes produce thorns, and there are exceptions."

"That is correct. A wise man, your father," Gaston murmured loudly enough for Andrew to hear. "You need to ensure that all information you count on is truthful and consistent with its source."

Gaston opened a photo album and tapped his finger on one black and white photo of several men sitting around a large table. He rested his finger on one person. "This is Bistro, an old friend." The picture had been taken in the boardroom of the President of France, in the garret suite on the top floor of the Élysée Palace. In the foreground was a window through which the top of the Place de la Concord Luxor Obelisk could be easily seen on the right bank of the Seine. The anonymous photographer had included the whole photo image in front and behind the camera lens. Not captured had been any feelings of impunity about missions not yet executed. Andrew scanned others in the photograph, focusing more on those standing immediately to the left and right of Bistro. They could be close colleagues, he supposed.

"Influence, perhaps considerable," Andrew insinuated as he raised his eyebrows.

Gaston acknowledged his suggestion as his finger continued to rest on the same individual in the photo. "Memorize this face. It is Bistro," he whispered. "That is his *nom de guerre*."

Andrew leaned forward and stared in earnest at the man Gaston pointed to.

Gaston continued, "We grew up together. He is now retired. When the Nazis invaded, we both became apprentice crew on the barges together, and subsequently members of the *Maquis* together. He is the only person I have been able to depend on absolutely after all these years. He helped smuggle your father back to England in 1944. I told him about you. If anything mysterious happens to me and you need any assistance, contact him at the Brasserie du Bac in the shadow of Caudebec-en-Caux cathedral. He is the proprietor. To initiate contact with him, ask: *Is this a bistro?* If he replies, *Oui,* then mention your father was a former RAF pilot. If it is safe, he will give you a menu. If he replies, *Non,* then it will not be safe to carry on with a conversation at that time. Order a cappuccino in a paper cup and leave without any fanfare. Return at another time. One last point. It is imperative that you follow these instructions explicitly. Remember that the war is not over equally for everyone." Gaston hesitated for a moment before asking for confirmation. "Do you understand, young Andrew?"

Andrew nodded. "Understood," he replied. He leaned over the photo album and concentrated on the photograph for several more moments.

"Question," Andrew prompted Gaston. "What strategies could the French communists use to attack Monique and me? If you were to go on the offensive, how would you set a trap to catch them? What would you do or not do?"

Gaston stared warily at Andrew as a sorcerer would look upon an apprentice. "Be very careful young Andrew with that line of thinking. You are well out of your league. I commend you on your initiative but better for you to leave that to people like Natalie and her friends. Assuming you cannot be identified and remain anonymous, you could best serve the cause as a *flâneur.* Master the art of becoming a practised observer, a connoisseur of life. You do not want to leave my Monique without a trusted and loyal partner before you formally become her partner."

It was Andrew's turn to quietly nod at the senior senator. He could watch and record. He had experience in that vocation having been a member of the Watcher Service for the Royal Canadian

Mounted Police while attending Laval University in Quebec City during the FLQ crisis in October 1970. His father had coached him in the art of surveillance in order to gain experience for future employment. He could now put those skills to good use in his *flâneur* observer role.

"Second question," he followed up. "It relates to the unsuccessful attempt of the French communists to abduct Monique. How would they have known that Monique would be taking a walk with Langue? It might have been pure luck, but highly unlikely. I think there must have been a leak."

"Perhaps. All questions relate to the same strategy. The wartime strategies of the *Maquis* have always been to ambush, retreat and hide. Hiding often involved taking cover in plain sight, like going back to work. As a young boy, I worked on the Seine barges. So, I returned to the barges. I had the added advantage of being a young lad, appearing younger than my actual years. I was less likely to be suspected as a member of a *Maquis* cell.

"Larger missions tended to involve a great deal of planning with contingencies for alternate tactics if their primary plan had to be changed. There was invariably little or no time to practise blowing up railway tracks. *Maquis* actions would usually be carried out by one or two working together, not platoon-sized groups. One would be a look-out while the other carried out the plan. You came with the knowledge and skills regarding explosives and fuses, for example. The only actual training would be for new recruits to learn advanced skills. On the first or second mission, the new recruits would be employed as the look-out. Many *Maquis* preferred to work by themselves. That reduced the chances of the missions being unsuccessful because of leaks of plans to unknown Nazi collaborators."

Andrew interjected before he forgot. "What strategies did the

French communists use during the war? Today, would they use something different to get their hands on the document?"

"The primary tactic of the French Communist *Maquis* was to infiltrate our *Maquis* cells. That was why *Maquis* cells rarely worked together. In addition, one *Maquis* member rarely worked with or shared information with someone they did not know well. We only trusted fellow *Maquis* members we had known for years, ideally our entire lives."

"Like your childhood friend, Bistro?"

Gaston acknowledged this with a gesture. Andrew was becoming more proficient at detecting Gaston's innuendoes.

"Even then, some became turncoats and betrayed their colleagues. Others broke under the pressure of torture. It was hard to blame them. That was why we used a *nom de guerre* and not our real names."

CHAPTER 37

"I need to show you a photograph," Natalie explained to Gaston. He looked up abruptly. "Where did you get it?" he asked. His glare suggested he was familiar with the woman lying awkwardly face-up on the ground.

"Her body was found under boards covering a stall in the stable-garage on Andrew's urban estate adjacent to his house lot."

Gaston took a deep breath and squinted at it. "They are getting closer. Does Andrew know, and my Monique?"

"They do now."

"And others?"

"In addition to Alexandra and Paul, the Police nationale. Their ident section took the photo along with others at the scene. We do not believe the deceased was chasing after Andrew and Monique or was even aware they were living next door. She was focused on getting her hands on the cash and other treasures allegedly stolen by SS Gestapo Oberstleutnant Hans Dietrich."

"How did she get past security?"

"She had an accomplice we believe is associated with DGSI, la *Direction Générale de la Sécurité Intérieure.*"

"Luc Moreau?"

"We believe so but have not been able to contact him to confirm, not that he will admit to any involvement or knowledge. You know his reputation. The ministry is not talking, not even to Daan Segers at the European Union Intelligence Unit or Yolina Lambert at the EU Commission in Brussels. Can you confirm her identity?" Natalie repeated.

"Louise Dietrich. She is or was a ruthless member of the French Communist Party – one of their enforcers. She often exhibited sociopathic behaviour. Word has it she duped her husband,

Manfred, to get to the treasure that his father, SS Oberstleutnant Hans Dietrich, supposedly stole from her parents. The parents themselves deceived Jewish residents of Paris into surrendering their savings to them for safekeeping. Her parents were subsequently sent to concentration camps through Fort Queuleu on the orders of SS Oberstleutnant Dietrich. Somewhere enroute to the Auschwitz death camp they were murdered. By whom, I cannot verify, much like others who had collaborated with the Nazis and ended up floating in the Seine within weeks of the end of the war or decades later." *Like Théo Cartier and others who ended up floating in the Honfleur estuary or were unceremoniously buried in unmarked graves elsewhere*, he mused with a gleeful inward smile.

"Thank you for the confirmation," Natalie replied. "We suspected as much."

"The French communists tended to always work in pairs during the war and still do today. Have you captured her partner? If not, have you been able to identify him? I say *him,* because the French communists continue to work in male-female teams?"

"Unfortunately, not as of today. Rest assured, though, all our resources are focused on that objective," Natalie replied.

"Please keep me informed. In the interim, I will call on my *Maquis* colleagues," Gaston confirmed. *In addition to a select few others*, he contemplated.

"If you do find out, please leave it to us to take him into custody. We need to question him. Please," Natalie emphasized as she stared solemnly at Gaston. She was well aware of his reputation for taking matters into his own hands.

On his own initiative, he had dealt with threats to his Angelique and his children without leaving a trace. On other occasions, he had been contracted by the Ministry to take care of business that permanent employees, including some agents could not, for which he had been well paid and compensated by other means. They had afforded him considerable latitude for services rendered in addition to other services to be completed should the targets' heads rear up from their lairs in the quagmires of the underworld.

CHAPTER 38

" *J'écoute,*" I'm listening, the electronically generated voice message advised whoever was calling the unlisted number on the throw-away phone. Few had the number. Fewer still had ever called or been called. The benefit of maintaining the clandestine communication device to ensure anonymity outweighed any other cost.

The reply was clean and concise. *"Merci."* A warning that a trap was being planned was appreciated and would be rewarded in kind.

"Thank you for taking the time to meet here at the EUI Unit office overlooking Place de la Bastille in the 4e arrondissement. I never get tired looking out at the Colonne de Juliet topped with the *Génie de la Liberté,*" Daan commented.

"Appropriate scene given the reason for us to meet," Alexandra added. "We are not storming the Bastille but defending the Republic, which is under threat once again."

Daan continued. "Natalie, you have not met the most recent member of our team, Emma Bauer who is on loan from the German Federal Criminal Police Office, the BKA. She uses the *nom de guerre*, Yana. We were together when Louise stabbed Manfred," Daan explained to the others. "Subsequently, we searched Manfred's house on rue de Petit Champé in Metz. That was where Yana located SS Oberstleutnant Dietrich's diary in Manfred's bookshelf. That discovery revealed intelligence regarding Gestapo tactics we had only suspected before. It also confirmed that SS Oberstleutnant Dietrich was instrumental in the theft of money and art treasures from Jewish residents of Paris before shipping them off to concentration camps. More germane to our motivation for gathering here today, it relates directly to the security of the document that Andrew and Monique rediscovered only recently."

"Brilliant bit of investigative work," Paul complimented Yana. "Thank you all for your efforts thus far," Daan said. "If you have not already surmised, the unearthing of the document has created a frenzied reaction at the highest levels of government. Numerous former politicians and senior bureaucrats are named, many of whom are currently retired and serving on influential committees and boards. The publication of these names would bring a flood of embarrassment to the current and previous governments. Natalie, what is the latest on the primary suspects?"

"We know for certain that the French Communist Party has issued a contract to two individuals to find the document with the sole purpose of toppling this government by making the names public. One is deceased, Manfred Dietrich's former wife, Louise, whose body was discovered in a cavern under the floor boards of the first stall in the stable-garage lot adjacent to Andrew's urban estate. We do not know for certain who murdered her but suspect Luc Moreau, the former occupant and agent for DG Internal Security, may be connected. That brings us to the second suspect, the government, particularly the Direction Générale de la Sécurité Intérieure, and/or the Direction Générale de la Sécurité Extérieure. They are often at odds. Perhaps to our advantage, they do not always share information."

"Regardless, they are formidable foes for Andrew and Monique," Daan confirmed. "That brings in a third player, Gaston Abreo, Monique's father and former member of the *Maquis*. I use the term *former member* prudently because he maintains strong ties with other former members of the French Resistance. Virtually all garner considerable influence with former and current senior politicians residing in or associated with the Élysée Palace."

"Well, that makes for interesting bedfellows," Yana commented. "And I thought just German politics were incestuous with all the tentacles reaching into the former Third and current Fourth Reich among other players. Since the fall of the Berlin Wall and the re-unification of East and West Germany, the Cold War continues, with individuals having swapped employers but not necessarily their old allegiances. There are new alignments and new players emerging, with each needing to hold the other in check."

Daan nodded in agreement with Yana's analysis. "As far as we can determine, only the French communists are prepared to kill Andrew and Monique if necessary to get their hands on the document. Ironically, the EUI Unit now has the original. Andrew and Monique hold a copy. I doubt the French communists would care one way or the other given their *raison d'être* to make the document public in order to topple the current government. That just leaves the DGSI and DGSE who would not want blood on their hands. Worse, they would not want to have to deal with Gaston and his colleagues. It comes down to a matter of damage control for them, preventing political Armageddon, curtailing the worst-case scenario from becoming a calamitous reality."

The air pressure in the room seemed to drop as everyone took a deep breath and glanced at each other. They stared out the window at the Colonne de Juliet in the centre of Place de la Bastille with traffic rotating around it. None of the drivers appeared to be consciously paying homage to those citizens of the 1789 revolution who had taken up arms against the tyranny of King Louis XVI.

"That brings us to the purpose of our meeting," Daan stated, not as a summary of facts but an invitation for further contribution. "We need to come up with a strategy to safeguard the contents of the document and, most importantly, to protect Andrew and Monique. One option would be that we could just destroy the document. Alternatively, we could retain it for the opportunity it provides – intelligence that can be employed to turn those named into confidential informants for the European Union Intelligence

Unit. I prefer the expression 'confidential informant' rather than blackmail by another label."

"Regardless, we need to involve both Andrew and Monique in the conversation and soon," Natalie suggested, not as a preferred option but as an obligatory condition. "I share this with you because Andrew approached me with the idea of making the document public. He figured if the content was made known, the French communists would have no reason to hunt for him and Monique. The names would be out there. Hence, there would be no need for 24-hour security. The French communists would be pleased because the government might topple and no blame could be attributed directly to their involvement."

"A second consideration," Alexandra noted, "is that we have approval with funding from Brussels to proceed with the sting operation to identify who else, besides Louise, has been contracted to get their hands on the document that Andrew and Monique have. It would be opportunistic for us to confirm the identity of this second resource, this fast gun for hire, particularly if this person is associated with the Saint-Denis or Marseilles organized crime network."

Daan turned to Natalie. "Would Andrew abandon his idea, even temporarily, if you asked him personally?"

She did not have to think long before responding to Daan's question. "Now, no. He is not just a naïve tourist any longer with aspirations of becoming a *flâneur*. He has an insatiable fixation, almost a quest to establish the provenance of his urban estate. The probability of him setting that pursuit aside, if the request came from me, is so infinitely small you might as well say never. He believes that making the document public will reduce the danger to him and Monique from some quarters. He has been speaking with Gaston in private and is confident that Gaston will not only back him up but will provide him with all the support he needs, including introductions to *Maquis* colleagues."

"Good to know," Daan acknowledged.

"Having said that, if the request came from Gaston for Andrew to abandon or at least suspend his idea of making the names public, there would a greater probability that he would comply because of Gaston's relationship with Andrew's father. Andrew has great respect for both men. For those of you who are unaware, as a member of the *Maquis* in 1944, Gaston helped smuggle Andrew's father back to England as an RAF pilot after his father had been shot down by the Nazis near Rouen."

"A second reason equally compelling," Paul interjected, "is that Andrew and Gaston share a mutual love of Monique – Gaston as her father and Andrew as her intimate partner. Again, for those of you who don't know, Andrew and Monique fell in love as teenagers when Andrew first lived in Paris with his father about thirty-five years ago. That flame has never been extinguished. On the contrary, it has grown stronger since he returned to Paris recently and they reunited."

"Monique helped Andrew claim his lottery windfall," Alexandra added. "That was another intensely emotional event in Andrew's life. It is important to note that emotions can be the most significant motivators."

"I repeat, good to know," Daan acknowledged as he transferred his attention to Natalie. "Should I or should you approach Gaston with this request?"

Natalie hesitated, contemplating the best thing to do. "With all due respect, Daan, my first choice would be me because my relationship with Gaston is lower key. Despite that, I am confident the request coming from you would make a greater impact because of your professional status as the Director of the European Union Intelligence Unit. I know for a fact that Gaston holds you in the highest regard for the respect you have shown him as a member of the *Maquis* with a distinguished war record."

"I will take on that task," Daan confirmed. "Thoughts on asking Yolina Lambert to accompany me?" Daan asked.

Natalie's response was immediate and emphatic. "No. The discussion needs to be warrior to warrior."

"Agreed," Daan replied immediately. He looked at everyone around the table in order to confirm their agreement. It had been a long time, too long, since he had sat down with Gaston and engaged in conversations that mattered to both of them and the organizations they represented. Gaston was a wealth of information and experience. He could also be a bit of a loose cannon, more an independent actor than one who discusses his strategies with others before acting. Daan understood why and was prepared to work with him.

"Final point," Daan confirmed. "We proceed immediately with the sting operation to lure the French communist agents who have been assigned to capture the document at whatever the cost. Confirming the identity of Louise's partner is our primary objective if we are to safeguard Andrew and Monique in the short term. It's important to note that a replacement agent for Louise may have already been assigned. Confirming potential members of the organization's crime networks and their affiliates from the Paris region, especially Saint-Denis, in addition to Marseilles also has considerable merit."

"Are there additional resources available?" Paul asked. "I ask because this mandate and the territory is growing in complexity."

"I appreciate that," Daan acknowledged. "Yana is a new face. Thus, the probably of her being recognized is low. She also has a proven track record with multi-faceted missions. Most importantly, she has in-depth knowledge of Louise and Manfred, in addition to SS Oberstleutnant Dietrich and his damning diary with perhaps even more damaging details than the document unearthed by

Andrew and Monique. Accordingly, we will employ Yana in the planning and execution phases of this operation."

Daan's reference to SS Oberstleutnant Dietrich's diary caused Yana to shiver from the recollection of the statements of cold fact in the diary. How could her fellow German citizens treat other human beings with such callous contempt? The potential was there for it to happen again with the recent rise of the Fourth Reich and neo-Nazi sympathizers among other right-wing groups in the general population both young and old.

The smile on Paul's face confirmed the sentiment shared by Alexandra and Natalie. Yana would be a welcome addition to the team.

CHAPTER 39

The multi-phase sting operation with different drop points was confirmed. As previously sketched out, the first would be the abandoned warehouse close to the T8 Tramway station in Saint-Denis. The second drop point would be Gate E on the east side of the Stade de France, a twenty-minute drive away in good traffic, which rarely occurred. The third drop point would be beneath the south-east end of Avenue Laennec overpass, an approximate twenty-minute drive from the second.

The tight schedule would require different people to be on standby in order to retrieve the second and third envelopes. The first would contain a photocopy of a partial page in the document listing a few names, in addition to instructions for drop point two. The second would contain a photocopy of a few more names and precise directions for the third and final drop point. The third envelope would contain photocopies of the entire document listing all the names. Alexandra would coordinate the surveillance of the first drop point, Yana the second and Paul the third. Drop point two was the most straightforward with the easiest access. Hence, it was assigned to Yana because she was less familiar with traffic patterns in Saint-Denis, in the event a change in instructions had to be undertaken.

Natalie was pleased with the final draft of the plan to entrap the French communists whose primary objective was to capture the document at whatever the cost including the death of Andrew or Monique. Their raison d'être since becoming a *Maquis* cell in the early months of the Second World War was to destabilize the democracy of the French Republic which Natalie had proudly sworn to defend as a member of the Police nationale. She had no time for those who behaved with contempt toward patriots of the Republic such as Gaston who had fought valiantly, and for others who had given their lives.

The Police nationale had informed their mole from the Marseilles Mafia who had infiltrated the Saint-Denis organized crime network. This informant passed along the details of the drop point near the T8 Tramway station to the French communist contact suggesting there might be a second drop point. Alexandra, Yana and Paul had set up their surveillance in advance. There was a ransom payment being demanded by the anonymous individuals who had the entire document, but the amount was manageable for the French communists given the prospect of getting their hands on the entire document. The communists were not happy with the rather cumbersome instructions but would comply reluctantly. If the roles had been reversed, they would have done the same.

"Double-check your surveillance systems," Daan advised. "The French communists rarely agree outright. Instead, they usually barter for conditions, like Algerian rug salesmen in a flea market. Even merchants in higher-end markets such as those in Place des Vosges on the boundary of the 3e and 4e arrondissement do not accept a first offer. It is part of their culture to haggle for a final price." The fact that they agreed outright triggered Daan's acid reflux.

"Natalie, reconfirm with the Police nationale that the information from the Marseilles Mafia mole is still current." Daan wasn't second-guessing her ability to achieve a flawless outcome. In fact, he always questioned his own rationale and the accuracy of his stratagem. The more moving parts, the greater the potential for error.

Natalie's reply was conditional. "My contact is as confident as any could be, given the fact they were dealing with criminal informants. It is always a fine balance between nurturing confidence as relationships grow. Some of these folks can be fickle from the outset as you know."

"Understood," Daan responded. He remained uneasy yet masked his concerns as best he could, not wanting to upset his agents, most of whom were aware of his apprehensions about their safety. "All dedicated eyes are to scrutinize the monitors of the electronic surveillance systems set up at each drop point. In addition, reiterate your instructions to all those boots on the ground. They are to maintain painstaking vigilance before, during and after the actual drops."

Staff in his operation communications centre would concentrate simultaneously on all positions' monitor displays from a macro perspective. Redundancy was an advantage on this type of mission.

"The first drop appears to have followed our instructions accurately," Alexandra announced from her vantage point. "As suspected, the person picking up the envelope appears to be a low-level soldier, not one of their contracted agents. He seems to lack the cognitive bandwidth to understand the broader scope of what he has become involved in. He didn't scan for surveillance systems or backup enforcement. He just read the instructions and dialled a number on his cell phone. I suspect he was told to pass along the instructions to a central operator."

"Anything out of the normal?" Daan asked. He much preferred to deal with adversaries who had the authority to make decisions regardless of their integrity – the organ grinder rather than the monkey so to speak.

"Not looking around, not being aware of his environment might have been instructions to the first soldier so as not to appear guarded. Once he had completed his task, he would need to bring the envelope to a designated location immediately," Alexandra suggested. "That would have left me feeling uneasy."

"But you are not a low-level soldier," Daan commented.

"True," she acknowledged. "I would surmise that even a low-level soldier would be alert if for no other reason than for his own safety. We are following this first soldier and will arrest him as soon as the final envelope has been delivered to drop point three and has been picked up by the final soldier."

"Copy that," Yana confirmed.

"Likewise," Paul reported.

"Pass that along to your surveillance team, Yana," Daan directed. "Paul, I suspect your pick-up soldier will be hesitant in approaching your location, perhaps more observant. Once this person has the envelope in hand, they will skedaddle fast."

Yana's voice crackled on the airways in a monotone. "Someone approaching drop point two. Unlike the first, they are visibly scanning Gate E and the parking areas. They are certainly treading cautiously. I sense they do not like being out in the open, possibly feeling vulnerable."

"Copy that," Daan replied.

The barely audible thump of an object striking a solid surface reverberated ominously over the telecoms channel. It was like the muffled sound of a boat gently bumping against a wharf in a dense fog bank. "Sniper fire, sniper fire, sniper fire," Yana barked repeatedly. "Soldier has been shot, on the ground not moving."

"Are you hit?" Daan asked, clearly concerned. He had been on too many missions serving with the Belgian military, United Nations missions including the Former Republic of Yugoslavia and more recently with the European Union Intelligence Unit, when those words were precursors of the worst kind of information. Too often, the wounded could not be rescued easily or within the golden hour or critical minutes.

"I'm safe. My team is also safe," Yana confirmed.

Daan breathed a sigh of relief. "Anyone have eyes on the shooter?" he followed up immediately.

"Negative. No one at drop point two has reported a sighting," Yana said.

"Electronic surveillance monitors report," Daan directed, formulating tentative contingency plans based on the initial intelligence reported and the options available.

"Nothing," the team from the surveillance monitors replied. "The shooter was outside the scan of our cameras."

"Everyone remain under cover while continuing to scan your arches of fire," Daan directed.

"The soldier is not moving," Yana updated. "He had the envelope in his hand when he was hit. It is lying on the ground beside him. He had not read the instructions or made a phone call. We can only conclude the third soldier has not received instructions for drop point three."

"Copy that," Paul confirmed. "Not observing any unusual movements or abnormal behaviour. Standing by for further instructions."

"I have directed my team tailing the first soldier to arrest him immediately," Alexandra reported.

Natalie called her contact at the Police nationale and provided an update. "Strongly recommend you advise your mole from the Marseille Mafia. He may want to keep his head down for the foreseeable future. Will advise update soonest."

"Paul, remain vigilant for the next hour. Then shut down your operation," Daan directed. "Likewise, Yana, advise all your people to remain in situ and watchful for anything suspicious. If nothing in the next hour, Paul and Yana, extract your people strategically following rules of withdrawal with cover and backup. All, debriefing 1600 hours, my location."

The next hour seemed like a day. Radio silence did not have to be imposed. It reflected the vigilance. No one moved from their surveillance positions. All eyes continued to scan their individual arches of fire with meticulous scrutiny for any abnormal activity. If anything, it was almost too quiet.

Alexandra, Yana and Paul directed the strategic withdrawal of their team members. They then debriefed each team member individually and finally as a group.

CHAPTER 40

"So much for having Yana at Gate E in order to make it the easiest of the three drop points. The logic being, an incident would be less likely," Natalie admitted reluctantly with a sheepish grin. "What is it about the expression written by Robbie Burns – *the best-laid schemes o' Mice an' Men Gang aft agley?*"

"There is some truth in that," Paul uttered in jest. "Our EUI Unit CCTV surveillance cameras identified nothing because their focus was narrow, mostly on the drop point. To our advantage, the Stade de France security cameras had a broader sweep. They picked up someone dressed in a black hoodie walking quickly away from a structure near the parking lot. This person was clearly carrying a reinforced elongated case that we suspect contained the sniper rifle. Bottom line, we could not make any positive identification of the shooter, not even the gender. We can only confirm average height and weight."

"What went wrong?" Daan asked with a degree of frustration. He had learned not to hide but instead to express such emotions with his team as a tactic to motivate them to reflect and reply with fact-based suggestions and recommendations. "Whoever it was, they had detailed knowledge of the operation well in advance. So, where is the leak?" Only those in this room had access to this precise level of detail." Even the Marseilles mole did not know.

Daan had complete confidence in his team. They had worked together on numerous cases, some highly sensitive. All except Yana, he mused. She had come with the highest recommendations from the German Internal Security and Intelligence organization. He had verified her references personally in addition to his own independent sources, some of whom he had worked with closely when employed with the Belgian Military Intelligence Service. He gazed around the room making eye contact equally with everyone so as not to suggest the leak came from within the team. His pause was not baited purposefully. Instead, it was an invitation to all to reflect and make recommendations.

Alexandra was the first to respond. "Could the source of the leak be an electronic listening device planted to eavesdrop?"

"A possibility," Daan acknowledged. "It wouldn't be the first time and it wouldn't be the last. Our own technicians sweep this office on a regular basis, as they do other facilities we use, but not on a set schedule. They were here last evening. Thus, anyone trying to plan around our routine would be hard pressed to do so. That begs the question: where have we been when sharing details, even preliminary tactics?"

Natalie looked around. Her pensive manner did not escape Daan's notice. He raised his eyebrows in response as if to say: care to share what is on your mind?

"Recommend we sweep Andrew's house," she stated emphatically, not as an option for discussion but as a recommendation based on thorough analysis. "Gaston confirmed that Andrew's house had been bugged by the Paris *Maquis* on the eve of Nazis marching arrogantly into Paris down the Champs Élysées in 1940 as a prelude to their perceived One Thousand Year Reich. In doing so, they goose-stepped on the essence of French culture, a symbol of blind obedience." Natalie rarely hid her disdain for the Bosch when talking about their impertinent presence in her City of Light.

"Please explain," Daan invited. Without background information, he was careful not to endorse any follow-up action or deny it outright, instead wanting to encourage all suggestions.

Natalie looked up in careful contemplation. "Luc Moreau came to Andrew's house at my request to discuss any provenance information with Andrew. He lived there as the previous owner of the property and knew the layout of the rooms better than Andrew or me. In reflection, his manner was cocky from the moment he approached the front door and ambled in until he departed. Without an invitation by Andrew, he strode into the parlour and then into the living room ahead of us. I can honestly say he was not in my sight all the time. He could have covertly left an electronic eavesdropping device. I had no reason to suspect he would do so." She paused, "Or would not secretly plant a bug. As a second unbiased opinion, for what it's worth, Langue growled all the time he was in the house."

"Interesting," Daan responded. "Thank you. I will ask our technicians to sweep the house. They will be in contact to confirm a convenient time and place."

"Luc's name keeps popping up. Why?" Paul pondered. "It's not a rhetorical question."

"Keep this incident involving Luc Moreau on the front burner in the context of my next question," Daan directed. "Who are our primary suspects? Who would want the names in the document released and who would not want them made public? The same people but under different circumstances?"

"Top of the list would be the government, the DG Internal Security. A close second would be the DG External Security," Paul proposed. "In addition, several prominent ministers and senior mandarins have vested interests, and would want to keep the names out of the public eye, perhaps their own names," he said as an afterthought.

"And there is Luc Moreau who works for the DG Interior Security," Daan suggested. "I am not saying he is our primary suspect. I am merely stating an observation."

"Second on the primary list but not too far behind the government would be the French communists?" Natalie proposed. "On every occasion I have chatted with Gaston, he has reminded me to always be suspicious of their activities. I am well aware of his deep dislike of them from his time with the *Maquis* as a teenager in Honfleur and other places in Normandy."

"They could both benefit and suffer from the consequences of a premature release," Alexander added. "Speaking about the French communists, there could be a traitor with a vendetta or a mole within their ranks who would use the list of names to discredit this or another organization, or for their own benefit."

"I don't mean to repeat myself, but there is Luc Moreau lurking in the background as an agent of DG Internal Security whose on-going mission it is to engage in politically motivated espionage," Daan implied. "Just a thought to consider."

"On the top of the secondary list and a lower priority would be affiliates of the French Carlingue Gestapo or affiliates of the former SS Nazi Gestapo," Yana interjected. "Perhaps correlated, there are the Nazis who never formally demobilized or returned to Germany after the war ended. Instead, they took off their black forage hats adorned with a skull and cross bones and put on Parisian berets. They remained in France where they slowly blended into the general population while re-establishing ties with the Fourth Reich. I had been working on that file with the German Internal Security and Intelligence organization before I was seconded to the EUI Unit."

"Other possible suspects?" Daan looked around.

After a period of silence, he posed a related question primarily to Alexandra. "What is the status of the low-level soldier who received the first envelope?"

"He was taken into custody and questioned after the shooting. As suspected, he has said nothing, at least not yet. His photograph is on file with the Police nationale which has linked him to the Saint-Denis crime network. He was kept under surveillance immediately after he left the first drop point. He only made one short phone call. He did not hand over the envelope to anyone.

Nor was he seen leaving it anywhere for someone else to retrieve. When he was arrested, he still had the envelope in his possession. Accordingly, we can safely conclude that the French communists have not seen the photocopy of the first list. Hence, they are none the wiser," Alexandra advised.

"Good intelligence linking French communists and Saint-Denis crime network," Daan congratulated all. "The complete document with all the names now gives us the opportunity to contact each person named and strongly suggest they become our informants. We suggest they talk with us openly about the French Communist Party or have their names turned over to the communists to do with as they see fit. Basically, talk to us or relinquish their ability to talk at all. As a bonus, we gain sources in government should any of them decide to become our confidential informants. Comments, ladies and gentlemen?"

With no further input, Daan summed up. "We have our work cut out for us. I will get back to you by tomorrow morning for follow-up action." On the top of his own list was having a conversation with Gaston. Hopefully, Gaston would be able to provide him with any lingering links between the French Carlingue Gestapo, the SS Nazi Gestapo and the French communists born out of the seeds sown by others during the war, the Fourth Reich being just one. As Gaston had repeatedly warned, the war was not over.

"One final thought, question," Yana offered.

"The floor is yours," Daan confirmed.

"If the purpose of killing the low-level soldier was to divert our attention from surrendering the names listed in the document, or something else, what would that be? What is looming on the horizon?"

Paul responded resolutely, "Every what has a who behind it. So, who is the who in this case, regardless of whether or not the shooting was a diversionary tactic?"

CHAPTER 41

Andrew entered the Brasserie du Bac in Caudebec en-Caux. "Is this a bistro?" he enquired in a low voice of an elderly gentleman behind the bar, following the instructions exactly as given to him by Gaston.

"Oui." The gentleman gestured to Andrew, suggesting he go to a private meeting room accessed from an alcove storage area adjacent to the bar. Once alone, Andrew followed up, "My father was a former RAF pilot."

Bistro merely nodded slowly without further acknowledgment. The intensity of the feelings of respect Andrew experienced had been forged in the crucible of those events long ago. Had it not been for the actions taken by Gaston, and more than likely Bistro and other members of the *Maquis*, his father might not have survived the ordeal and Andrew would not be here. For all he knew, his father could have sat at the table he was now gazing at. He had never considered the connotations of the word *surreal*. His presence at this moment seemed almost dreamlike as verbal keys opened doors to his past.

A lady followed them into the room with one *thé vert* and a snifter of brandy on a silver serving tray. She presented herself as mid-fifties but was appreciably older. Like most women in her milieu, she appeared courtly and correct, consistent with the reserved atmosphere of the café in this out-of-the-way sleepy fishing village on the Seine, known more for its ancient cathedral than its cuisine. Her thoughts, worn by grief and tragedy, took flight at the mention of Andrew's father like pigeons in a village square at the approach of a cat. She disappeared as discreetly as she had come in.

"My wife, Gisèle," Bistro whispered. "Like Gaston and Angelique, Gisèle and I survived the war years as children older than our years only to be plagued by nightmares of those precarious times. We are not alone. Gisèle cringes when any mention is made of those who survived the war, like your father, because others did not, their names fading but not our memories of them. One day, acknowledgement of even their names will be limited to moss-covered letters etched in granite tombstones."

Andrew scanned the room more out of curiosity than any other motivation. The décor was spartan yet eclectic and unconventional. For reasons Andrew could not fathom, the unflustered almost mundane tone of Bistro's voice spurred him to think back to the photo Gaston had shown him of Bistro and others taken in the boardroom of the President of France in the Élysée Palace. Seeing Bistro in person jogged his memory. The person standing beside Bistro in the photo might have been a younger Luc Moreau.

A slight smile crossed his face as he recalled advice once given to him by his father. He should examine any photograph from the outer edge first and then move in to the subject at the focal point in the centre. This would allow him to put the subject in context. Had he followed this sage suggestion when Gaston pointed to Bistro, he would have recognized Luc Moreau sooner.

"Have you seen or heard from Gaston?" Andrew enquired. He was uneasy about Gaston's absence from his Parisian home in the 1re arrondissement and anxious because he hadn't responded to emails or voice messages.

"Not recently," Bistro replied. "Why do you ask?"

"He seems to have gone AWOL, again. I am not worried but concerned."

"Not uncommon for him." Bistro commented. "He tends not to announce his agenda to others. A holdover from the war." He hesitated without expression before continuing. "I am certain you can appreciate his reasoning, young Andrew."

The name Bistro used, *young Andrew*, surprised him. Only

Gaston had ever referred to him in this way, most recently but only in a social sorcerer-apprentice context. *Thé vert*, two other words. Only the server at Les Deux Magots had repeated these other two words after he had used them when with Natalie at their first meeting. *Curiouser and curiouser, cried Alice.*

"Is there anything else I can help you with?" Bistro asked, changing the tack of the conversation slightly.

"Gaston told me that if ever I couldn't get hold of him, I was to contact you."

"Do not worry yourself, young Andrew," he said reassuringly. "If I see or hear from him, I will mention that you were enquiring."

Young Andrew. He wasn't young, just younger than Gaston and Bistro. He recalled his father on several occasions referring to him as young man and young lad. Had he used that term when speaking with Gaston about his future?

"Thank you," Andrew acknowledged. "If you see him before I do, can you ask him about the status of the barge used to transport my father to Honfleur? Has it been reduced to marine scrap?"

Several barges built at the turn of the century and no longer used for transporting produce from Normandy to Paris had since been refurbished as boutique cruise vessels on the Seine. Perhaps he could take one of these high-end luxury tours. Perhaps one had been the barge his father had been smuggled in enroute to Honfleur as a final layover in the safehouse before returning to England. Perhaps Monique could join him on such a river cruise. Before doing so, he would first need to enquire with Gaston.

"I will," Bistro replied in a neutral tone as if there was nothing significant about his question or what a response might reveal.

Andrew finished sipping his green tea and contemplating the curious atmosphere of the café before leaving as he had entered. He smiled in Giséle's direction. She gave the slightest acknowledgement of his courteous gesture. He sensed she wished him well and a safe journey back to Paris. Perhaps they would meet again under different circumstances, at which time she would answer questions he had not yet asked but should consider, advice only a mother could bestow upon a son about to leave the safety of the hearth to journey along perilous paths. He sensed no immediate threat to himself, should he return.

"Thoughts regarding young Andrew?" Gaston asked Bistro as he sauntered into the room adjacent to the bar, much like John Le Carré's sleuth character, George Smiley, had done so many times entering and leaving his own safe houses.

"I vaguely recall his father as a downed RAF pilot we helped return to England. I remember him better from our meetings in the early 1960s. Andrew shows considerable promise, as you suggest. Well worth following up," Bistro remarked. "I will contact my colleague to ensure he comes to no harm. He has a credible cover story made to measure – a financially independent retired foreign national, now a property owner and resident of the City of Light acting out his *flâneur* dreams." Andrew was not provincial by any standards, which would have been less desirable. Instead, he was Roman – educated, cultured, a citizen of substance.

There were a few outstanding issues to be taken care of first, Bistro recognized. He was confident that resolution was close at hand.

"And a devoted companion to my Monique. *À bientôt*, see you soon," Gaston gestured with a grin conveying his sense of satis-faction as he left the café through the back door as he had done many times before. He was convinced Monique and Andrew would complement each other well now that Claude was no longer alive. Abusive spouses tend not to listen to prudent advice: if you live by the sword, you die by the sword.

Bistro sent his encrypted communiqué to his colleague saying what he meant to say without having to describe it explicitly. In doing so, he directed the contact to befriend Andrew to ensure no harm came to either him or Monique. He was to be a quasi-mentor to Andrew, not so much a guiding light as a lighthouse to warn unsuspecting ships' captains away from hidden shoals. Instead, as a guiding shadow, his benign influence was perceived but not seen, much like Andrew's father had been on all those occasions when quiet father-son dialogues had taken place.

"We have a common interest," Bistro advised. His eyes were elsewhere, focused on old images projected on his mind.

The recipient of Bistro's communiqué confirmed, "at least one and perhaps more or less common interest, but certainly worthwhile talking about and coming to an agreement regarding strategies to be employed and procedures to be followed."

Never is a very long time, Bistro mused. The war had become an emotional Berlin Wall as envisaged by Moscow. Once physically erected, it was never to be torn down. Yet it did crumble and fall under the sledge hammers of imprisoned citizens, like the walls of the Bastille two hundred years before. For those whom it had affected, it was to remain a constant reminder of events that had influenced countless decisions and subsequent actions. Many dated back to 1919 and the Treaty of Versailles, and before that to the 1917 Russian Revolution.

CHAPTER 42

"I asked Jean Belliveau from the European Union Anti-Terrorist Cyber Unit to conduct a thorough sweep for electronic eavesdropping devices in all the facilities we use. He was to include Andrew's house specifically," Daan announced. "He has done so. Nothing was discovered."

"How then did the leak regarding details about the sting operation occur?" Yana asked with a tinge of frustration in her voice.

Jean responded to her question. "Good news, as Daan mentioned – there were no bugs located. Bad news – there is a new next-generation of Artificial Intelligence e-bugging system out of South-East Asia. We strongly suspect China. I had previously mentioned the Dark Web which is where cyber criminals tend to conduct their business. What we are facing currently is different yet equally threatening. AI hacking has been spread simultaneously using the Dark Web into the European Union. Artificial Intelligence software programs, like TD-Gammon, have learned to play backgammon at a high level, just below that of the top human players. Clearly these AI advances are being used now for nefarious purposes – including intercepting e-communications. Cell phone viruses and eavesdropping are the primary means of operation from various staging platforms in North Africa. We suspect from Egypt and Morocco to the Marseilles Mafia as a preferred distribution network."

"Sorry for interrupting. When you say different yet equally threatening, are you referring to the Basque operation?" Alexandra interjected. At the end of that case she recalled committing to spending one-on-one time with Jean to upgrade her knowledge of the cyber world and skills. She never did. She would now.

"Correct," Jean confirmed. "We broke that particular version of the code in the middle of that operation but not before some perpetrators had been killed."

"In addition to two innocent children killed and one of our agents wounded," Daan clarified. The loss of one member of the team, even wounded as was the case with the Basque file, caused his acid reflux to erupt.

It was unfortunate that one low-level soldier had been killed on this mission at the Stade de France. At least, it wasn't one of his own agents. That had always been his worst-case scenario.

With a go-ahead nod from Daan, Jean elaborated, "Like this previous case, we have been able to upgrade the code for the new prototype since the previous e-generation was implemented. This earlier generation had a single source. This recent one is multi-sourced. Thus, it is now exponentially more difficult to identify its origin without signatures. With this generation, no human voice can be traced to a person. To the disadvantage of its creators and to our advantage, the absence of a human voice is a signature in itself because all digitally created voices have unique cyber codes. We can say with confidence that the first cell phone encrypted with this software is a throwaway device recently tracked to someone in the French government. Again, to our advantage, the digitally created code has been partially broken. I can confirm that someone was recently shot fatally at your second drop point. As a direct result, this latest sting operation was stopped in its tracks." This revelation gave him pause. "That is the leak."

"Thank you, Jean." Daan scanned those sitting around the table. "Perhaps not what we wanted to hear but what we needed to hear before we review our plans for the next phase. Any last-minute questions before Jean concludes his presentation?"

No one responded. They contemplated with horror the knowledge they were at the mercy of the programmers roaming freely in the cyber cosmos.

"In the final analysis," Jean summarized, "your electronic communications on this recent operation had been compromised. No one could have anticipated this level of electronic spying. This is the first case in which we have been able to identify this generation of the Asian software. We strongly suspect the Marseilles Mafia sold a copy to the French communists. If it is of any consolation, our unit is in the process of developing our own software for cell phone application to counter this off-shore threat to the European Union." He looked around. "Have no doubt, it is a real and tangible threat to European Union security," he confirmed.

The first thought that came to Daan's mind was the need to have Jean attend all future planning sessions for operations and all debriefings regardless of success or failure. Clearly, the role that advanced electronics was playing had increased exponentially since the Basque file was concluded only a few months earlier.

Jean held his stare. "Welcome to the cyber battlespace, a war declared without any formal declarations and a foe without identifiable uniforms, traditional borders and what military strategists used to refer to as clearly identified forward edges of the battle area. This is unlike the previous war which we continue to fight half a century later and, for some, even longer as Gaston and his *Maquis* colleagues continue to attest to. The cyber world of Artificial Intelligence is the most recent strategic position from which the battle for dominance of the world economy will define wealth and the fate of individual nation states and multinationals like the European Union, as the agrarian and industrial revolutions once did in previous centuries."

CHAPTER 43

" To take the wind out of the sails of the French communists named in the document, do we start at the top of the list, with the most senior bureaucrats or those who have the greatest influence and perhaps the most to lose? Or do we begin with the most likely to talk and possibly influence others?" Daan posed the question to Alexandra, Paul and Yana. "I will interview a select few." He looked over at Yana. "I don't want to involve you in this phase of the operation. Being the newest agent, I would prefer not to identify you as a European Union Intelligence Unit agent just yet."

"Understood," Yana nodded and smiled, indicating she was in complete agreement. She recalled Daan complimenting her on her interview techniques with Manfred Dietrich minutes before his wife stabbed him. Not only was she in her element in those solo roles, she enjoyed modifying her style when engaging in cameo performances.

In response to Daan's question regarding priority for interviews, Alexandra responded without hesitation, "Not an Either Or, but a Both And. I suggest the most senior because they have more to offer but also those who have the most to lose. Thus, they will be more likely to expose others in order to save their own unethical hides."

"Paul? Preferences?

"I agree.

"Confirmed then," Daan replied.

⊰ ⊱

ON THE HEELS OF ONE-ON-ONE interviews and revelations of their names on the list, many board members and other French

communists employed in influential ex-officio positions on committees and councils submitted their letters of resignation, having
first voluntarily indicated their intention "to retire to spend more
time with family" being the most common reason given. A few
discretely committed suicide while others simply disappeared. A
select few saw the advantage of accepting offers to become informants for the European Union Intelligence Unit, naming communist comrades in other EU nations. Yana referred names of several
candidates living in the Federal Republic of Germany to associates
in the German Internal Security and Intelligence organization.

"Is it wishful thinking or sheer gullibility on the part of some
senior executives of DG Internal Security and DG External
Security that they think they know everything there is to know
about Moscow's agents? Or is it their arrogance leading them to
draw that conclusion?" Alexandra asked Daan.

"I'm sensing some scepticism," Daan replied as he tried to hide
his smile.

She answered without answering, simply returning his gaze.
They knew each other well enough to read the other's mind.

Paul rocked his head back and forth several times. "If there is
one thing I have learned, it is the more I think I know, the more I
know that I don't know. And the more I learn, the more I learn that
I need to learn more. I would be naïve to think that those on the
list we have contacted thus far are the last French communists with
malice intent toward democracy."

"Let us put it in the context of when the document was drawn
up in the months after the first post-war French election in 1946,"
Daan proposed. "It was then that Moscow came to the realization
that the probability of forming a government in France was so infinitely small it was safe to say never. French internal security had
heard a rumour that a list existed but it wasn't until Andrew and
Monique re-discovered it several weeks ago and turned it over to

Alexandra, Paul and me, that the stark reality and implications of the contents became known."

"Fortuitous, given the fact Monique and Andrew first set eyes on the document in 1960 when they lived next door to each other in Saint-Germain-des-Prés," Paul reflected. "Even more so that they would have remembered it and the circumstances related to that discovery all these years later." He thought, *curiosity killed the cat.* "Curiosity can lead to unanticipated danger and misfortune, which it has."

"Agreed," Daan replied. "Having interviewed a few on the list myself, I am confident that some if not most of those named had more than likely forgotten about the existence of the document. The looks on their faces when I showed them their names clearly indicated the horror of the consequences, as did SS Gestapo members and guards of concentration camps when confronted by the Allied War Crimes investigators. Those who did remember the document assumed they were home free forever because of a statute of limitations or a false sense of privilege after successful careers in post-1946 France. Suffice it to say, *never* is a very long time. It is folly if not outright foolhardiness to believe otherwise."

For those who chose to end their own lives as a result of being confronted with the list of names or for other reasons, the murky River Seine became their watery grave. Gaston's forewarning that the war was not over was true.

⚞ ⚟

THE SOFT EARLY MORNING LIGHT revealed the harsh reality of yet another body found floating in the Honfleur estuary. He was identified from membership papers conveniently stuffed into his pocket as having been a long-standing member of the French Communist Party formerly from Normandy but more recently a resident of Paris.

The police concluded he had been killed silently. Unseen by anyone except his assassin, the body was dumped into the water sometime after twilight when the veil of darkness descended, shrouding any evidence of the offence. He was yet another casualty of D-Day, joining the SS Gestapo major who had tortured Gaston's Angelique on the eve of the Allied invasion, in addition to other Nazis whose corpses were also discovered floating face down stripped of all personal identification with the exception of unit insignia that condemned them to death by trial *in absentia*.

"The body was approximately 356 kilometres from Paris as the crow flies over the Seine," Daan confirmed. "Given the brief length of time between his interview and the discovery of his body beneath the Pont de Normandie, his death must have occurred close to the estuary. If killed in Paris or elsewhere, the route would likely have been the A13 roadway, an equally short trip from his Paris residence."

"Any idea who his assassin was?" Paul asked.

Daan continued, "Not yet confirmed by anyone we have interviewed. He is believed to be Louise's partner who had been contracted to stalk Andrew and Monique to secure the document, the list of names. His neck had been broken in the same vicious manner as Louise's. Curiously, the coroner reported that he had been stabbed recently. The wound was superficial, suggesting the blade had been deflected by the victim or the perpetrator was not strong, perhaps with a petite physique.

The French communist code of silence had been broken, at least by some. Those who issued the unwritten contract did not want anything falling back on them. As was the case with Claude, it appeared that if you lived by the sword, you died by the sword.

CHAPTER 44

The subject line on the email to Andrew read *Provenance*. He read further. "Can we meet to discuss? If so, may I suggest the Café de Fore at a convenient time and date." Andrew did not recognize the sender. He felt his heart rate increase and his palms become sweaty with anxiety.

"Forwarded for your comments and direction, please. I thought these new cell phones were supposed to be secure," Andrew's text to Natalie stated. He was confident she would quickly realize that he was beyond mildly annoyed.

"Where are you?"

"Les Deux Magots."

"Am fifteen minutes away. Have the waiter seat you," she replied.

Their regular table was occupied by other customers by the time Natalie arrived. The waiter apologized quietly as he tilted his head toward Andrew seated under the statues. He looked up from his *thé vert* as she approached. Their waiter followed shortly with a cappuccino on a silver tray as she was seated.

"Not certain who sent this message to you. By virtue of the fact he was able to do so suggests he has a high security clearance. I am assuming it is a he and not a she. I forwarded a copy to Daan, Alexandra and Paul. None of them sent the message to you. All agreed the sender had advanced security clearance or knew someone who did. My next step was to contact Jean. He traced the IPS and cyber link and could only say that it came from DG Internal Security. Jean recommended that you do not reply until such time as he verifies the identity of the sender. It should not take long."

"So, where does that leave me?" Andrew asked suspiciously. "I am okay with not replying, although I am intrigued by the subject line. That appears to be the bait. The only person other than yourself who knew of my interest in the provenance of my property was Luc Moreau, apart from your surveyor who has only communicated through you."

"Hold that thought." Natalie sent a request to her contact in DG Internal Security requesting that Luc contact her soonest. Before she had finished her cappuccino, her cell phone vibrated with an incoming terse single-syllable message. "Luc." Her reply was two words but equally succinct. "Client provenance?"

"Time, location?"

"Les Deux Magots, now."

"Twenty minutes. Café de Flore" Luc replied.

Natalie and Andrew walked to the door of Les Deux Magots where their waiter waved his hand indicating they could settle the tariff next time. They were seated and sipping their drinks by the time Luc arrived at the Café de Flore ten minutes late.

"Sorry for being longer than initially indicated. Heavier than normal traffic," he explained.

"You have information regarding the provenance of your former house," Natalie said as a statement of fact. She purposely did not mention Andrew or the text he had received.

"Yes, as a follow-up to our previous meeting *chez* Andrew. I crossed paths with my soon-to-be ex-wife, Estella. I mentioned your enquiry regarding provenance. She told me that in the garret suite, in the bottom dresser drawer she had found what appeared to be a blueprint of the house and property. The writing appeared to be in Old German script and dated 1871, the year following the Franco-Prussian War. There was no mention of 1814 or Napoleon Bonaparte. When Estella researched the surveyor cited on the blueprint, she found no record in France or Germany. Accordingly, she concluded it was false. The Nazis had a habit of doing that. Stealing property, destroying original records and replacing them with fraudulent ones. The blueprint was still in the dresser drawer when last she saw it. Just passing this information along for what it is worth."

"Thank you," Andrew replied warily.

"No problem."

"You have my email coordinates? I do not recall giving them to you?" Andrew stated bluntly. If not the tone then his bearing was sufficient to suggest he was suspicious of Luc's ability to access that classified information.

"I asked around." He then glanced at Natalie. "Like you, I left a message and like you, I received a confirming reply." He hesitated as he transferred his attention to Andrew before adding, "Rest assured, your confidentiality and source remain secure, young Andrew. I apologize if I seemed a bit short when last we spoke. I was in the middle of a sensitive case. It is almost concluded, thankfully. Stress is not good for the health," he added with a good-natured grin.

Andrew answered with silence. Luc did not appear to take offence.

He sensed that Andrew remained distant. He would need to bait him further if he was to gain his trust. "A few final matters of interest related to the provenance have come to my attention. SS Oberstleutnant Dietrich's hoard of stolen property grew in size and sophistication as the war came to a close. It was comprised mostly of gold ingots and bullion, in addition to smaller pieces of art, all more easily portable. It had been stolen with complete disregard for its provenance," Luc explained to Andrew.

"And other matters?" Andrew asked. He detected that he momentarily held the high ground in this exchange.

"Dietrich kept some money when he disappeared under cover of night as Paris was being liberated. He subsequently lived with Manfred while the son attended university. The gold and other monies he deposited in a Swiss bank in Davos. Now that both Dietrich and Manfred are dead, the latter without a legal will or identified heir, the ill-gotten assets remain in the Swiss bank. There was an abundance of wealth. Yet father and son perished from hunger for life like King Midas who died from starvation according to Aristotelian legend."

Andrew held his stare without saying anything. He presumed Luc had additional intelligence, perhaps information of little or no apparent value.

"After our first conversation, I became intrigued by your search for background details. As far as I can determine, there never was a door in the interior wall joining the two lots. Like you, I concluded that if there was no door when the Nazis moved in, they would have constructed one if for no other reason than efficiency which was in their Germanic blood."

Andrew doubted the truth of this latest bit of information. Luc was, after all, an intelligence officer, a master in the art of deceit and dishonesty. Validating this near truism could be a benefit of growing closer to Luc and engaging in conversations that mattered.

Andrew's attention went momentarily elsewhere. Gaston was the only person other than his father who referred to him as *young Andrew*. Then Bistro. Now, the previous occupant of his urban estate. What was the common denominator?

"If you would like to speak with Estella as a follow-up, let me know and I will ask her rather than giving her your email address. Although she has the same advanced security clearance as I do, the fewer who know your identity, the better. She knows some things that I do not. It comes down to a need to know."

"Thank you," Natalie acknowledged. She remained unsure of his sincerity or motivation given that his demeanour was appreciably different from the first time they met face-to-face at Andrew's house. Thinking back, she had never seen Luc or his wife during the real estate transaction, just their respective lawyers whom she knew from her days with the Police nationale.

Estella was known for her many disguises, including modifying her facial features. Perhaps Luc too had been trained by experts in the art and science of masquerades, a prerequisite for those who navigate the boulevards and less travelled pathways which define the arcane world of security and intelligence.

"On occasion, I find myself in Saint-Germain-des-Prés. I can ring your doorbell if you are serving thé vert." Luc spoke to Andrew but equally to Natalie, for her information. He was confident they would chat about this meeting.

Andrew remained neutral in response to his offer of developing a more congenial relationship.

After their first meeting, Natalie had been more suspicious, Andrew less so but still not fully at ease. The fulcrum appeared to have shifted by the time they parted company with Luc on this second occasion.

"Thoughts?" Natalie asked, clearly interested in Andrew's assessment of Luc's response and information regarding provenance details.

"It might be informative if we could speak with Estella, ideally without Luc's knowledge or involvement as an emissary."

"Something else appears to be on your mind," Natalie murmured.

"I am bothered by his ability to access my email so easily. If he can, does that mean French communists working in government or their informant colleagues can too? Luc could have contacted you through his lawyer as he did to confirm our first meeting. This information is nice to know but not a high priority. So why? He then concluded with an offer to be more sociable with the feeble reasoning he is often in the neighbourhood so he could easily drop in for tea."

"My thinking too," Natalie responded.

"Am I being paranoid thinking that there is more to Luc Moreau than he presents? I am well aware that if paranoia runs rampant, myths self-perpetuate. Then paranoia feeds off its own neurosis." Andrew hesitated for several moments before suggesting a possible link. "If I said Bistro, what comes to your mind?"

It was Natalie's turn to think about possible associations. She was confident Andrew was not conjuring up a list of places to sit at outside tables. "Not a what but a who?" she responded.

Andrew nodded. "Gaston showed me a photo of one of his *Maquis* colleagues taken in the boardroom of the Élysée Palace. He explained that if I couldn't get hold of him, Gaston, for any reason, I was to speak with this person. Standing beside this *Maquis* colleague in the photograph was what could have been a youthful Luc Moreau. You have been playing in this arena much longer than I have in addition to associating with Daan and his EUI Unit colleagues." Andrew stared more intently at Natalie without enquiring further.

"Interesting, anything is possible," she suggested.

"Just my intuition working overtime," Andrew added. "Is Luc solely on the DG Internal Security payroll or is he a character of another political stripe working for a second salary? He raised his hands with palms open. "Just asking."

"You are a natural at this game," Natalie replied in a quieter voice. "Are you certain you do not want another job in retirement, even part-time, while enjoying the Parisian *flâneur* lifestyle?"

"Not at this time," Andrew replied.

Natalie added, "The only thing that makes me doubt that Luc may be a double agent is the fact that Gaston thinks highly of him. If there was anyone I trusted one hundred percent, it would be Gaston." *But…* she entertained an afterthought.

"Thank you, good to know. On several occasions, my father

said much the same thing about Gaston. Having met him again now as an adult, I would have to agree. I just had to ask. So, what is Luc up to? What is motivating him to become more sociable? I hearken back to his change in behaviour to contact me directly rather than going through his lawyer to you. He must have known I would contact you immediately as my real estate agent. I repeat, WHY?"

"Good question. I don't know why. I doubt he would tell us if we asked him. I can safely say I didn't sense anything strange in his behaviour. My best explanation, in spy language, is that spooks can be spooky sometimes."

"Fair enough. But what about the fact that his fingerprints were lifted by the Police nationale identification folks from the crime scene where Louise's corpse was found. He told us he had never been in the stable-garage lot."

"I can't say for sure, only speculate."

Andrew stared at her as a prompt to give her best guess. *Speculation based on advanced knowledge he was not privy to*, he considered. He was becoming more attuned to her restrained expression.

"I suspect DG Internal Security was onto Louise. She told Manfred her parents were Jewish and had been sent to concentration camps. In reality, her parents were French Catholics. The parents befriended Jewish people and others labelled by the Nazis as dissidents under the guise they were helping them as members of the Paris *Maquis* to hide their valuable family possessions. Acting in cohort with Dietrich, they then stole the family treasures once Dietrich had shipped the rightful owners off to Auschwitz. Her parents were acutely aware of the dual account in the ledger of slaughter and survival. These deceptive antics had kept her parents temporarily in Dietrich's good books, yet ultimately to no avail. We understand that Louise was determined to find the cache of treasures that Dietrich had concealed under the floorboards in the stable-garage. She just needed to identify the access point. We can speculate further that on the direction of his employer, Luc guided her inside and killed her, or he purposely left the lane door open which made it plausible for someone else to follow them and kill her. Regardless, circumstances dictated that she be silenced, permanently."

"And the fingerprint?" Andrew pressed.

"A mistake on his part to leave a print. I was advised by a colleague with the Police nationale that these prints have since been misplaced. It happens even to professionals."

Andrew gazed at Natalie with a non-judgemental eye. He felt more secure with her speculation about himself and more so for Monique. He thought about his father for reasons he could not fathom. He recalled the occasions when his father provided a nebulous explanation of events Andrew never fully understood but accepted as the explanation. He concluded his rationalization with *c'est la vie, c'est la guerre.*

CHAPTER 45

From the moment Andrew entered the Brasserie du Bac in the shadow of Caudebec-en-Caux cathedral he was uneasy, unlike the first time he had arrived to meet Bistro. He allowed his emotion to percolate as he retreated into himself reflecting on potential scenarios, which could shed light on his consciousness of potential foreboding.

In the corner of the brasserie furthest away from the entrance, he saw a female sitting alone at a table with her back to him. A brunette ponytail flowed over her left shoulder. This was an odd occurrence in more traditional French culture for a petite female to be alone, unless she was waiting for the imminent arrival of a male companion. Alternately, she could be expecting a potential client, although her deportment and demeanour were inconsistent with the criteria for that trade craft. Nor did the Brasserie du Bac seem to be a venue for a liaison involving such business transactions. Two other older patrons sat at a table immediately to his left closest to the door seemingly speaking but strangely not ostensibly to each other. Andrew's intuition left him sensing they were dubious characters with questionable convictions unlike the female who projected an image of purpose, perhaps wary none-the-less.

Andrew had become conscious of his own heightened sense of concern, which had been triggered yesterday. He had attempted to contact Gaston at his home in the 1er arrondissement of Paris to follow-up on his suggestion that Andrew delve into Luc Moreau's background. He was unsuccessful in establishing contact. He had called Gaston on his secure cell phone but to no avail. He had then asked Monique to enquire as to her father's whereabouts. She had no further luck. She explained that Gaston tended to depart on business trips without notice only to return on his own schedule.

If the matter was urgent, she suggested that Andrew contact her father's colleague, Bistro, at the Brasserie du Bac in Caudebec-en-Caux. Andrew wasn't looking forward to the train ride from Paris to Caudebec-en-Caux but resigned himself to the reality. He was a retired Parisian gentleman on no particular fixed schedule. He would visit the cathedral while in Caudebec-en-Caux.

"Is this a bistro?" Andrew asked the female server who approached the table he had been sitting at for what seemed to be a considerable length of time. He recognized her as Bistro's wife, Gisèle, who had been reserved but guardedly friendly when they first met. Any indication of familiarity in her expression on this occasion was absent. He mirrored her distanced disposition, which did little to calm his growing disquiet.

"No," she replied in a polite but terse tone.

"Can I get a cappuccino to take with me?" he asked in a normal yet awkward tourist voice. "I plan on walking to the cathedral."

"No," she replied brusquely. "We do not have any disposal cups." She turned immediately and walked away. Her stature screamed of a need for caution.

As he stood to leave, he noticed Bistro entering the bar area from the alcove and backroom where they had previously met on his initial visit. Luc Moreau followed close behind Bistro yet seemed to stop abruptly on seeing Andrew who he did not acknowledge openly. Instead, Luc made eye contact briefly with an apprehensive glare, what Andrew interpreted as an ominous gesture. Andrew hesitated without gazing at anyone, including Luc who withdrew back into the darkness of the unlit hallway. Andrew then paused before departing the Brasserie du Bac as cautiously as he had entered.

On the sidewalk, he gazed left and right along Quai Guilbaud in order to re-establish his bearings and assess the safety of his surroundings. The serene flow of the Seine reflected the quietness of the quai along the river front. A solitary man approached from the right and strolled in front of him with his head down, his beret sloping low over his creased forehead obscuring his identity.

"Follow me," the man whispered, his lips remaining still like a ventriloquist.

Andrew hesitated momentarily before complying with Gaston's hushed instructions. Although the sole purpose of his trip to the Brasserie du Bac was to speak with Gaston, the circumstances leading up to this rendezvous were far from routine. But nothing thus far about this journey appeared normal. He would not have been surprised if Natalie appeared in one of her many disguises.

He trusted Gaston without any doubt. He trusted Bistro as a result of Gaston's unwavering endorsement as his oldest childhood friend and fellow member of the Maquis. Then there was Luc again appearing beside Bistro in the brasserie as he first noted their potential relationship in the photograph that Gaston had pointed to. That caused him to ponder once again: Is Luc a double agent, a Soviet spy who subverted the DG Internal Security or vice versa? An ill-omened shiver ran the length of his spine. Or is Luc a loyal agent of France who had successfully infiltrated the French Carlingue Gestapo in addition to the French KGB cell, recently rebranded as the FSB. All appeared to be linked and facing off against the Cerberus, the monstrous three-headed hound of Hades. The call of the Russian bugle or, perhaps, another nation's trumpet, was sounding in the distance.

Andrew recalled his father saying that the Cold War had become a nuanced force. Winning this conflict between East and West would be based on your ability to exploit tactical opportunities, mostly undetected like the Nazi submarine wolfpacks had accomplished during the early years of the Second World War. Gaston's wary warning reverberated, "the war is not over." What new undetected wolfpacks might have recently been lurking in the murky depths of the Brasserie du Bac in Caudebec-en-Caux?

CHAPTER 46

Gaston trundled along focused on his mission yet appearing nonchalant as if in silent contemplation. Andrew followed at a discrete distance, close enough to keep him in sight but not so close that someone might construe that they were together. At the traffic round-about, Gaston curved left along rue de la République and turned left again on rue de la Vicomté. He quickly stepped into the entrance way of a quaint relatively new two-storey house on the left. He ensured the front door remained slightly ajar after he entered.

Andrew calculated this house was directly behind the Brasserie du Bac. Their back entrances would be conveniently a stone throw apart yet obscured by a high wooden fence that impaired any direct line of sight. Andrew followed Gaston with equal agility closing the door behind him. He almost expected to hear the click of an electronic door lock behind him as would occur at his urban estate in Saint-Germain-des-Prés that he had purchased from Luc and his wife, Estella. All was quiet except for Gaston's welcoming invitation to the home of Bistro and Gisèle.

The décor was tasteful and the furnishings of excellent quality. The business of operating a brasserie must have been profitable years before, Andrew conjectured. Yet on both occasions he had visited there were less than a handful of patrons only sipping cappuccino. Perhaps the evening clienteles were numerous and chose from a more replete menu of local French cuisine regardless of the tariff. That would require a full-time master chef and serving staff with considerable salaries.

He doubted his assumptions were correct. Something was awry. Bistro must have had a second more lucrative and steady income. The Brasserie du Bac could be a front for a business similar to

Gaston's covert associations. He stared up beyond the ceiling, marshalling his thoughts. Not every entrepreneur met with colleagues in the board room of the garret suite at the Élysée Palace in the 8e arrondissement of the French capitol. The octopus had a ninth tentacle that reached into the hallowed halls and backroom of the clandestine tradecraft of security and intelligence, he concluded.

"And what brings you to Caudebec-en-Caux? It cannot be just the tourist attractions or the vistas of the Seine?" Gaston asked.

"When last we spoke, you encouraged me to more fully explore the background of Luc Moreau. I attempted to contact you in Paris at your home, by phone and with the assistance of your daughter, all to no avail. Monique suggested I come here." Andrew lingered as he smiled ever so faintly and canted his head in an inquisitive manner.

"That I did," Gaston acknowledged Andrew's motivation for once again leaving the relative security of his Parisian urban estate.

"I saw Luc briefly beside Bistro shortly after I entered the brasserie. He gave no impression that he wanted to acknowledge me. In no uncertain terms, Gisèle warned me away by stating that the brasserie was not a bistro. Accordingly, I concluded that it was not safe to be there and I should depart promptly."

Gaston responded without responding. Instead, he nodded subtly in agreement of Andrew's decision to depart. The backdoor to Bistro and Gisèle's house opened. Gaston gazed fleetly past Andrew. He then returned his focus. "You can pose your questions to Luc personally."

"Ah, two of my favorite Parisian colleagues," Luc responded. "Please excuse my lack of hospitality. I have no Pinot Noir to offer you as this is not my home, young Andrew."

It was Andrew's turn to reply without saying anything. He was learning the gestures of the tradecraft. Instead, he paused in his introductory conversation with Gaston who gestured to both to join him at the kitchen table.

Gaston then focused his attention on Andrew. "I owe you an explanation, Andrew. What I am about to tell you is still classified as secret and for your attention only. Lives will depend on your absolute silence. You will find a personal link." He hesitated as he looked at Luc who seemed to tacitly grant him permission with a nod to reveal details he had not yet disclosed in previous conversations.

Gaston continued. "Let me take you back to the late winter and early spring of 1945. The German high command knew the war would be over by summer. The Nazis would not be the victors. The Reichsbank in Berlin had been bombed and its contents of gold, cash and other valuable attributes of wealth were being moved to numerous locations, the largest being the salt mines at Merkers. By April 1945, the remaining gold reserves including gold bars and boullion, cash, precious stones and a hoard of other valuable stolen property were being transported to mines in Bavaria where the Nazis were preparing to defend the *vaterland* against the onslaught of Allied air and ground forces."

Gaston gestured to Luc to continue.

"In the final week of April 1945, one load of the final shipments of gold bars never made it to Bavaria. One Nazi transport plane was diverted to Brest, on the Atlantic coast, where the gold bars were to be hidden. Its purpose would be to fund the rise of the fourth Reich after the surrender was signed. Andrew, that night your father was returning from a bombing raid when he came under fire from Nazi anti-aircraft fire west of Rouen. He was shot down as was the Nazi transport plane within a kilometer of each other." With a hint of sarcasm, Luc stated, "the Allies did not register flight plans with the Luftwaffe and vice versa. Certainly, not the members of the Nazi Gestapo who were involved in this heist of the gold."

Gaston interjected in Luc's comic hiatus. "My Maquis cell rescued your father. Unfortunately, his navigator had been killed. That was when your father and I first met. You know the details of his eventual escape back to England on a fishing boat from Honfleur. What you do not know is the connection to the Nazi Gestapo major who had captured Angelique and started to torture her on the eve of the D-Day Allied invasion. This Nazi major was part of the conspiracy to steal the Reich bank gold. He dispatched German troops to locate and secure the transport plane. Unbeknown to the major, these Nazi troops secured the site of your father's Mosquito plane, not the transport plane. In the interim, members of the French Carlingue Gestapo found the transport plane. They grabbed the gold and hid it. All but one was killed in the process by members of our Maquis. This single survivor kept the location a secret, only disclosing it to a colleague on his death bed years later."

"That is when I became involved," Luc added. "I was a junior agent with DG Internal Security assigned to find the cache of gold bars. Initially, we thought the French Communists might have been involved but soon ruled out that scenario. My partner and I were following a suspect when he was murdered as he was about to disclose the location of the cache to us. We believed this assassin was a member of the Fourth Reich. Sadly, my first partner was also fatally shot at that encounter. My second partner joined me a year ago. We had a lead on another confidant. He was in the Brasserie du Bac this afternoon when you entered, one of the two men sitting at the table by the door. We suspected the second man was that same member of the Fourth Reich who had killed our previous informant and my first partner."

"That was why Bistro's wife, Gisèle, warned you away," Gaston added. "These two men departed shortly after you."

Luc continued. "I had followed them into the brasserie. Hence, there was an increased probability they might have seen me. We knew in advance that they were meeting here. They did not know my partner was already seated at another table. When they departed after you, she followed them. We had backup who kept her under surveillance when I snuck out the back and came directly here so as not to compromise the operation." Luc explained.

"I have said and continue to warn all that the war is not over," Gaston interjected. "When the Honfleur Maquis killed the Gestapo major along with other Nazis on D-Day, they eliminated potential leads as to the whereabouts of the gold recovered from the truant Nazi transport plane. Their deaths are one of the several reasons the French Carlingue Gestapo continue to this day to fight the Second World War. The resurrection of the Fourth Reich is another."

"Thank you," Andrew acknowledged as he slowly bobbed his head not wanting to endorse the details but merely to acknowledge them.

Gaston further explained, "every Nazi was someone else before March 1933 when Hitler was elected Chancellor of Germany. Many remained different after the war. One only has to look at all the Nazi conspirators involved in this heist of the gold bars as proof. Ironically, none got to reap the benefits from their nefarious scheme with the exception of the one survivor. He kept one gold bar. Unfortunately for him, this bar was 24 carat gold. Thus, he experienced considerable difficulty converting it to cash because the only source of pure 24 carat gold in that quantity was melted-down gold fillings from the teeth of prisoners of the Auschwitz and other concentration camps. Even the most unscrupulous traffickers in precious metals were hesitant to be caught in possession of large amounts of the 24-carat gold."

Andrew sat overwhelmed with the sheer volume of information that had been shared with him, especially intelligence related to his father. Gazing at Luc, he acknowledged, "I now understand why you had been standoffish when you came to my urban estate in

Saint-Germain-des-Prés to discuss potential provenance and why you had failed to openly acknowledge me in the Brasserie de Bac only minutes before."

Andrew also understood why and how he had been surreptitiously groomed for this career trajectory by his father and Gaston all those years ago. The thought crossed his mind that Natalie might also be a part of this covert recruiting endeavour.

"Eto pravil'no, tovarishch – that is correct, comrade," Luc confirmed.

Andrew no longer had any doubt regarding Luc's loyalty to France. Clearly, he was not a double agent on two payrolls, one being Moscow. Fate had brought his father, Gaston, Monique, Philippe, Luc and himself together, in addition to a host of other scripted lesser characters in this Athenian theatrical drama.

Luc continued to check for any phone messages from his partner regarding the status of the surveillance and her location. There was none. Waiting was the most stressful aspect of this case. His second partner was an exceptionally capable agent. Regardless, he was concerned for her safety and the progress of the case.

"I would like to walk to the Caudebec-en-Caux cathedral," Andrew explained. There he hoped he could find peace in the solitude of this place of worship. Silence wasn't always synonymous with peacefulness and certainly could not guarantee it. But he had relied on his faith more than once to help calm his unsettled soul. It was times like this that he so missed his wife. He paused. He had just referred to Lynette as his wife and not by her first name? That caused him concern for reasons he could not fully fathom.

CHAPTER 47

Andrew lit a votive prayer candle, then sat alone in a pew at the back of the cathedral. There he hoped to process all the information Gaston and Luc had passed on to him. He had once thought that he was reasonably well informed having been the son of a military attaché who had quietly listened to banter between his father and his colleagues, some information classified that he knew was not to be repeated. Of particular interest at this juncture in his life was the serendipitous role his father and his Mosquito plane had played in the escapade surrounding the shooting down of the Nazi transport plane carrying the gold bars acquired in the heist leading up to D-Day.

He had asked himself on many occasions, why does anyone kill? He had a good idea. In its basic sense: for fear of loss or opportunity for gain, primarily in the arena of love, lust, power and control. Money is invariably connected.

Gott mit uns – God is with us, had been inscribed on military belt buckles since the formation of Prussia until the end of the Second World War. Yet Germany's enemies also insisted that God was backing their side. At their most basic, an individual's moral quandry and the geopolitical conflict were both about power. After 1945, the power battle revolved around the Cold War, the rise of the French Communist party and the Fourth Reich. It was the literal spoils of war – the heist of the stolen gold bars from the Reich bank – that linked Andrew to this duplicitous and potentially dangerous life through his father.

A naïve answer to his pressing question was the weaving of a complicated garment that defined geopolitical events of the last half of the twentieth century that he found himself having to navigate with increasing cautiousness. The life of a flâneur, a Parisian gentleman of leisure, seemed to be moving farther away, beyond his grasp. Ironically, his yearning for that simpler life was increasing. Wasn't that what retirement was supposed to be all about?

His thoughts were distracted by a gaggle of Chinese tourists who had entered the cathedral, all following a tourist guide and their leader carrying a troop flag. He huffed in disgust at their disrespect for the religious ambience of this sacred place of worship. Increasingly, he surmised other cultures like the Chinese seemed to demand respect yet were not prepared to reciprocate. More bothersome, the thread of his peaceful pursuits was gone like a caboose that had become uncoupled from the train and drifted away onto a siding.

Separate from this group was a female who sat a few rows ahead of him. Her dress and demeanor, in addition to her brunette ponytail that flowed over her left shoulder, caught his attention. She seemed eerily similar to the female he had observed sitting alone in the Brasserie du Bac less than a few hours before. Some males accompanying this tourist group seemed to disperse throughout the pews. One stood as he lit a prayer candle and awkwardly bowed this head all-the-while covertly scanning the environments. A few more fell in with the gaggle of Chinese tourists who had spread throughout with cameras focused and flashes bouncing off the interior walls, pillars and centuries-old renaissance works of art. He found his tranquil concentration further disturbed.

To his right, a priest dressed in oddly fitted vestments approached, head bowed, fingers intertwined as if in prayer. Andrew had spent many hours sitting in solitude observing the rituals of Catholic clergy. His father had encouraged him to do so in an effort to improve his observation and analytical skills. What had he seen? What had he thought? What had he felt? What had he sensed? Something about his priest was different.

The priest glanced at the female. A few moments later, he

glanced at Andrew who recognized his expression. Luc appeared to have as many disguises as Natalie. Definitely a differentiating trait perhaps of the surreptitious tradecraft, he concluded. "If you dress up intelligence with bullet-proof provenance, you can appear like a saint," Luc mumbled under his breath for Andrew's sake as he nonchalantly strolled past him.

This impersonating priest entered the confessional booth. A man entered on the other side to confess in penitents. Within moments, another man briskly walked away from the gaggle of Chinese tourists, while covertly drawing a semi-automatic pistol with a silencer attached from what appeared to be his camera case. He then fired several shots into the congregational side of the confessional booth. He then strode to the rear of the cathedral and exited. The man who had been standing with the candles pretending to pray followed in quick succession. The female with the brunette ponytail followed in close pursuit of both.

Luc exited the priest's side of the confessional booth. He deliberately opened the congregational door and leaned over the body that had tumbled to the floor, blood flowing from his chest. Luc discretely placed his face closest to the victim who whispered a few final words before falling limp.

Andrew became acutely aware of the transformation of this sacred place of worship into a crime scene with the cathedral's reverence being invaded by the sound of approaching police sirens. Noting that Luc had unperceptively departed the cathedral leaving the priest vestments on a pew beside the confessional booth, Andrew followed as if in line of stern.

CHAPTER 48

G aston and Andrew again sat around the kitchen table in Bistro and Gisèle's house behind the Brasserie du Bac. What had taken place in the cathedral had become a fuzzy chronology of events in Andrew's mind that spiralled seemingly out of control like a kaleidoscope on steroids. Had Alice experienced similar sensations as she travelled down the White Rabbit's hole into the fictional land of the Mad Hatter and the Cheshire Cat in addition to other characters described by Lewis Carroll in his children's novel, Alice's Adventures in Wonderland? How much was Gaston aware of what had transpired? It needed to be discussed, put into context, but not at this moment.

Most pressing for Andrew was his quest to put closure to this chapter in his father's life and to bring clarity to how it had molded his own. There was more truth in story than detail in fact. Gaston had provided many of the missing details for which he was truly thankful. Andrew needed to process the whole story.

"Can you take me to the location where my father's Mosquito plane had crashed?" Andrew asked Gaston.

Gaston nodded. "It is not far, a twenty-minute walk, now concealed by a grove of trees and shrubs that has grown over. The spot where the Nazi transport plane crashed is relatively close by but in a tangential direction."

"I am only interested in the location of my father's Mosquito unless the presence of the transport plane can shed more light on his exploits immediately following the crash."

Gaston led Andrew to the site where his father's Mosquito had crashed, identifiable by a prominent depression in the ground. Andrew bent down and picked up a fragment from the Mosquito. He then stood in deep solitude pondering as he delicately rubbed the tactile remanence of his father's life from a time beyond his own yet intrinsically woven. Its presence in his hand seemed surreal as did the experience.

His mother had told him a few details relating to the harrowing experience and then only scattered segments of stories his father had shared with her on rare occasions. His father only spoke to him once on the fiftieth anniversary of the D-Day invasion. It wasn't a discussion, so to speak. More so an unsolicited fleeting glimpse into a moment that appeared to overflow from his memory. Andrew felt deeply honoured, humbled. It seemed to be fictional as Andrew stared down at the remanences of that reality.

His father was known to a handful of strangers like Gaston and Bistro and other unidentified members of the French *Marquis*. There was greater safety in anonymity of names and faces. The tales of their daring exploits were true yet fictional akin to the anecdotes of Robin Hood and his band of merry men. In addition, there was his navigator, Flight Sergeant Andrew Drake after whom he was named. His father had related many harrowing experiences with Drake. But not the final moments of the last flight the two airmen had together, the night his beloved Mosquito was shot down west of Rouen within sight of the spires of the Caudebec-en-Caux cathedral Andrew had just visited.

Andrew had long sought this tangible connection to guide him. Yet now he seemed more unsure, without a compass. What thoughts had gone through his father's mind in those moments of his rescue by Gaston, knowing his navigator, Flight Sergeant Andrew Drake, was never to accompany him again? Who would help him to navigate through future missions?

How could Andrew have ever prepared himself for such a mental no-man's land? His father was gone, his mother was gone, his wife was gone. He was more alone than he could ever have imagined. Yet all three were speaking to him at this moment as he stood on hallowed ground. His lottery winnings had been the catalyst. Gaston had repeatedly said that the war was not over. His words never rang so true. He had never fought in the war yet he was a causality as much as Gaston and Angelique, Bistro and Gisèle, and all those others who had survived though not unscathed.

Thoughts seemed to come out of nowhere, flooding his mind like torrential rains and flood waters. His father had recited many proverbs, one to his mother as a budding author: *Verba volant; sola scriptura restat* – Spoken words fly away; only what is written remains. She had related this adage to her friends who were also aspiring authors on the occasions they gathered at Les Deux Magots in Saint-Germain-des-Prés when they lived in Paris decades before. As Andrew grew older, he would suggest that what is written, etched on the monitor of the mind, also remained in the form of a message transmitted across the cosmos and the intersection of time and space. Only shamans, druids and other truly spiritual mediums had mastered the ability to read and hear the implicit communiqués.

CHAPTER 49

G aston, Bistro, Luc and Andrew gathered in solemn contemplation around the table in the meeting room adjacent to the bar of the Brasserie du Bac. Late to join them was the brunette female with the ponytail.

"Successful day at the office?" Luc quietly enquired with a reed-thin smile as he tilted his head ever so subtly.

"Successful day at the office," she quietly confirmed as she nodded her head ever so subtly. "Talk later regarding the government's recent pollution control policy as it applies to the Honfleur estuary at the mouth of the Seine."

"Andrew, I would like to introduce you to my partner, Liesl," Luc said. "In addition to superior surveillance skills, she is an expert in all things cyber, especially counter-espionage electronic surveillance including cyber-hacking and code-breaking."

Andrew was acutely aware of what cyber security would bring to spy architecture as it pertains to offensive field operations. He wasn't certain why Luc had mentioned it. Perhaps as a distraction. But from what?

"Liesl, Andrew is the retired Canadian I mentioned who purchased my former urban estate in Paris. Well, the house and property in Saint-Germain des Prés that Estella and I owned." Luc lamented the fact that their marriage had become irreparably shattered. In the final months, they had lived parallel lives. Any words of reconciliation shared between them had rung hollow long before, no less real in its shared silence.

Andrew shook her hand. "Very nice to meet you, Liesl." She may be petite in stature and appear demure, however, she has a gorilla-like grip. He concluded she could captivate a target, either male or female, with her alluring charm and affable personality, and then break that person's neck with virtually no effort. A venomous viper under the control of the snake charmer, perhaps. But who fulfilled that role? He felt comforted to have been introduced to her as a friend and colleague of Luc under the guise of a recently minted Parisian gentleman of leisure.

Liesl remained reserved in response to Luc's preliminary introduction.

Andrew nodded faintly. "Last name?"

"Liesl is fine for now," Luc qualified promptly.

"Liesl, an Austrian or German name?" Andrew enquired further."

"Yes," she acknowledged with a disarming smile. She had correctly assessed his questioning approach to her introduction by Luc. She clarified with a light-hearted qualification. "But not to be confused with the young fräulein, sixteen going on seventeen, from the Hollywood movie, The Sound of Music. My family is actually from Strasburg."

"Beautiful city any time of the year but especially so during December with all the Christmas markets and decorations around the Grande Île, Place Gutenberg, and the neighborhood of rue de Vieux Marché Aux Poissons," he added with a tinge of warmth in his voice.

She replied without adding further clarification. Instead, she smiled and nodded pleasantly. He has travelled there or has reviewed a considerable number of photographs. Honest response, nonetheless, she admitted. Not overbearing like an increasing number of nouveau-riche Asians.

"My late wife and I travelled to Strasburg on a Rhine River Christmas market cruise from Amsterdam to Basel. We were so impressed we visited there again the following summer as a select vacation destination."

"Let me add to that introduction," Gaston interjected. "Luc

and Liesl are examples of modern-day French agents. Luc is fluent in Russian and English, and Liesl in German and English. As a team, they pose a formidable challenge to the two greatest foreign threats to France, Moscow and a Bavarian resurgence of Nazi Fourth Reich, which on occasion have been known to join forces or at least not outright oppose each other. Both the communists and the Carlingue Gestapo in France gained power as a result of the Second World War. Lately, Beijing has become a rising threat.

Andrew thought back to the gaggle of Chinese tourists that had entered the Cathedral and caused a disruption. For what purpose? he reflected curiously. How many of them were agents-in-training on a field trip all the while pretending to play the part of curious tourists.

Gaston continued. "If you had any doubts, I can assure you that Luc is a loyal French patriot and an ardent defender of the tricolour, as is Liesl. Occasionally, their methodologies can be perceived by some as unorthodox, which I sense you may have wondered. That is what makes them effective."

Luc has learned well from his sorcerer, Andrew surmised with a single subtle bow in homage. Or should I be comfortable in acknowledging two wise sorcerers, Gaston and Bistro?

A slim smile accentuated Gaston's face. "Your father has taught you well, young Andrew, as has your time with the RCMP Watcher Service been fruitful. Yes, I have briefed both Luc and Liesl on your background."

Without an introduction to create a context for Gaston's sake, Luc stated emphatically, "Unknown casualties of war. These were the words the man in the confessional booth had whispered to me."

Andrew gazed at Gaston for a reaction. There was none, not even a raised eyebrow. He would not be the first in those assembled to comment one way or the other. Instead, he remained stoic. Some details were best not mentioned, he concluded, like his father's identity on the night he had been rescued by Gaston and others from the local Maquis cell all of whom used a nom de guerre to mask their actual names.

"Before coming here," Gaston said. "I scanned names on headstones in the cathedral cemetery. One read: Unknown Casualties of War. There was a date, 14 May 1944."

"That was the date my father was shot down," Andrew interjected.

"A detail I might have neglected to mention," Gaston added. "The body of your father's navigator, Flight Sergeant Drake, had been removed from the crash site and stored in the outdoor crypt where it stayed until the Allied front line had moved across the Rhine River into the Nazi vaterland. His remains were then turned over to the British who transported him back to England with the bodies of other casualties."

"So, who was buried in the grave marked by the headstone: Unknown Casualties of War?" Bistro pondered outload. A silence filled the room.

"If I recall correctly, a member of the parish congregation had died a couple of days before and a grave had been dug," Gaston added. "I attended the funeral because the deceased was an uncle of mine. That is why I remember. I thought it strange because the body had already been lowered into the grave and most but not all of the dirt covered the casket."

"Unknown Casualties of War, casualties as in plural," Luc repeated with a questioning tone. He glanced at Liesl, his eyes squinting, his lips pursed, his head tilted.

"Thoughts, partner?" Liesl asked.

"Has it been under our noses all along?" he replied.

"The unknown casualties of Auschwitz and other concentration camps whose gold fillings from their teeth had been melted down and turned into the 24 carat gold bars. Is that what you are thinking?" Andrew asked as much as he suggested as a possible explanation. The fog started to clear and with it the trappings of the vagueness of his father's plane crash.

"Do we want to go there?" Bistro asked, not implying a judgement decision that needed to be made.

"If we dig up the grave and find the missing gold bars, we will have to act one way or another. Either we re-bury it or turn it over to the appropriate government department for disposal. What good would that do beside add to the coffers and force reluctant politicians to make decisions they desperately want to avoid?"

"The souls of the casualties of war, some certainly Jewish by faith, have been laid to rest already in mass graves in concentration camps with the Star of David inscribed on a tombstone," Liesl uttered not as a debating topic but instead as a statement of obvious fact. The cathedral here in Caudebec-en-Caux is Roman Catholic as is the cemetery, not Jewish by faith, not even ecumenical.

Gaston looked up as if seeking an elusive thought that was suspended in the air. He then waved his hand in a maître d' motion. "If we do not dig, no one will be the wiser. It is only conjecture, supposition at this point." Silence was absolute. It spoke for all those assembled, each pondering in their own careful reflections, each face a façade giving nothing way. Even with bad choices there were invariably worse ones.

The sensed but unseen mist that had plagued the clarity of Andrew's raison d'être appeared sharper. He found the peace he had sought in the sanctity of the Caudebec-en-Caux cathedral and hallowed ground concealed among the tall trees and low shrubs that outlined the depression and remanence of the downed Mosquito his father had piloted that fateful night. The latter had unknowingly defined him more than he realized. He looked forward to returning to the solitude of his urban estate in Saint-Germain des Prés, to Monique and Langue. Especially, he looked forward to further fashioning his new life as a Parisian gentleman of leisure while in the company of interesting acquaintances doing interesting things in interesting places.

CHAPTER 50

"**M**onique, I need some legal advice, assistance in dealing with a minor but important matter related to the disposition of my lottery windfall."

Andrew was in her law office, seated across a polished mahogany desk from her.

"Absolutely. If I cannot help you, I am confident that someone else in my law firm will be able to."

Where have I heard that before? It must run in the family. Andrew chuckled to himself.

"And?" she enquired good-humouredly.

A simple smile lingered momentarily on his lips before he got to the point. "I asked your father if he knew the whereabouts of the barge he had worked on as an apprentice deckhand during the war – the barge used to secretly transport my father to Honfleur after he had been shot down."

She leaned across, sensing he had put considerable thought into what he was about to ask her. Being in the company of someone who asked for her advice and respected her opinion was new to her. Claude never had. She caught herself pulling back physically and emotionally, then questioning her reaction. After years of abuse, she understood why but wondered whether she could ever change. How long would it take before she would stop defaulting to Claude?

"As promised, Gaston got back to me regarding its whereabouts. It is now a houseboat in Paris permanently moored on the right bank of the Seine along the Quai des Tuileries. The current owner and occupant is the son of the captain from the time Gaston worked on it as an apprentice deckhand."

"Nice to know. So, how can I help?" Her expression and tone of voice mirrored her interest.

"According to Gaston, after the war, the government department responsible for veterans made a one-time payment to have the barge converted into a houseboat and towed to its current location where the captain lived out his final days. This payment was in compensation for actions the captain had taken so far above and beyond the call of duty to save so many downed Allied aircrew. He did not want public recognition for his heroic actions for fear of reprisal from die-hard Nazis and their collaborators who remained in the region, some of whom the captain knew from his experience as a member of the *Maquis*. That was when he and Gaston forged their close bond. Like Monique and Philippe, the son learned of his father's wartime record years after the barge had been refurbished and moored along the Quai des Tuileries. On his death, his only son inherited the captain's entire estate including the houseboat. Unfortunately, the son can no longer afford to keep it."

"I think I know where you are going with this and what you would like me and my law firm to do – somehow pay to return the barge to its restored state after the war."

Andrew nodded in acknowledgement. "I have put considerable thought into how I can best financially honour my father, the captain of the barge who helped save his life, and France."

"That is a relatively simple task," Monique responded. "We can make a one-time stipend payment on your behalf for immediate repairs and upgrades. Thereafter, we can set up monthly or quarterly honorarium payments for as long as the son is alive and the barge remains his permanent home. I can set up an escrow account from which payments can be drawn. This way, the partners in the law firm will not think I've not been working all this time," she chuckled.

"I doubt they would. But if any are in doubt, you can advise them in the strictest confidence that you have been approached by a new client to handle future financial requests similar to what I have just described regarding the barge."

Monique smiled in deep appreciation of his unconditional commitment to her career. The subsequent thought escaped her before she could intervene. She lowered her head to hide her emotions.

Claude had never supported her. In fact, he had gone out of his way to criticize her in public with demeaning comments and in private with physical abuse. Each assault would require more makeup to hide the bruises and abrasions in addition to mascara to distract those who stared at her. It was apparent who had caused the injuries yet no one offered to assist.

She needed to seek psychological counselling before these flashbacks interfered with her growing relationship with Andrew.

"One final request," Andrew asked. "After the repairs have been completed, I would like permission from the son to board the barge and examine the location of the concealed compartment in the bow where my father and other Allied aircrew had been smuggled to Honfleur."

She forced herself to look up at him and smile confidently. "I am sure we can arrange such a visit."

"No fanfare, no fuss, no media, absolutely no negotiations on this final condition," Andrew emphasized politely but with determination. "No one is to know about my lottery windfall."

He reached for her hand which he held as a heartfelt smile filled his face. He never wanted her to think that he would ever be anything but completely supportive of her. He might never know how much his gesture supported her.

Natalie was not a psychologist but she had helped Monique to short-circuit her downward spiral of depression before Monique and Andrew recently reunited, to acknowledge the source but more importantly to take control to move on.

⊣ᆯ ᄐ⊢

M<small>ONIQUE</small>'S EYES SCANNED ALL COMPASS bearings, stopping momentarily as if trying to capture a misplaced thought. She stood still, then walked deliberately to the library with the floor-to-ceiling bookshelf. When alone and hiding in the house before Andrew purchased the urban estate, she had spent hours sitting in the high-backed leather chair reading mystery novels. As a child, she had been a prolific reader of romance books.

Langue raised his head curiously, then followed her immediately once she had turned into the library. He gently rubbed against her as a reminder that he was there and would protect her again if circumstances dictated.

Off to one side of the main bookshelf was a much smaller single shelf containing oversized books. She drew her index finger along the spine of several, stopping on one that appeared to be oddly out of place by height and width, protruding as an atlas would among smaller reference books. This book bulged as if containing fold-out pages. She recognized it as a first edition of the Michelin Travel Guide dated 1900, now a valuable collector's copy. Although not a professional antiquarian, she admired the literary excellence of authors and the craftsmanship of publishers and book binders. Today, it was hard to find that level of excellence. Being careful not to damage the binding or soil the individual pages any more than they already were, she delicately riffled through the pages more out of curiosity than to review its details.

She looked down at Langue with a smile. Her memory was not as crisp as it had once been as a teenager when she and Andrew first met but it was still accurate. On occasion, certain memories just needed more time to rise to the forefront. She whispered, "Our landlord will be pleased with what we are about to show him. I think you'll receive a special treat in gratitude."

"Andrew," Monique called out from the dining room.

"*Oui, ma Cherie*," he replied as he entered and stared at the blueprint spread out on the table. His eyes skimmed the document first then settled on the outline of the house and finally the stables. He had to look a second time, not believing what he had before him. He reached over and wrapped his arms around Monique, snuggling his face into the nape of her neck. He then kissed her and gave her another long hug. "You may never know how much this means to me," he whispered. "Where did you find it?"

"In the back of this 1900 first edition of the Michelin Guide." She held it up. "Shortly after Natalie moved me in here to escape Claude, I looked through the books in order to pass the time. I just now recalled scanning through this one but never made note of the contents because it was of little interest to me."

The date, 5 November 1864, in addition to the name and address of the surveyor had been written above the legend. Other notes mentioned that the blueprint had been prepared based on the 1815 description of the construction, and after Georges-Eugène Haussmann had completed the vast public works program in the mid 1850s to create the boulevards and parks in Paris. Other minor marginal notes commented on lesser features not identified on the blueprint itself because they had not been completed, including reference to a door in a wall. Mention of the mysterious access point caused Andrew's heart rate to increase. Just a mention without a location increased his frustration. His search for this mysterious door was now rewarded beyond its being a rumour.

CHAPTER 51

While strolling the tree-lined boulevards and parks as a gentleman of leisure, the thought again crossed his mind that he needed to decide whether to sell or keep the property. Both had their pros and cons. The value would increase with even partial proof of provenance. He experienced mixed emotions.

By the French law governing real estate, he could not simply sell the lot without declaring that a murder had taken place there. He knew he would have to cleanse the soil of the violence regardless of his decision.

Either way, he would have the stable-garage torn down and replaced with groves of apple, plum and Maribelle trees, in addition to cobblestone paths between planter spaces for vegetables and herbs. He would invite his neighbours to come together to adopt a planter space in the spring and harvest the produce each fall. Perhaps that would help to soften memories of the atrocities committed against neighbours of Saint-Germain-des-Prés. Some had been edited out of family narratives, yet not forgotten by those who survived. All had been associated through death with previous occupants of his property.

He made his decision. He would remain with Monique and Langue in his urban estate. He would plant a much larger rose garden and mount a discrete brass plaque on the trellis with the name "Lynette" carved on it. The thought caused him to reflect in earnest. It was hard to believe something as beautiful as a rose could exist in this place.

He could now waft through retirement as a *flâneur* – detached but fascinated – the life he had always imagined back in Canada, yet had rarely spoken about to anyone except Lynette. As he strolled the tree-lined boulevards and parks in the evening, holding hands with Monique and with Langue by their side, he contemplated what the garden would look like once complete. For now, it would be a work in progress. He was confident that Haussmann would have had similar thoughts during the planning and construction of his mighty work.

They would pass by Luc Moreau on occasion and nod in acknowledgement. Langue would growl in a low tone that warned them to be prudent if not cautious of this DG Internal Security agent. Andrew could never completely trust anyone who was trained to be deceitful and dishonest as his default mode.

He and Monique made reservations at Au Pied de Cochon restaurant for dinner in the secluded alcove on the second floor in recognition of so many events that had transpired since the day she had helped him claim his lottery ticket and deposit the winnings. They extended an invitation to Philippe to join them if his schedule permitted time away from his mythical kingdom of Camelot and the Knights of that Round Table in his office.

—FIN—

www.ingramcontent.com/pod-product-compliance
Lightning Source LLC
Chambersburg PA
CBHW042144170626
46815CB00006BA/302